W9-ABA-153

Cherished Mercy

Books by Tracie Peterson

www.traciepeterson.com

*with Judith Miller **with Judith Pella ***with Kimberley Woodhouse

TRACIE PETERSON

BETHANYHOUSE
a division of Baker Publishing Group
Minneapolis, Minnesota

Published by Bethany House Publishers
11400 Hampshire Avenue South
Bloomington, Minnesota 55438
www.bethanyhouse.com

Bethany House Publishers is a division of
Baker Publishing Group, Grand Rapids, Michigan

Printed in the United States of America

Library of Congress Cataloging-in-Publication Data
Names: Peterson, Tracie, author.
Title: Cherished mercy / Tracie Peterson.
Description: Minneapolis, Minnesota : Bethany House, a division of Baker
    Publishing Group, [2017] | Series: Heart of the frontier ; 3
Identifiers: LCCN 2017012333| ISBN 9780764213441 (hardcover : acid-free paper) |
    ISBN 9780764213298 (softcover) | ISBN 9780764213458 (large-print softcover)
Subjects: LCSH: Frontier and pioneer life—Fiction. | GSAFD: Christian fiction. |
    Love stories.
Classification: LCC PS3566.E7717 C44 2017 | DDC 813/.54—dc23
LC record available at https://lccn.loc.gov/2017012333

Scripture quotations are from the King James Version of the Bible.

This is a work of historical reconstruction; the appearances of certain historical figures are therefore inevitable. All other characters, however, are products of the author's imagination, and any resemblance to actual persons, living or dead, is coincidental.

Cover design by LOOK Design Studio
Cover photography by Aimee Christenson

17   18   19   20   21   22   23   7   6   5   4   3   2   1

In memory of Phillip DeShazer

I was joyfully there when you came into the world
and sadly was there when you departed.
You were an amazing young man,
and I know you will be missed by so many.
I look forward to seeing you again one day, sweet nephew.

Chapter 1

OCTOBER 1855
OREGON CITY, OREGON TERRITORY

Push, Hope. You have to push," Grace commanded.

Mercy Flanagan wiped her sister's forehead as she labored to give birth to her baby. After ten hours of intense pain, Hope had clearly weakened.

Looking to their eldest sister, Grace, Mercy grimaced. "I thought you said second babies come faster." Hope had given birth two years earlier without a lengthy labor, and they had all presumed she would do the same again.

"They usually do, but the one thing you must remember about babies is that no two births are ever identical. They are as different as the babies being born." Grace turned her attention back to Hope and the unborn child. "Your baby is almost here. Now give me a big push. Bear down with all your strength."

"I haven't . . . got any . . . strength . . . left," Hope replied, falling back against the pillow.

"Mercy, when I tell you, I want you to help Hope sit up.

7

Support her shoulders and push her forward." Hope grimaced and cried out. Grace nodded at Mercy. "Now."

It wasn't easy, but Mercy managed to slip in behind Hope and raise her up at the same time.

"Push, Hope. The baby is coming now."

Mercy felt Hope tense as she did her best to obey. Grace took hold of the baby's head as it emerged and then rotated the baby as the shoulders emerged. After that, the infant slid easily from Hope's body.

"It's another boy," Mercy whispered against Hope's ear.

"A boy? Truly? Sean will have a little brother."

"This farm is going to be overrun with children if you and Grace keep having babies," Mercy teased. Already she was aunt to Grace's two children, Gabe and Nancy, and there would be a third in the spring. Now Hope had brought another boy to join her two-year-old son, Sean.

Grace cut the cord, then lifted the baby by his heels and smacked him on the bottom. He started to cry almost immediately.

Mercy smiled and brushed back Hope's damp hair. "He's got a great set of lungs."

"That he does," Grace agreed. "Mercy, I want you to care for him. Hope, you're not quite done yet, as you well know."

Birthing was hard work, but so too the aftermath. Mercy had been present at the delivery of all but one of her sisters' babies and would no doubt help in Grace's third in March. She came from a long line of women who practiced healing arts and midwifery. Mercy had never thought herself all that interested in learning such a craft, but over the past few years, she had found it more and more appealing, and Grace had patiently taught her all she could.

Mercy took the towel-wrapped infant from Grace even as Hope called out. "I want to see him."

The baby cried even louder—if that was possible. "Let me make him presentable first."

"He's more than fine just the way he is," Hope replied. "Please."

Without waiting for Grace's approval, Mercy took him to Hope. There was no hesitation as Hope reached for him. She pulled him close and pushed back the towel to examine every inch of him.

"He's beautiful," she said, a sob breaking from her throat.

"He is," Grace agreed, "but you have to let Mercy tend to him. There are things that must be done to ensure his health."

Taking the baby in her arms, Mercy smiled down at her nephew. "What are you going to call him?"

"Edward, after Uncle Edward," Hope murmured. "And Flanagan for our maiden name. Edward Flanagan Kenner."

Mercy nodded. "Hello, Edward." She frowned. "That seems like much too formal a name for a baby. I'm going to call him Eddie."

"Lance will like that. He has a good friend named Eddie."

The baby began to calm. He looked up at Mercy with eyes the color of sapphires—eyes like his mother's. "Come, Eddie, let's clean you up."

"Uncle Edward will be touched you chose to call him that," Grace said.

"Well, we named the first one Sean Howard after both our fathers, so I thought it only right. Uncle Edward did so much to help us after we came to Oregon City," Hope replied.

Mercy nodded and began to wash the baby. "Indeed he did." Eddie didn't care for the procedure at all and began to kick up a storm. "Gracious, I think he's going to have your temperament, Hope." She glanced over her shoulder with a smile, then turned her attention back to the infant. "I will soon be done, Master Kenner, and then you will feel so cozy with warm clothes and a blanket."

Mercy continued her tender care, using generous portions of vinegar water, as she had done with other newborns. Her mother and grandmother had been firm believers in the multiple curative powers of vinegar, and it was something they had handed down to their daughters.

Once she had Eddie properly bathed, Mercy put an herbal salve on the stub of umbilical cord, then secured a band around it. After this she diapered and dressed him.

"There you are, little man," she said, lifting him carefully. She wrapped a blanket around him, lest the damp autumn air cause him to catch a chill. The baby calmed and looked up at her, his blue eyes open fully. "You really are quite handsome." She took him to Hope and lowered him into his mother's arms. "He's finally ready to be with you."

"And I'm finished as well," Grace declared. "So you may invite Lance to come meet his new son." She rose and began collecting the bloody towels and afterbirth pan.

Mercy smiled. She loved bringing in the father almost as much as caring for the newborns. She left her sisters and went downstairs to find Lance. It wasn't hard to locate him. He sat with Sean on the floor of the living room, playing with wooden blocks. At the sight of Mercy, however, he jumped to his feet.

"Is she all right? Is the baby all right?"

"They're both fine." Mercy gave his arm a pat. "You may go see her now, and your new son."

Lance grinned. "Another boy?" He looked down at little Sean, who was doing his best to stack one block atop three others. "You hear that, Sean? You have a baby brother."

"Brudder," Sean repeated, but his mind was clearly on his task.

"Go on now. I'll stay with Sean." Mercy didn't have to tell him twice. Lance all but ran from the room. No doubt he'd take the stairs two at a time.

She knelt down beside the handsome little boy and brushed back his brown curls. "Would you like to eat?" Her own stomach felt empty, and she knew it was well past lunchtime.

Sean abandoned his blocks and threw himself into Mercy's arms. "Eat now, pease."

She laughed and got to her feet, shifting Sean to her hip. "Well, since you are so polite, I think we can arrange that. Let's see what your mama has in the kitchen."

Lance and Hope had continued to live on the Armistead Farm, as it was called. The house and outbuildings surrounding it belonged to Grace and Alex, but both were keen to keep their family close. After marrying, Hope and Lance had taken up residence in the small log house where they had all lived before Grace and Alex built their larger farmhouse. Mercy had always been grateful that Alex cared for her and Hope as if they were his own sisters. It had saved both of them from having to seek out husbands before they were ready. Far too often Mercy had seen her friends marry young, and not always happily. Her former best friend, Beth Cranston, had married the preacher's son, Toby Masterson, at the tender age of fifteen. This had happened after Mercy refused him. Toby had begged Mercy to marry him so that he could claim additional acreage in the Donation Land Claim Act. Mercy had turned him down, and in that one move, lost her two dearest friends. It hadn't been easy to bear.

"But that was five years ago," she reminded herself.

Sean grabbed her dress collar and began pulling it toward his mouth. Mercy laughed and pried it away from him. "Dresses aren't for eating, Sean."

Balancing him on her hip, Mercy found the bread and butter. There would no doubt be jam as well. The sisters had canned over two hundred pints of apple, berry, and pear jams and jellies that summer. Opening the cupboard, she found an open jar of apple jam.

"Here we go. This ought to be good for a start." She put the food on the table and went back to retrieve a knife.

"I want some bread," Sean declared.

"I know you do." Mercy settled herself at the table with Sean on her lap. "That's why I'm making this piece just for you." She paused to give him a quick peck on the cheek, then went back to her task.

Once the bread was properly slathered in butter and jam, Mercy cut it into quarters and handed one to Sean.

"What do you say?"

"Fank you."

She chuckled. "Close enough."

Sean quickly devoured his piece of bread and held his hand out for more. "Pease."

"With a sweet face like yours, how can I refuse?" Mercy handed him another quarter.

"Where is everybody?" Alex called from the front of the house.

"Sean and I are in the kitchen, having some bread and jam." Mercy heard the patter of feet running across the room and knew she'd soon have two more mouths to feed.

"Mercy!" nearly five-year-old Gabe declared. He barreled into her and wrapped his arms around her. Luckily it wasn't the side on which she held Sean. Even so, the younger boy wasn't happy at having his eating interrupted and gave Gabe a sticky-fingered push.

"Go away!" he commanded.

Gabe raised his head and stuck out his tongue. Sean countered by imitating his cousin. Mercy shook her head while Alex laughed.

"Do you see those naughty boys, Nancy?" he asked his daughter.

The beautiful little girl shook her head, making her long dark hair sway against her back. "No."

This only made Alex laugh harder. "She likes saying *no*. I remember when Gabe went through that for a time."

Mercy laughed. "I imagine all children do. Is it all right if I give them some bread and jam?"

"Of course." Alex put Nancy on one of the chairs while Gabe climbed up on his own. "So do we have a new arrival finally?"

"Yes. Another boy. They've named him after Uncle Edward, but I'm calling him Eddie. Edward sounds far too stuffy." She fixed two more pieces of bread and cut them in fours as she had with Sean's.

"That ought to please Edward and Lance." Alex helped Nancy with her bread while Gabe stuffed an entire quarter into his mouth at once.

Seeing this, Sean tried to follow suit, but Mercy was ready for him. "No, you don't. Gabe's mouth is bigger than yours. Stop trying to copy him."

"As for you," Alex said, fixing Gabe with a disapproving look, "no more stuffing big pieces of food in your mouth. Be a gentleman. Take a bite and swallow before you take another."

"Can I chew it?" Gabe asked quite seriously.

Mercy put her hand to her mouth to contain her laughter while Alex rolled his eyes. "Of course you can. I want you to chew it before you swallow it."

Gabe smiled and went back to his bread. From his smug expression, Mercy wasn't entirely sure the question had been innocent.

"I didn't know you were here," Grace said, coming into the kitchen.

Alex turned from the table and pulled her into his arms. "How are you two doing?" He put his hand to her slightly rounded abdomen.

"We're very tired. I need a hot bath and a nap."

"We could all use a nap," Alex said, kissing her forehead. "These hooligans have been up since five."

13

"Good thing it's a Sunday. We may have missed services, but we won't miss an afternoon of rest." Grace yawned.

"I apologize for not giving them something more appropriate to eat." Mercy got to her feet and placed Sean on the chair so he could finish eating.

"It's not a problem," Grace said. "I have stew at home for all of us. It only needs to be heated."

"I've already put it on the stove," Alex interjected. "I figured as long as it was taking to deliver this baby, you'd need some sustenance."

Grace smiled. "That was very thoughtful." She turned to Mercy. "Why don't you bring Sean, and we'll all eat at our house?"

"That sounds good. I'm hoping for a nap myself."

Grace nodded. "Alex, would you mind going upstairs and letting Lance and Hope know that Sean is with us? Oh, and tell Lance I'll fix them a tray if he wants to come get it."

Alex placed another kiss on her forehead as Grace yawned again. "I just hope you can stay awake long enough to eat." He started to go upstairs, then paused. "I nearly forgot." He pulled a letter out of his coat pocket. "Jed Drury brought this letter. Said he picked it up on Friday with his own mail and thought to bring it over, but then forgot until today. When he saw we weren't at church, he decided to stop by the farm on his way home."

"Who's it from?" Grace asked, taking the missive in hand. "Oh, it's from Eletta. I'm so glad. I haven't heard from her in so long. I was beginning to worry." She ripped open the letter then began to read. "Oh my! She's expecting a baby! Isaac must be beyond joyful." She continued to read and began to frown.

"What's wrong?" Mercy asked.

"She's been very ill. Her condition doesn't agree with her, and she's been unable to keep food down. She thought it would pass after the first few months, but she's still suffering and only able to eat or drink a tiny bit."

"When is the baby due?" Alex asked.

"The same month as ours—March." She read aloud, "'*I know that you and Hope are both busy with your own children, but I wonder if Mercy might come and help me. I know you will worry because of the Rogue River troubles, but I assure you our people in the immediate area are not up in arms.*'"

Mercy knew that the Rogue River Indians were at war with the whites. Having lived through captivity at the Whitman Mission in November of '47, she was apprehensive about putting herself in harm's way again. The Whitman Massacre had resulted in most of the men being murdered and over fifty women and children being held hostage for a month. Mercy and Hope had been among their number. The women had been treated abominably by the Cayuse Indian men. Hope had managed to protect Mercy from being molested. Mercy had been twelve years old, and other girls that age had been abused, but given her petite stature, Mercy looked much younger and was thus saved from harm. At least for the most part.

She still had to live through the nightmare of having people she cared about cut down and violently murdered. She lived through the wailing and sorrow of the women and children who were held captive alongside her. She had come through the entire affair scarred, but not defeated. Her mainstays had been Hope and God. She had studied the Bible and prayed so much during that time that her spiritual life had grown by leaps and bounds.

"'. . . *and as I said, the fault is mostly on the part of the white men.*'"

Mercy realized she'd missed part of the letter. "I'm afraid I wasn't paying attention. What is the fault of the white men?"

Grace looked up from the letter. "Eletta says there have been many attacks along the Rogue River. Some of the worst were far inland, over the mountains from where they live. She said that the militia has adopted a plan of extermination. They intend to kill every Indian who puts up any kind of fight."

"I don't understand. A fight about what?"

"About being removed from the region and sent to live on a reserved area of land elsewhere. The government apparently is rounding up the various tribes and forcing them to relocate to a place southwest of here along the coast."

"What else does she say?" Mercy motioned to the letter. "Go ahead and read. I'm paying attention."

Grace nodded. "*There is a terrible spirit of hatred here for the Indian people, but I wouldn't ask Mercy to come if I feared her to be in danger. Being white, she won't be harmed by those who are bent on murder. The native people are mostly taking to the hills and mountains and doing their best to avoid being captured or killed. Our people here at the mission have been peaceful throughout the time we've been here, so the government has not worried themselves yet with their removal. However, sadly, I know that this will be the order of things. If Mercy can come, please try to arrange for her to be in Port Orford by the first of November. Isaac has plans to be there at that time, and he can bring her back to our mission. He will be there for a week, and if she doesn't come in that time, then we will know she was unable to join us.*'"

"That's all she has to say," Grace said, lowering the letter, "besides a few words about their mission work." She looked at Mercy. "I can't possibly ask you to do this, and frankly I'm surprised that Eletta would. She knows what you went through. All I can figure is that she must be very sick."

Even with the memory of the massacre in the back of her mind, Mercy felt a strange peace about the matter. She had been fervently fasting and praying that God would show her what she was supposed to do with her life. She felt certain this was His calling.

"I don't think it sounds wise to put Mercy in the middle of a war," Alex said, looking grim.

"Nor do I." Grace fixed her with a look. "I don't want you to go. That's very far away, and I would be frantic with worry."

"I want more bread and jam, please," Gabe requested.

Mercy didn't look away from her sister's gaze. "I'm going to pray about it."

"Do you seriously think God would want you to go?" Alex asked. He went to where Nancy was teetering on the edge of her chair and helped her down.

"As you both know, I've been praying night and day for God's direction for my life. I admit this wouldn't be my first choice, but I also feel strangely drawn—perhaps called—to this purpose."

"But the dangers are clearly there," Grace countered. "You know very well how violent it can be."

Mercy nodded. "I do." She heaved a sigh. "But if God is calling me to go, then I can hardly worry about that. We both know that faith isn't faith unless it's tested. In spite of what happened at the Whitman Mission, I don't hold the Indians any grudge. God calls us to forgiveness. You've said as much to me on more than one occasion."

"Yes, but . . ." Grace fell silent and looked up at Alex.

"I think Mercy's right. We need to pray about it." He sounded less than convinced. "I'll go let Lance know about lunch and meet you at the house." He headed out of the kitchen with a frown on his face.

Mercy helped Sean from his chair. She took his hand and then held out her free hand to Nancy. "Come on. I'll walk with you back to the house, but you have to help me by holding my hand."

The children were happy to comply, and even Gabe followed

her. "It's too bad God only gave us two hands," he told her. "If we had three, then you could hold my hand too."

Mercy laughed. "Well, at the rate of nieces and nephews being born in this family, I would need at least half a dozen hands, and that would just be silly."

"Spiders got eight legs," Gabe offered. "Papa showed me that."

Mercy paused as she reached Grace, who stood frowning. "'Take therefore no thought for the morrow: for the morrow shall take thought for the things of itself.'" She quoted Matthew six, verse thirty-four, as Grace had often done.

Grace's frown only deepened. "As I recall, there's more to that passage."

Mercy nodded and gave a sigh. "Yes. 'Sufficient unto the day is the evil thereof.'"

Chapter 2

Grace shook her head as she gathered up Hope's dirty laundry. "I don't want her to go, but I know Eletta. She wouldn't have asked for help if her situation wasn't dire. I fear she must be terribly ill."

Hope sat in the rocker nursing Eddie. She knew very well her sister's apprehension regarding Mercy setting off for the Rogue River. It matched her own.

"Mercy says she feels confident it's what God wants her to do, but I still have no peace about it," Grace continued. She put the final piece of clothing in her basket and straightened. "I don't know what to say or do to change her mind."

"I don't think we will change her mind. I spoke to her as well. She told me she likes the idea of helping at the mission. She has wanted to teach school for some time and figures this might be where God would have her do that."

Grace sank down on the edge of the bed. "She's twenty years old and has always had sound judgment."

"Much sounder than my own, I have to admit," Hope agreed.

"I know we can't keep her here forever . . . not that I'd even

19

want to. She needs to find a husband and start a family of her own, but I don't see that happening anytime soon." Grace glanced around the room as if expecting someone to be listening in. "Eletta feels confident that Mercy and Adam might hit it off."

"Adam is Isaac's brother, right?"

Grace nodded. "She's been praying for a good wife for him and said in her letter that it came to her one day that Mercy might very well be the right woman. Still, given she's refused all the men around here, I wouldn't hold my breath."

Hope knew what Grace was talking about. Mercy had rejected would-be suitors left and right. She was always sought out at church socials and town dances, but no one piqued her interest.

"Maybe God doesn't plan for her to marry and have children of her own. Some folks are called to remain unmarried," Hope said after a long moment of silence. "We can't know what God plans for her, nor can we live her life for her."

"I thought you were as much against her going as I am."

Hope nodded. "I am. No one fears the Indian wars more than I do, but the Indians are warring all around us. The Yakama are fighting just to the north across the Columbia. It's not like the Rogue River Indians are the only tribes warring. I don't want my sister endangered by throwing herself into the middle of the fight, but I know Mercy. You do too. She's made up her mind, and we can either offer our support and make it as easy on her as possible, or we can be an obstacle in her way."

Grace sighed. "I know. I know too that Eletta is in great need and I would go to her myself if I could. And, of course, there's Faith."

Hope had thought of little else since the idea of Mercy going to the Browning Mission had come up. Faith. The daughter she'd given birth to as the result of being raped at the Whitman Mission by one of the Cayuse.

There were times, like on Faith's birthday, when Hope couldn't help but wonder about her. Was she happy? Was she pretty? Eletta wrote to say she was, but as her adoptive mother, she could hardly do otherwise.

Eletta had been childless and desperate for a baby, and Hope had happily given her Faith. But the miles and years couldn't stop Hope from feeling as if a tiny part of her was missing. She'd said nothing of this to anyone save Lance. She wasn't at all sure how she could explain it to Grace. From first realizing she was with child, Hope had wanted nothing more than to be rid of the baby, and when she couldn't get Grace's help in that matter, she had planned her own death. Suicide had seemed better than bearing an Indian baby conceived in violence.

"Did you hear me?" Grace asked.

Hope shook her head. "No, I'm sorry. I'm afraid I'm rather tired. Once I finish feeding the baby, I'm sure we'll both have a nice long nap." She smiled. "What did you say?"

Grace shook her head. "It wasn't important." She got to her feet. "Get some rest. Sean is doing fine with our bunch. He thinks it quite novel to get to sleep over at the big house."

"I'm sure he does. Thank you for all you've done."

A smile finally edged its way onto Grace's face. "You've done the same for me and will again, no doubt."

"Especially with Mercy off to the south with Eletta."

"I hadn't thought of that." Grace heaved another sigh and picked up the laundry basket. "I suppose I haven't begun to think of what her absence will mean to us."

⁓

Mercy moved the Armistead sheep from one pasture to the other with the help of two collies and Gabe. The boy wasn't nearly as much help as the dogs. In fact, Mercy often thought she should train the dogs to herd Gabe.

21

"I like the sheep," Gabe said, striding alongside Mercy as the last of the large flock passed through the gate.

Once they were safely in the fenced pasture, Mercy closed the gate and secured it. "I do too." She paused a moment to look over the flock as the collies, Buttons and Bows, came to Gabe for attention. With him occupied by the dogs, Mercy gave some serious thought to what leaving would mean to her.

Since coming to Oregon Territory, the flock had grown considerably and now numbered over five hundred animals. This had always been Grace's dream. Her sister had originally seen the sheep as a means of supporting themselves, and they had served them very well. Mercy enjoyed working with the sheep, as did Hope. There was something very calming about being with them. Some of her best hours in prayer had been spent with the flock.

She smiled to herself. Life here had been good. The prospect of taking herself off to the wilds of the Oregon coast was intimidating, but also invigorating. She hadn't realized it until now, but there was something very stagnant about her life here.

"You won't forget me, will you?" Gabe asked out of the blue.

Mercy looked down at him. Buttons and Bows were seated beside him, looking content. "Why would I ever forget you?"

"Because you're going far away. I heard Mama tell Papa that you might be gone for a long time."

She hadn't considered how her going might affect the children. Kneeling, she smiled. "Gabe, I could never forget you. You're in my heart."

He frowned, confused. "But I thought Jesus lived in my heart."

Mercy chuckled and wrapped him in her arms. "Of course He does, but when He's there, it makes our hearts all the bigger, and our love for others grows too. So there's plenty of room for the people we love, and you are one of the ones I love the most."

She hugged him close and tried not to think about how much she'd miss him—how much she'd miss all of them.

On the twentieth of October, after much discussion and prayer, Mercy found herself on a dock, waiting to board the steamer that would take her along the Willamette and Columbia rivers to Astoria, where she'd catch a ship to Port Orford. Alex stood nearby, consulting with one of the porters. Grace hadn't wanted Mercy to travel alone, and Alex had agreed to go with her as far as Port Orford, where Isaac Browning would meet her. Secretly, Mercy had been relieved. Her biggest fear had been of traveling alone, especially since there would be delays and changes of ships.

Movement off to her right caused Mercy to glance up. Beth Masterson was making her way down the street past the dock area. They'd once been so close but now rarely even exchanged greetings. Since she was leaving the area, Mercy felt an urge to go to her one-time friend.

"Beth!" Mercy waved as the young woman turned. Mercy left the dock and hurried to where Beth had stopped. "I haven't seen you in so long. How are you?"

Beth shook her head, looking bedraggled. "I can hardly tell. I'm so busy." She motioned to her very large abdomen. "This is number four and due next month."

Mercy smiled. "You must be very happy. I'm sure Toby is."

Beth frowned then quickly recovered. "The children are quite dear. Toby says the three boys will be a great help in farming the land when they're older. He hopes this one will be a boy too."

The Masterson children ranged in age from four to not yet a year old. Beth had been expecting a child pretty much every year since her marriage to Toby in 1850.

"What about you, Beth?"

"Me? What do you mean?" She looked surprised.

Mercy was overwhelmed with compassion for her former friend. Beth was her own age yet looked a dozen years older. She was unkempt, her hair barely pinned in a bun, and her brown eyes had lost their luster.

"I meant how are you doing with all that responsibility?"

Beth looked away. "Mother Masterson helps with the children when I come to town. That's where they are right now. I was on my way to purchase some flannel. We need to make more diapers." To Mercy's surprise, tears came to Beth's eyes.

Seeing Beth so distressed, Mercy couldn't help but reach out to touch her arm. "What is it, Beth?"

"I'm sorry." She shook her head and choked back a sob. "I'm just so tired."

Mercy wasn't at all sure what to say. She and Beth had barely spoken to each other in years, and now here she was, falling apart. "Is there anything I can do? I'm leaving shortly to go south to help a friend of the family, but I hate to go seeing you so troubled."

Beth shook her head again and struggled to regain her composure. "I've treated you abominably all these years, and I'm sorry. Toby wouldn't allow—" She fell silent and shook her head. "I should have listened to you, Mercy. Being married isn't at all what I thought it would be. Not only that, but—" She again stopped midsentence. After a moment of looking at the ground, she glanced up to meet Mercy's eyes. "Toby doesn't even love me."

Mercy was stunned. She felt such sorrow for her old friend that all she could do was pull her into her arms for a hug. "I'm sure you're wrong," she whispered against Beth's ear.

"No." Beth pulled back. "He doesn't. He told me so. He said he only married me to get the extra land."

It was just as Mercy had suspected. Toby had proposed to

her for the same purpose. It was the very reason she had tried
to stop Beth from rushing into marriage.

"I'm so sorry to put all of this on you," Beth said, wiping
her tears with the edge of her shawl. "I suppose everything just
overwhelmed me today. The baby has been sick, and I haven't
been sleeping well."

"Beth, I know we haven't been close for a while, but I've never
stopped caring for you. I admit I haven't been very faithful to pray
for you, however, and I vow here and now to change my ways."

"I miss our friendship," Beth admitted. "I miss the fun we
used to have dreaming about the future."

Mercy hugged her again. "We'll always be friends."

"Mercy, it's time to board," Alex called from the dock.

She gave him a quick wave, then turned back to Beth. "I'm so
sorry things are difficult, but you know God can work miracles.
Let's agree to pray that He provides one for you very soon. I'll
try to write, although I'm going deep into the remotest part of
the territory, and I don't know how easily I can send or receive
mail. Nevertheless, you'll be in my prayers."

Beth nodded, and her eyes again filled with tears. "Thank
you."

The look of regret on her face was almost more than Mercy
could bear. She choked back her own tears and hurried toward
the dock. Alex looked at her oddly but said nothing. Instead he
offered her his arm and helped her onto the boat.

Mercy stood at the rail and watched as Beth continued along
the road that followed the river. She wished so much that things
could be different for her friend.

"Are you all right?" Alex asked, coming to join her at the rail.

"I am, but she's not." Mercy shook her head. "I tried to tell
her five years ago that marrying Toby Masterson was a mistake.
Now, with three children and another soon to join the family,
she's starting to realize the truth of it." She turned to face him.

"Oh, Alex, it's such a mess. She's so sad and . . . she says that Toby doesn't love her. I knew he didn't when he proposed, but I hoped he'd come to love her."

Alex put his arm around her shoulders. "You can't let yourself get in the middle of it, Mercy. God has joined them for better or worse. When folks try to meddle in that, it only causes more problems."

"I know, and I don't intend to meddle. Obviously I'll be far from here and won't even know what's happening, but I feel terrible for her."

"You tried to warn her, and she made her choice."

Mercy stepped out of Alex's embrace and turned to face him. "Yes, but maybe if I'd told her the day they announced their engagement that Toby had proposed to me just the night before . . . well, maybe she wouldn't have gone through with it. I said nothing because I didn't want to sound petty, but now I wish I had."

Alex smiled. "You have no way of knowing that would have made it better. Put it in God's hands, Mercy. He's the only one who can make things right."

She nodded and looked back at the shoreline as the boat began to steam down the river. Beth had disappeared from sight, leaving Mercy feeling a terrible sense of void.

Please, Lord, please help her. She's so miserable. Please give her strength to endure and make Toby realize her value. Help him to love her.

They transferred to an oceangoing vessel a week later. Mercy had always wondered what it might be like to travel on the ocean, and now that she was actually aboard, she found it even more delightful than what she'd imagined.

As they sat down to dinner that first night at sea, Mercy

marveled that the dining room was as finely appointed as any restaurant back east might have been.

"You look completely enraptured," Alex teased.

Mercy laughed. "I am. I find this to be such a surprise and delight. Just look at this—fine linen napkins and tablecloth, beautiful china and silver. And look at the chandeliers! I feel like a queen."

"It reminds me of a place in New Orleans that was a favorite of my parents," Alex replied. "Hopefully the food here will be just as good."

Other travelers soon joined them at the table, and before long, the meal was served and conversation filled the air. Mercy sampled the appetizer—grilled clams in a ginger-lemon sauce— as the men across from her shared the latest news.

"Word came down last night that the Puget Sound Indians have gone to war," one of the men said as he dug into his food. He was not at all afraid to speak while chewing.

"It's true," the other replied. "There's a hunt on for the Nisqually Indian leader Leschi. I know little else, but there's been trouble up there for some time."

His companion nodded. "That's because the government has put its foot down and is rounding up the tribes to put them on a reservation where they won't cause any more problems. I say keep their women and men separate and don't allow any more heathens to be born."

"Maybe their children should be taken and raised elsewhere. They need to be taught white ways, not Indian ways. Otherwise this problem is never going to end."

Mercy nearly choked on her tea. She coughed as quietly as she could into her napkin, but no one seemed to care. Except Alex.

"Perhaps there is a better time and place for such discussions," Alex said, nodding toward Mercy. "This is hardly a conversation for mixed company."

The men didn't seem to notice. "It would seem we're surrounded by warring tribes. That's one of the reasons I'm heading to San Francisco. It's booming, and with the large influx of people since the gold rush began, there's no thought of Indian troubles."

"Once the government gets enough militia on the payroll, they'll nip the problem soon enough."

The older of the two men wiped sauce from his beard and nodded. "With the drought in the south-central part of the territory, they'll have little trouble recruiting down-on-their-luck miners."

"That area is certainly suffering from the Rogue River Indians. They're fighting up and down the river."

Mercy saw Alex's eyes narrow. "Gentlemen, I tried to ask nicely, but now I'm going to tell you outright. This isn't the kind of conversation I want my sister-in-law to have to endure. Please refrain from discussion on this matter until you're in the smoking cabin."

The waiter appeared with the next course, a creamed soup with a heavenly aroma. He placed a bowl in front of Mercy and then Alex, while another waiter on the opposite side of the table serviced the stunned gentlemen.

"We meant no harm," one of the men said as the waiters departed. He had the decency to appear embarrassed. "We're very sorry, Miss."

The older man nodded at her. "We didn't mean to offend."

Mercy gave a slight nod in return and focused on her dinner, although she'd lost her appetite despite the inviting appearance and scent of the soup.

Maybe I've made a terrible mistake. Maybe I shouldn't go to the mission. Perhaps we could just remain on the ship and send word to Isaac. But even as she considered all of this, Mercy knew she couldn't refuse Eletta's cry for help.

She continued to consider all that she'd heard as she picked at her dinner. When Alex was finally finished, she put her napkin aside as well and rose from the table without a word. They said nothing as they made their way back to their cabin, but once they were behind closed doors, Alex asked Mercy to sit.

"I think it's best we talk about this. I have no idea what is truth and what's exaggeration regarding the Indian wars, but you and I both know there's been ongoing trouble, and so long as the government is bent on this campaign of exterminating the Indians, there's going to continue to be trouble."

"It's not just going to go away, I know that." Mercy picked at some lint on her skirt. "But I also know Grace and Hope will be worried sick when news reaches them. Even so, Alex, I don't feel it's right to abandon Eletta. She has Faith to worry about, and Isaac can't be both there and out trying to minister to the Indians. Of course, that's probably a moot point if things are truly as bad as those men say."

Alex pulled out his bag and opened it. "I was going to wait until we reached Port Orford, but Hope wanted you to have this." He produced Hope's Colt pocket revolver.

Mercy looked at the gun for a moment. "I don't know if I could ever shoot someone, even if they were attacking me."

He smiled. "I told Hope and Grace the same thing. We all know how tenderhearted you are. Still, it might be enough to scare off an attacker. In the worst situation, you could always aim to wound them so that you could get away. You do know how to handle it, right? Hope said she'd taught you."

"She did, and I know well enough. I still don't know that I want to take it."

"It would give your sisters considerable peace of mind if you would. It's one of those things you might never need, but if the situation is bad and you do need it . . . well, I think you'll be glad Hope thought of it."

Mercy tried to imagine herself in a situation where she might need the revolver. She knew she'd rather die than kill someone or even wound them.

"I'll take it, but I don't foresee myself using it." She took the revolver and felt the heaviness of it in her hand. It seemed such a small thing, and yet it could end a man's life in the blink of an eye. The weight of this thought burdened her. It was a responsibility she wouldn't take it lightly.

Chapter

3

I saac, I think you're making a mistake." Adam Browning watched his brother closely. They sat together at the table in the mission house. "Bringing a city girl here to help is going to be more trouble than it's worth."

"Mercy is hardly a city girl. She endured the Oregon Trail and a great deal more. It's true I haven't seen her since we left Oregon City, but I'm sure she's capable."

Adam ran his fingers through his coal-black hair. "But what if she isn't? What if she's all lace and frills? We don't need that here. None of us have time to watch over her. Besides that, I can't imagine many white women living comfortably in the midst of the native people. She might come here with all sorts of prejudices and cause our hard work to be completely upended."

Isaac looked at him with an amused smile. "You sound mighty worried about this."

"I am. Bringing this woman here is bound to spell trouble. She'll be more work for all of us."

"Look, I prayed this through. Eletta needs someone to help her until the baby is born."

"But the Tututni women are happy to help. The tribe has been good to Eletta—to all of us."

"Yes, but Eletta knows Mercy and her sisters, and it would give her added comfort. Maybe when you have a wife of your own, you'll understand."

Adam frowned and turned his focus back to the slate boards he was cleaning. "I just hope she won't prove to be silly and scared of her own shadow."

Isaac laughed. "I've never known any of the Flanagan sisters to be frightened of much, nor were they fussy or ridiculous. Although the middle one, Hope, was flirty and a bit silly when she was young."

Adam shook his head. "We especially don't need flirty."

This made Isaac laugh even harder. "Who would she flirt with? You? Maybe that's what's got you all bothered about having her here."

"I'm not worried about her flirting with me. I just don't want to be surrounded by silly women. You know as well as I do that this is a hard life." Adam stood and put the stack of slate boards away. "If she comes here only to find life too difficult, then she'll fuss and fret until you take her back to her people. We haven't got time for that."

Isaac sobered and pulled on his coat. "I appreciate your concern, Adam, but I assure you that Mercy Flanagan won't fuss and fret. Besides, we don't even know if she'll be able to come. By now she could have gone and gotten herself married. News travels slow around here." He opened the door. "I'll be gone for at least two weeks. I know you understand what's needed while I'm away, but I want to show you a couple of projects we need to address before the cold sets in."

Adam nodded and took up his own coat. "I know there's plenty to tend to."

Isaac was talking about the tasks they would need to accomplish, but Adam's mind was on the young woman who might join them soon. He didn't know why the idea struck him as such a bad one. Usually he trusted his older brother's decision making, but this time Adam couldn't help but feel concerned. Life at the mission was a hard but good life if you didn't mind its more primitive setting. Even he had found adjusting to the isolation a little difficult. Coming from back east, where towns were plentiful and well supplied, life on the Rogue River had been a rude awakening. Here, no matter what you needed, you had to make, grow, or find it for yourself. Supplies could be had, of course, but they had to be ordered well in advance and then picked up downriver on the coast. He couldn't imagine most women being content without stores and conveniences to make their lives easier. Mercy Flanagan would find her work cut out for her here, and Adam hated to think of what would happen if she proved to be too weak or ill-tempered to be useful.

He sighed and shook his head. He just had a feeling that this Flanagan woman was going to cause a great deal of upheaval. As far as he was concerned, she already had, and she hadn't even arrived.

Mercy hadn't known what to expect of Port Orford. As the only main port between Astoria and San Francisco, she had imagined it to be larger than most coastal towns. Instead she found a series of docks and a small number of buildings that constituted the "town." Beyond this were numerous houses and tents, but overall the place was rather disappointing . . . and very dirty.

But it's better than being on the ship.

The weather had turned stormy, and their last day at sea had left her feeling queasy. Thankfully the seas had calmed and the winds died down just long enough for them to make their destination, but already the weather was worsening, with a cold steady rain soaking them to the skin.

"Looks like the customs office is this way," Alex said, raising his voice as the wind began to blow.

Mercy nodded and bent her head toward the ground. She kept her eyes on the back of Alex's boots to avoid rain blowing in her face. The building was close to the dock as expected, but not near enough that they could avoid being soaked clear through by the time they reached it. Mercy was thankful for the refuge and was even more grateful when the man in charge led her to the stove so she could warm up and dry out.

"We're looking for Isaac Browning," she heard Alex tell the customs agent as she held her wet gloved hands toward the stove.

"He's been here several times today," the man replied. "I expect him back almost anytime." He paused and pointed out the window. "In fact, here he comes now."

Isaac was just as Mercy remembered him, albeit a little older. He was tall and muscular with broad shoulders, but it was his kind face that she remembered most. His was a gentle, welcoming expression that had always made her feel at ease. She smiled when he came to greet her.

"I'm so glad you've come," he said. "I heard from some of the volunteer militia that the ship was due in. I'm surprised you made such good time, what with the storm."

"I think it actually got us here faster," Alex said with a smile. He shook the water off his hat. "It was a rough passage this past twenty-four hours, and we weren't even sure we could make it into port."

"Well, you're on solid ground now. I was going to arrange for my people to canoe us to Ellensburg, but the seas have been rough for weeks."

Mercy was intrigued. "You have canoes capable of ocean travel?"

"Indeed, Miss Mercy. Long canoes created exactly for that purpose." Isaac paused and shook his head. "Goodness, but just look at you all grown up. You were just a little girl when I saw you last."

"It has been several years." Mercy felt chilled to the bone, and the stove was doing little to warm her up.

"We'd best get out of here. No sense drying out only to get drenched again." Isaac went to the door where the customs agent was speaking to one of the dock workers. "Would you please have their things delivered to the Hulls' right away?"

Both men confirmed this request, and Isaac led Mercy and Alex out into the rain.

"We have a regular army fort, of sorts," Isaac told them, pointing across the small group of buildings. "The Third Artillery are here to keep peace. There's also some Dragoons stationed here, and of course the civilian militia. Every miner who failed to strike it rich has joined up. Big money has been promised to any white man willing to slaughter Indians. Apparently the government is paying for murder now."

"What of the danger, Isaac?" Alex asked.

He shrugged. "The entire territory is in danger of attack. Nothing new about that, as you well know. If you're asking about the dangers for Mercy, I'd say they're minimal. Our people are loyal to us. It's not like things were at the Whitman Mission."

"That was exactly my concern," Alex said, sounding worried.

Isaac continued. "We've been here long enough to prove to them our support and truthfulness. I have no concern there. Some of the other area tribes are questionable, as they're known to war amongst themselves, but given the pressure put on them by the government, many have fled deeper into the mountains."

"You said other tribes." Mercy held the brim of her bonnet as the wind picked up. "I thought they were all Rogue River Indians."

"That's just a name given them by the whites. They call them Rogues or even Rascals. In truth, there are several tribes represented in the group called the Rogue River Indians. There are Shasta, Tututni, Takelma, Coquille, and Tolowa just to name a few, and within those tribes are subsets. The government finds it easier to just call them all Rogues."

"And what of your people?" Mercy lost her footing in the mud, but Alex righted her before she could fall. She smiled her thanks, and Alex gave a nod and smile in return. Isaac didn't seem to notice that anything was amiss and continued talking.

"Our people are the Tututni, with a few women from other tribes having married into their number. They treat us with great affection. Of course, that didn't come about overnight."

Alex looked skeptical. "Still, there's a lot of fighting going on, the way we've heard it."

"There is, but the reason I don't think Mercy will be in much danger is twofold. One, the worst attacks and killings are being done by the whites. No white man is going to harm a white woman, even in a mission setting where she's working with the Indians. And second, the area soldiers and militia know our people are peaceful, so there's no need for attack. Even with the tribal roundup, the officials have allowed our people to stay put. Eventually they'll force them to go north to the reservation as well, but for now they're leaving us alone.

"Not only that, but the really bad fighting is taking place on the other side of the mountains. That's where the army really started the roundup. There's a reservation there called Table Rock, but as I understand it, there's been nothing but difficulty in keeping the peace. Even so, the army makes regular treks upriver and throughout our area. So I'm not overly concerned about our safety."

Mercy took in this information and considered the days to come. Having overheard more than one conversation on the ship, she knew that the government leaders were set on containing the Indians so the whites could spread out and take over the land wherever they pleased.

"What about getting back to your mission?" Alex asked, bringing Mercy's attention back to the conversation. "Aren't the dangers increased if you travel by land?"

"I've arranged for us to go south with the army. We'll travel under heavy protection and large numbers, so I doubt there will be any danger. Alex, honestly, I wouldn't have agreed for Mercy to come had I thought there would be any real threat to her well-being. The government claims to have this situation all but wrapped up. They tell us that by spring, all of the tribes will be en route north. Eletta and I plan to go north as well. We intend to minister on the reservation. We can bring Mercy with us and arrange to get her home from there."

Alex looked around the tiny town. "I don't suppose there's a decent hotel here."

Isaac smiled for the first time. "I have something better. Friends who own a store and live on the backside of it. They have a couple cozy rooms over the store they've set up for guests. Seems someone is always coming or going and needs a room. If you'll follow me, I'll introduce you."

Sadie and Ephraim Hull were a generous and lively couple in their fifties. They welcomed Mercy and Alex as if they were long-lost relatives and treated them with great affection. Sadie's first order of business was to get Mercy dry and warm, and for that reason if nothing else, Mercy adored her. Now, an hour after their arrival, Sadie satisfied Mercy's remaining need by feeding them a hearty supper.

"Child, you need to eat more than the small bit you took," Sadie said, ladling more stew into Mercy's bowl.

"I've had so much already, but it is delicious." Mercy picked up her spoon again as Sadie turned her attention to Alex.

Alex made no protest at being given more food. "This is the best I've had since starting this trip," he told Sadie.

She laughed and gave him a wink. "Don't you go sweet-talking me. There's no need. I'll continue to put food on the table until you've had your fill, whether you praise it or not."

"It's her way," Ephraim said, as if anyone needed an explanation.

Sadie reclaimed her seat. "Any friend of Isaac's is a friend of ours."

Mercy appreciated the kindness more than she could say, but she was so tired, and the bed that awaited her upstairs was all she could think of.

"How's that brother of yours?" Sadie asked Isaac.

"Adam is doing well. He's taken to life at the mission as if he were born to it." Isaac turned to Alex and Mercy. In this setting, he was much more relaxed and lighthearted. "My younger brother Adam joined me a year ago last May. He felt God's calling to preach the gospel to the various Indian tribes here."

Mercy nodded. "Eletta said that in one of her letters earlier this year."

"He's been a tremendous help. There are often times when I must leave the mission, trips like this one either to retrieve supplies . . . or people." He smiled and continued. "I feel confident leaving Adam with Eletta and Faith. He, however, often travels into the surrounding areas to preach to some of the other tribes."

"What happens if you both need to be gone from the mission at the same time?" Alex asked.

Isaac took a drink of the hot coffee Sadie had served before answering. "I have had to leave the girls there alone, but the Tututni provided safety and assistance in every way. I'm not afraid to leave Eletta and Faith there when it's absolutely necessary."

"That truly speaks to your confidence in the natives there," Alex said. "I can't imagine you leaving them if there was a threat."

"Indeed no." Isaac turned back to Sadie, smiling. "Adam sends his love and a request for your sourdough bread. And he said if you were feeling particularly generous, he'd love some of your shortbread as well."

The older woman chuckled. "I guess I'd best get to baking."

"The army won't be ready to leave for several days," Isaac reminded her, "so I think you'll have plenty of time."

"I'd love to help you." Mercy wasn't sure if Sadie would welcome her offer or not, but she felt compelled to make it all the same. "This sourdough bread was delicious, and I've never made shortbread. I'd love to learn your recipe."

"Your help and company would be much appreciated. Adam can eat his weight in shortbread," Sadie replied. "We'll get started on it in the morning."

"Tell me more about this brother of yours," Alex said to Isaac, finishing off the contents in his bowl. He picked up a piece of Sadie's sourdough bread and sopped up the remaining broth.

"He's grown up to be quite a credit to our family. He graduated from Harvard after studying theology and European history. After that, he returned to our native Georgia, where he immediately went to work with a longtime friend of the family."

"Doing what?" Alex asked.

"Preaching. He has a definite passion to see the lost brought to salvation," Isaac replied. "Adam's brilliant, much smarter than I ever was. He earned top marks in all of his classes and memorized a large portion of Scripture. Not only that, he has a way of speaking and teaching that draws folks to him. His love of the Word is evident in all of his sermons."

Mercy covered a yawn, then asked, "Is he your only sibling?"

"No. We have two sisters between us. Adam and I are bookends, our mother used to say. Our sisters are married with children of their own. They both still live in Georgia." He shook his head. "I haven't seen them in nearly ten years."

"And your folks?" Alex asked, pushing back his bowl.

"Both are gone now."

Fighting another yawn, Mercy bowed her head. She didn't want to be rude, but if she didn't excuse herself soon, she was going to fall asleep at the table.

"I think our young gal here needs a bed more than a piece of pie," Sadie declared. "Am I right?"

Mercy looked up and nodded. "I do apologize. I didn't sleep much last night, what with the storm. However, I don't want to leave you to clean up by yourself."

"Nonsense." Sadie got up from the table. "You come along with me. I'll show you the washroom and where the privy is. You have a basin in your room if the need arises in the night."

Following on feet that felt leaden, Mercy bid the others good night. Sadie rambled on about the house, but none of it made a bit of sense to Mercy. After a few minutes, Sadie seemed to realize this and just smiled.

She picked up a lighted candle in a decorative tin from a small table in the hall and handed it to Mercy. "Get on upstairs with you, and don't you worry about waking up any too soon. There will no doubt be plenty of ruckus going on in the store, which is right under your room, but we won't open until seven, so you should have plenty of time to get your sleep out."

"Thank you so much. I appreciate all that you've done."

"Pshaw! Ain't nothin' to it. Just doing what the Lord would have us do. Feeding the hungry, giving drink to the thirsty."

Mercy smiled. "And a bed to the exhausted."

A week later, Alex prepared to board *The Calliope* and return to Oregon City. The weather had been bad enough to keep everyone under cover, but now that the worst seemed to have passed, everyone was eager to get on with their business. With the sun warming the air and drying out the ground, the army too was anxious to be on the move.

Mercy hated to admit it, but Alex's plan to return home made her uncomfortable. She knew he longed to be with Grace and the children, and to get back to his work at the lumber mill. No doubt Uncle Edward missed his help. Still, it was hard to see him go. Sadie and Ephraim had been wonderful company, and Isaac was always kind and considerate of her needs, but Alex was her last connection to her sisters. At no time in her life had Mercy been separated from both of them as she was now.

She didn't want to worry Alex. He'd been so good to come this far with her. She would just have to be strong. Tears threatened, but she was determined not to cry. "Don't forget to give Hope and Grace their letters from me."

Alex patted his pocket. "I have them right here, along with the shortbread you made."

She swallowed the lump in her throat. "Tell them I'll be home in the spring."

He smiled and put his hand on her shoulder. "You're going to be just fine. I might have had questions coming down here, but I've been praying about it, and God's given me peace. I think you're going to be amazed at what He shows you here."

"I'm sure you're right. Oh, I nearly forgot." Mercy reached into her pocket. "This letter is for Beth. I tried to write her some words of encouragement. I'd like you to read it, Alex. If you think it the wrong advice, then just discard it. Otherwise, I'd appreciate it if you could deliver it to her."

"I will." He reached into his coat and put the letter with the others. He gave Mercy a smile. "Don't look so forlorn. God's got you right where He wants you."

"Looks like they're ready for you to come aboard, Alex,"

Isaac announced, coming to join them. "Tell your wife and sister-in-law that Mercy is in good hands. Between me and Adam, she'll be well cared for."

Alex and Isaac shook hands, then embraced almost as an afterthought. "Mercy's not nearly the trouble her sisters are," Alex declared. He threw her a teasing smile. "She's the calmest of the three Flanagan sisters."

Isaac actually laughed. "I know it well. Thanks again for all the supplies you brought down. Adam will be glad for the McGuffey Readers, and Eletta will cherish the flannel."

"We're glad to help." Alex turned back to Mercy to embrace her. "I love you, little sister. You'll be in my prayers."

Mercy stood nodding as he let her go. She knew Alex was right. She was where she needed to be—where God wanted her. Now if she could just get on with the job of caring for Eletta and Faith, Mercy knew she'd finally feel settled.

Chapter 4

The army was ready to march two days later. Mercy had heard one of the soldiers say it was only about twenty miles to Gold Beach as the crow might fly, but it would be much longer on foot. There were hills and rocky crags to be managed, not to mention thick forested land that looked like no man had ever gone there before. Isaac had thought they might be able to board a shallow draft schooner and sail to Gold Beach, but then the weather turned cold and rainy again, with winds that drove the dampness into one's bones.

Mercy was grateful for her heavy wool coat and sturdy boots. She had very carefully chosen the things she brought with her, and was glad now that Grace had insisted she take gloves and a scarf. She feared that as the days passed, the temperature would continue to drop.

"Looks like they're ready to head out," Isaac said, returning to her side after speaking to one of the officers. "The army's found a place for your trunk, as well as all my supplies."

Mercy had put her most needed possessions in a knapsack that she wore slung over her shoulder. In it she also carried

Hope's revolver, figuring it wouldn't be much use to her if it was packed away in her trunk.

"Some of the Gold Beach militia are heading back with us." Isaac motioned to several men with packs and rifles on their backs. "They can be a rowdy bunch, so I'd avoid contact with them if I were you."

Mercy noticed that one handsome bearded man seemed to be watching her. When her eyes met his, he grinned. Mercy looked away.

"How long will it take to get back to the mission from Ellensburg?" She could feel the warmth in her face despite the cold.

"That'll depend on arranging a ride up the river. There's always someone going up the Rogue. Miners or militia usually, but it shouldn't be too hard to trade goods for a ride. Especially since I can help paddle. Once we're on the river, it shouldn't take us much more than a day."

She nodded and tried to keep her thoughts focused, but the man who'd smiled at her was making his way toward them.

"Mr. Browning," he said, reaching them, "remember me? I'm Billy Caxton."

Isaac stiffened. "I do. I see you and your friends are heading back to Ellensburg with us."

"Yeah, we got picked to retrieve supplies. Store there was out of most everything. Especially ammunition."

Mercy could tell that Isaac was being guarded with his words. Billy, on the other hand, had no difficulty speaking his mind.

"I saw you standing here with this pretty little gal and figured I should come and make her acquaintance."

Isaac cast a sidelong glance at Mercy. "This is Miss Flanagan, a good friend of our family. She's come to help my wife. Mercy, I believe you heard his introduction. This is William Caxton."

"Billy to my friends." He swept off his hat and gave a bow. "Miss Flanagan, this is purely a pleasure. I do hope you'll stay for a long while. The mission isn't all that far from one of our camps."

"Mr. Caxton." She gave him a nod but refrained from saying anything more. She had no desire to mislead him or make him think her a flirt. It was bad enough he'd caught her looking at him. Worse yet was the sense of danger that seemed to accompany him.

"I have to say, we haven't had a pretty gal like you around for some time," Billy continued.

"Billy, you'd better get back over here and tend to business," one of his cohorts called from across the yard.

Mercy breathed a sigh of relief when Billy tipped his hat and turned to go. She was about to speak to Isaac when Billy stopped and whirled back to face her.

"I plan to see to it that we become good friends." He grinned in his self-confident manner then finally rejoined his friends.

Mercy looked at Isaac, who wore an expression of distaste. "Is something wrong?"

He shook his head. "I've never cared for that young man. He's trouble, and I hope you'll steer clear of him."

"You needn't worry. I have no interest in Mr. Caxton whatsoever." She felt some satisfaction in having her feeling of danger confirmed. He might have a handsome face, but it was the heart that mattered. Her grandmother used to say, *"Handsome is as handsome does."* Only time would tell if Billy's dashing good looks came with an equally good heart. Mercy didn't hold out much interest or hope. Isaac didn't like him, and there had to be good reason.

Unfortunately, in the days to come, despite her guarded response, Billy Caxton seemed anxious to deepen their acquaintance. He often appeared in step beside her on the trail, regaling her with stories of his adventures in the wilds of Oregon and California. Because of the bad weather and poor trails, the journey seemed to take forever.

"There's plenty of gold to be had," Billy told her for the tenth time. "When we get this Indian trouble under control, we can get back to doin' what we came for."

Mercy didn't want to encourage the conversation but found herself questioning him before she gave it much thought. "What is your part in these 'Indian troubles,' as you call them?"

"Plenty. My friends and me are part of the private militia. Government's payin' us good money to kill Indians."

She had tried to keep her thoughts and feelings to herself on this trip, but his comment sent a shiver down her spine. Billy mistook it for fear.

"You don't need to be afraid, Miss Flanagan. I'll protect you."

"I'm not afraid. I find your attitude distasteful."

He frowned. "So I suppose you're an Injun lover like your friends the Brownings?"

"I neither love nor hate them."

"That's because you haven't experienced what they can do. If ever you see up close how they steal and murder, you'd change your tune."

She stopped and fixed him with a look of disdain. "Mr. Caxton, you know nothing about what I have or haven't experienced. I urge you to keep your judgments to yourself." She picked up her pace again, hoping he'd get the idea and leave her be.

"No, I don't know much about you," he said, easily matching her stride, "but I want to. I think I've plum lost my heart to you. Fact is, I'm dyin' of love for you." He leaned in as if to steal a kiss.

She gave him a push so hard that he landed on his backside. "Well, do your dying somewhere else." She walked away as Billy's companions laughed.

Isaac hurried to her side, casting several backward glances at the militiamen. "Is there a problem?"

Mercy looked over her shoulder just to make sure Isaac hadn't seen something she'd missed. Billy was back on his feet, but he stared after her with a look of shock and anger. Given his handsome looks, Mercy figured he wasn't used to rejection.

"No. No problem. I was just replying to something Mr. Caxton said."

"If he's bothering you, Mercy, I'll have a talk with him."

She looked up and smiled. "That isn't necessary. He's not saying anything I haven't heard before. I'll be glad when this territory starts bringing in as many single women as they do sheep and cattle."

Isaac laughed. "I'm sure Billy Caxton feels the same way."

"He's not shy about sharing his feelings, that's for sure. He holds the native people a grudge."

"And do you feel the same?"

It was an honest question, and coming from Isaac, Mercy knew the intent was only to learn her heart on the matter. Not to condemn or approve her one way or the other.

"At one time I did truly hate them for they'd done to us at the Whitman Mission." She frowned and pushed aside the memories that were ever at the back of her mind. "But I can honestly say that God has helped me to better understand their plight. The trial five years ago to condemn the men responsible for the massacre left me with a sour taste in my mouth where revenge is concerned. I can't see that it helps anything, and instead I actually pity the Indians. I suppose that's something Mr. Caxton will never understand."

"No, I don't imagine so," Isaac replied, sobering. "A friend of his was killed down on the Rogue River. It was a misunderstanding over a bottle of liquor, as I understand it, but the man who shot his friend was a Shasta brave. It set Billy on a path of revenge, I'm afraid."

"So that's why he's trouble?"

"That and other things I've heard. He doesn't respect folks, and he certainly has no interest in God. In fact, he seems to pride himself on thwarting God and our efforts for peace. He's put out rumors among the tribes that we're only here to steal their children and souls."

"I figured as much." She hugged her arms close to fight the chill of the damp wind. "I hope we can have a fire tonight. I'm nearly frozen."

Isaac glanced around the wooded area they were marching through. "I doubt it. The captain said there's been trouble just to the east. I'm sure they'll want to keep a cold camp so as not to attract attention. A fire might bring some Indians to see what's happening. If they're hostile, they might make trouble. And if they're friendly . . . well, Billy and his friends will make trouble."

Mercy could see the worry in Isaac's expression. For all his talk about their safety, she knew he was concerned. She glanced at the dark woods, wondering what dangers lurked there. She couldn't help but think back to the Whitman Mission. It had been this same time of year when the massacre took place. She shivered again and bit her lower lip. Would she soon find herself in the same situation as she'd been in that November?

She'd only been a child—still recovering from a bout of measles. The same measles that had taken the life of so many of the Cayuse people. Especially the children. Dr. Whitman had been unable to save very many of the Indians, and they blamed him. In fact, Chief Telokite had accused Whitman of actually poisoning his people. It was this that had led to the attack—at least it was the excuse given.

Determined not to focus on such horrors, Mercy began to pray. As always, she prayed that God would protect those she loved and that somehow the Indians and whites could learn to live in harmony. It didn't seem like too much to ask. After all,

God had created both, and He was all-powerful. Surely He would want them to live in peace as well. Wouldn't He?

~~~~~

Gold Beach was not that different from Port Orford, just smaller. Businesses and unpainted homes left little doubt the whites had established the area for themselves. Here, Mercy found even more miners turned volunteer militiamen and an ever-growing hatred of any and all Indians. Two men had even taken it upon themselves to start building a fort with an earthen barrier for protection, although most people in town thought it unnecessary.

The townsfolk seemed friendly enough. There were a few families in the immediate area, and still others on farms nearby. The greater part of the population, however, were men who had come to mine the area for gold. Mercy had more than her share of attention and was relieved when Isaac told her they'd immediately head upriver. She was less enthusiastic, however, when she found out that Billy Caxton would be traveling with them. In fact, it was Billy and his friends who had the canoes and had offered to transport Mercy and Isaac for free. One of their volunteer militia camps was set up at Big Bend, not all that far from the Browning mission, so it seemed only logical to accept their offer.

"I would prefer other company." The look on Isaac's face said it all. He shook his head. "But the army isn't heading upriver for a couple more weeks, and I feel we must get back to the mission. Eletta is ever on my mind."

Mercy understood and assured him it was the right thing to do. She could endure Billy's attention a bit longer if it meant putting Isaac's mind at ease.

With the constant rain and wind, the river was difficult to navigate and made travel arduous. At least this kept Billy too busy worrying about paddling to bother Mercy. If there were any reason to thank God for a storm, it was this.

Mercy spent most of her time huddling under a waxed canvas cloth. The cloth helped keep her dry and warm, but only marginally. Still, as she looked out on the banks of the river, she found herself captivated by the changing landscape. Flat fields and marshy grounds gave way to rolling hills and steep banks. Large rocks and occasional rapids gave the boatmen plenty of obstacles. At one point, things became so difficult that Billy and his men decided to make camp along the river and wait out the storm. Mercy wasn't happy at this, but no one consulted her on the matter.

To avoid Billy, Mercy remained faithfully at Isaac's side. Thankfully, Billy seemed focused on other issues. The men were concerned about Indian attacks and each took turns standing guard over the camp in case of trouble. The rest slept with their rifles at their sides.

The next morning, the weather had calmed, and the militiamen reloaded the boats. This time Billy gave Mercy plenty of attention and told her stories of his exploits on the river. At least he no longer spoke of his love for her.

"Just up there a ways," he told her, "was where I found my first gold. This whole place is just a gold mine waiting to be gleaned. I'm telling you, Miss Mercy, a man can make his fortune here."

"But at what price, Mr. Caxton?" she asked even though she hadn't wanted to engage in the conversation.

"Well, any price is worth what a man can haul in from the river. The gold is there to be had, and if not for the Indians, I'd already be a rich man, and you might agree to court me."

"No amount of riches would entreat me to court you, Mr. Caxton. I'm only here to help at the mission, and then I'll return home." She turned from him. "I believe I'll rest now." She pulled the canvas around her and closed her eyes. Billy didn't challenge her.

When they finally reached the place where one of many creeks poured into the Rogue River, Isaac announced that they were home. High up on the bank, Mercy could see native women and children. It was her first glimpse of the native people here save the Indian women who had been married to the white miners back in town. She put her hand to her brow to search for Eletta, but there was no sign of her. Of course, given all that Isaac had told her, Eletta was probably too weak to come and welcome them.

Isaac helped Mercy from the canoe and handed over her knapsack. "Just leave the trunk and crates here on the bank," he instructed the militiamen.

"We'll help you out," Billy volunteered. He hoisted Mercy's trunk onto his shoulder as if it weighed nothing. "Boys, lend us a hand and bring those supplies," he commanded, looking back at the men in the canoes. He turned to Isaac and Mercy with a smile. "See there? All settled. Now lead the way."

Mercy didn't like Billy having anything to do with her trunk. It made her feel obligated to him, and she definitely didn't want that responsibility.

Isaac took hold of Mercy's elbow. "The climb's a bit steep, but it's a comfort to be up there when the river floods."

"I'm sure. I've lived in river towns most of my life, so I know very well the dangers." She hoisted up her skirt and began the climb.

It proved to be rather slippery due to the rain, and Mercy lost her footing more than once. Isaac took it in stride. He was obviously used to it and managed the path with little trouble. Once they reached the top of the bank, Mercy gazed around her in wonder. Tall evergreens, oaks, and red alder surrounded the clearing. There were two log cabins to the right, one bigger than the other. Beyond that were multiple Indian dwellings—houses of long wood planks built half underground. Mercy had never seen anything like it.

"This is our home," Isaac said, pointing to the first cabin. "The smaller one is the church, which we also use for the school. It's mainly just one large room, but we attached a small room on the back for Adam."

"Where do you want this trunk?" Billy asked. He glanced around with an expression of disgust but said nothing.

"I'll take it." Isaac handed Mercy his pack and took the trunk from Billy. "Thanks again for getting us home and for toting this up the bank. We're obliged." Isaac motioned to the men who followed with the mission's supplies. "Have your men just leave the crates here." With that taken care of, he headed for the house.

Mercy started to follow, but Billy put himself between her and Isaac and gave an exaggerated bow.

"I was happy to help. Where there's a pretty gal involved, I like to make myself useful. Especially when they pack a punch like you." His expression was approving as he looked her over from top to toe. "I like aggressive women with fire in their bellies."

Mercy frowned. "I hope you find one." She walked around him and headed to the house.

Thankfully, Isaac waited for her at the door. He wore a look of annoyance that matched Mercy's feelings. "I'm going to have to talk with him, I can tell."

"Don't bother. He's all noise and feathers, as my grandmother used to say. Like a rooster strutting and crowing to get the attention of the hens."

"Yes, but roosters have spurs and can be mighty dangerous. We have one here that will take after you in a heartbeat if you aren't careful. It's wise to carry a big stick." He grinned. "You might need it for Billy too."

Mercy smiled. "I'll try to find one."

Inside the cabin, Mercy marveled at the homey arrangement. The large front room held a kitchen on the left side and a sitting area on the right with a stone fireplace and large rag rug. A bench was positioned on one side of the hearth and two chairs on the other. Here and there were shelves holding a variety of books and personal items. On the back wall were two doors. Both were open.

"That's our bedroom," Isaac said, pointing to the right. "Yours will be with Faith over there." He led the way to the left door. "I imagine Faith is over at the school. They should be about done for the day." He put her trunk just inside the room. "I'll let Eletta know we're home."

"I'd really like to see Eletta, if I may."

Isaac nodded. "Why don't you unpack and familiarize yourself with the house first? I'll go see how she's feeling and let her know everything that's happened."

"Of course."

Isaac left her, and Mercy turned to survey the room. There were two neatly made rope beds on either side of a small, oval rag rug. Positioned between the head of the beds was a wooden chest with two drawers. Atop the chest were several candle stubs and tin holder, a wooden cross, and a hairbrush. One bed had been made up with a crazy quilt of many colors. A small doll lay upon the pillow. It was the only sign that the room belonged to a child. The other bed had a simple quilt of greens and blues in star patterns.

Figuring this to be her bed, Mercy pulled her trunk close and sat down. Looking around the log room for a moment more, she wondered what the future held in store. She thought of her sisters so far away and waited for a sense of sadness to wash over her. When the feeling didn't come, she smiled. It was proof once again that she was exactly where she was meant to be.

She had just set her knapsack on the bed when Isaac appeared at the door. "Eletta wants very much to see you."

Mercy got to her feet. "Of course. I'm glad she's feeling up to it."

She followed Isaac to the couple's bedroom. Eletta sat propped up in bed with a smile on her pale face. Mercy returned the smile and moved to her side.

"I can hardly believe you're little Mercy Flanagan," Eletta said, shaking her head. "I remember you as just a little bitty thing when we were coming west."

"Well, that was eight years ago. I've done a lot of growing up since then."

"Of course you have, and look at how pretty you are. Grace must be so proud of how you've turned out. She said you were a tremendous help to her. I hated that you should have to leave her to come here and care for me."

"It's all right. I was in need of an adventure." Mercy glanced toward Isaac. "I want to make myself as useful as possible to both of you, so just let me know what needs to be done."

Eletta sighed. "Most everything. I can no longer teach the children, and although Adam has been filling in for me, he's anxious to be out ministering."

"I'd be happy to take on the teaching. The household chores too." Mercy smiled. "And Grace has sent me with all her best concoctions, so we'll soon have you as right as rain."

Eletta smiled, but it didn't quite reach her eyes. "That is my deepest desire."

Chapter 5

"Adam, Papa's back. Bright Star told me." Seven-year-old Faith all but danced around the schoolroom as she made her announcement.

Having dismissed school early that day, Adam was surprised his niece had returned. "I thought you were spending the afternoon with your friends making baskets at Red Deer's house."

"I was, but she sent me to get the rushes from Bright Star. When I went to her house, she told me there were canoes downriver, and Papa was in one of them."

"Thanks for letting me know." He cleaned off a piece of slate he'd used to teach English words. "And what about Miss Mercy? Was she with them also?" He almost wished the child would tell him no.

"Bright Star said there was a lady with him, so I think it must be Miss Mercy."

Adam smiled, refusing to let Faith see his apprehension. "I've almost finished here. What say I leave the rest for later, and we'll go greet them?"

Faith gave an enthusiastic nod. "I know Mama will be happy. She's been feeling so bad."

Adam knew only too well. He usually slept here at the school, but with Isaac away, he had been compelled to stay in their house. He was more than a little worried about Eletta, who had only grown weaker in Isaac's absence.

He walked with Faith to the larger cabin, hoping Isaac was right about bringing Mercy Flanagan in to help. It wouldn't do any of them any good if she turned out to be flighty and silly. He couldn't abide women who displayed either of those traits. But to be honest, over the last few years, he hadn't abided women at all.

"Papa!" Faith stormed into the cabin like a whirlwind. "Papa, where are you?"

Inside, Adam was surprised to find their visitor already at work in the kitchen. She'd rolled up her sleeves and had an apron on over a simple brown cotton dress. Her shapely figured moved with grace as she tackled one thing and then another. It was clear she was used to such tasks. At the sound of Faith's bellowing, however, she stopped to watch.

Isaac stepped into the main room, which elicited a squeal from Faith. She ran the short distance and threw herself into her father's arms. He lifted her into the air and whirled her around. Adam smiled. He often did the same when greeting her.

"I missed you so much," Faith said, giving Isaac several kisses on the cheek as the twirling stopped.

"I missed you too. And I brought you a present." He reached into his pocket and pulled out a peppermint stick. "Mrs. Hull said I should give this to you. I've had a dickens of a time keeping it dry."

"Thank you, Papa! I love peppermint."

He smiled. "I know." He chucked her under the chin and put her down. "I have some other things for you in our supplies, but they'll have to wait. First I want you both to meet someone very special."

Adam turned to their visitor and was startled to find her watching him with great interest. When Isaac and Eletta had first mentioned Mercy Flanagan, he had worried about her character and ability to work hard. But he'd also figured her to be a stodgy old maid, homely and perhaps unkempt. After all, she was twenty years old and unmarried. There were few single women in the territory, so he figured there had to be something wrong with her if she was still single. But seeing her now, Adam realized just how wrong he had been. He felt dumbstruck. She was beautiful.

"Adam, Faith, this is Miss Mercy Flanagan."

Mercy stepped forward and flashed a smile. "I'm pleased to meet you both."

"My mama says you were just a little girl like me when she first met you," Faith said.

"I was a little older, but she's right. We met on the trail west. It was a very long walk, to be sure, and your mama and papa became our very good friends."

Faith nodded. "And now you can be my good friend."

"I'd like that very much."

Mercy looked up and met Adam's gaze. He'd never seen eyes the color of hers before. They were like the turquoise stones he'd seen in Indian jewelry when he'd been in the south on his trip here.

"Miss Flanagan, it's nice to meet you." He tried to keep his voice formal—aloof. He didn't want to appear overly friendly. Women could be such strange creatures and often read far more into a smile than was ever intended.

"It's very nice to finally meet you both. But please just call

me Mercy. I can't see that formalities will be at all useful here."
She smiled and looked back at Faith. "That goes for you too.
Just think of me like a big sister."

Adam could see that Faith was happy about this, but in his
own mind he couldn't imagine thinking of Mercy Flanagan as
his sister. Not when she had the face of an angel and eyes that
he could lose himself in for hours.

*This is much too dangerous and will only lead to trouble if
I keep letting myself think this way.*

Adam knew his loneliness and disappointments of the past
were working against him where Mercy Flanagan was concerned. He was definitely going to have to guard his heart, or
he would find himself in the same predicament he had back in
Boston—and no one wanted that. Especially not him.

"That was one of the best meals I've had since Eletta took
sick," Isaac said, patting his stomach. "I've always loved veni-
son stew."

"Well, Mrs. Hull's sourdough bread was the real treat,"
Mercy said, clearing away some of the dishes. "I'm glad she
sent me with a starter so I can make my own." She looked at
Adam with a smile. "Good thing you made the request, or I
might never have learned to make it. Or the shortbread." She
held out her hand for his bowl.

"You helped make the shortbread?"

He'd been aloof all through the meal, so his question surprised Mercy. "I did. I hope you liked it."

He said nothing, instead lifting his coffee mug and taking
a long drink. Mercy didn't know what to make of him. Adam
Browning was certainly nothing like she had envisioned. For one
thing, he was much younger. For another, she hadn't expected
him to be quite so handsome. She'd never considered Isaac

handsome and had presumed his younger brother would be of similar looks. But while there were similarities, there were also differences. Adam was leaner, more muscular. His eyes were a dark hazel color, where Isaac's were brown.

"How about that, Adam? If we can get the butter, you can have shortbread whenever you like." Isaac got up from the table. "I'm going to check on Eletta and see if she's ready yet to take a little food."

"Can you make pies?" Faith asked, helping Mercy clear the table.

"I can. Do you like pies?" She smiled at the young girl. She enjoyed Faith's vivacious spirit. It livened things up considerably.

Faith nodded. "So does Adam. His favorite is blackberry."

"I—" Mercy started to say that it was her favorite as well, then stopped. "Do you have blackberries here?" She thought Adam might answer, but he continued to nurse his coffee.

Faith nodded. "Mama planted them when I was just a baby. She said there are some wild berries too, but she wanted her own bushes. They're all picked now, but I'll show you where they are, and next year you can help pick them too."

Mercy didn't want to point out that she wouldn't be here come late summer when the berries would be ripe. Instead, she gathered the remaining dishes and motioned to Faith. "Can you help me wash up?"

"Yes. I always help." Faith stood next to Mercy in front of the tub of boiled water and lye soap.

"I'll wash and you dry. How about that?"

Faith giggled. "That's just like I do it with Mama and Adam."

Mercy nodded. "Good. Just give me a minute to set up a bucket to rinse them in." She was reaching to pick up the bucket of hot water on the floor when Adam appeared next to her.

"Let me." He hoisted the bucket up onto the counter. With that done, he took several steps back, away from her. "I'll take my leave now. I hope you don't find our accommodations too primitive, Miss Flanagan. I'm sure after living in a proper town, you'll be disappointed in our meager fare."

His comment took her by surprise and set her on the defense. "I've lived in places more primitive than this, I assure you." She hadn't meant to sound offended, but it clearly came out that way.

Adam frowned. "Then I'll be on my way." He headed for the door.

"Uncle Adam, you didn't kiss me good night."

He stopped and turned back to hold his arms out to Faith. Mercy focused on the tub of dishes. Adam's actions and open affection for Faith puzzled her. He seemed so hardened otherwise. In fact, he bordered on rudeness, and it brought out the worst in Mercy. For a moment she considered apologizing, but then decided against it. She was tired from her day's travel and longed only to clean up and go to bed. Maybe her negative perception of Adam was based solely on her state of exhaustion. Perhaps he was tired too.

When she heard the door close behind Adam, Mercy turned to see where Faith had gotten off to. Spying the open door to Eletta and Isaac's bedroom, she figured Faith had gone to see her mother. Eletta's illness and Faith's concern for her reminded Mercy of when her own mother had been dying. Mercy had been so afraid to be left alone with her mother for fear she'd die when no one else was around. Faith, of course, had no need to fear her mother's death. Eletta was only expecting a baby, and they'd soon have her back on her feet.

In a few minutes, Isaac and Faith came from the bedroom. "Eletta said to come see her when you're done," Isaac told Mercy. "She wants to discuss some things with you."

Mercy did her best to not look as tired as she felt. "Did you get her to eat anything?"

"A piece of shortbread." He shrugged. "I guess it's better than nothing. Now, if you'll excuse me, I need to speak to some of the Tututni men and let them know the state of things regarding the fighting." He pulled on his black coat and took his hat from a peg by the door. "If you have any questions, I'm sure Faith can help you."

"Thank you." Mercy looked at Faith and smiled. "I'm sure she can."

Once Isaac was gone, Mercy turned her attention back to the dishes while Faith took up a dish towel.

"Tell me about your school here. Your mama said she needs me to teach, so it might be nice to know what your classes are like."

"We have ten students," Faith replied. "They're all Tututni except for me. Oh, and two of the mothers come to learn too. Bright Star and Red Deer. Mama's been teaching all of them to read and write."

"I see. And do you like to read?"

Faith giggled. "I read a lot. Mama taught me when I was just a baby."

Mercy looked at the child in surprise. "A baby?"

"I was just two years old. Mama said I learned so fast she could hardly keep up with me." The little girl's smile widened. "I can read the Bible, and every day I write down words and look them up in the dictionary."

"Well, I've never heard of a child who learned to read so young. You must be very smart." She rinsed a plate and handed it to Faith. "Are you good at mathematics as well?"

"Not as much. I don't like numbers. I like stories."

Mercy agreed. "Stories are my favorite too. I've brought several books with me, in fact."

"Oh! May I read them?" Faith's eyes were wide in anticipation. "I haven't seen any new books for a long time."

"Of course. I think you'll enjoy them. Two are biographies.

One is about George Washington, our first president, and the other is about the old kings and queens of England. I have some others, but those two would perhaps interest you the most. I think it's always fun to read about other people."

"Me too." Faith stacked the dried plates and bowls.

Mercy hesitated a moment. She wanted to ask Faith about Adam but didn't want to appear overly curious. "Are you and your folks the only white people around this area?"

"Just us and Uncle Adam. Well, sometimes the soldiers and militia come here. I don't like them, though. They're always mean to the Tututni."

"I heard about the fighting when I was still back home. I suppose the soldiers have their orders from the government."

"Some of them aren't real soldiers," Faith added. "They're volunteers, and they can be very mean. They hate the Indians."

"I know. I ran into some men like that on our trip down here."

"You don't hate Indians, do you, Miss Mercy?"

"No. I used to when I was young, but that was because they killed some of my friends."

"So why don't you still hate them?" Faith watched her as if trying to figure out Mercy's heart.

"Well, I suppose the biggest reason I no longer hate them is that I learned to forgive and give all of my anger to God."

The little girl nodded. "That's good. The Tututni are very nice. I think you'll like them a lot. Adam says both sides of this fight have a lot to forgive and forget."

"Your uncle sounds wise."

Faith smiled. "He is, and he's so much fun. He's been teaching us at school since Mama took sick. He makes up all sorts of games to help the Tututni learn. He says it's important to help them understand our ways, but also for us to understand theirs. He spends a lot of time with them."

"And what do they think of that?"

"They love Uncle Adam! He's always helping them and talking to them. They invite him to eat with them all the time, and that's an honor. They don't invite just anyone to come into their house, and they only share meals with friends."

Mercy considered that for a moment. The man Faith described was nothing like the staid man who'd graced their table earlier. He'd barely conversed and certainly hadn't extended much of a welcome.

In no time at all, they had completed their task without the conversation leading back to Adam. Mercy decided against asking Faith anything more. No doubt in time she'd come to better understand him.

She untied her apron and draped it on the back of one of the chairs. She would deal with the wash water after she talked to Eletta. "I'd best go see your mother now."

"I'm going to practice my sewing. Mama's teaching me to make quilt blocks."

"That's wonderful. I like to sew and spin yarn and knit. Can you do those things too?"

Faith began to hop on one foot and turned her face to the floor. "Mama tried to teach me to spindle spin, but I'm not very good at it."

Mercy laughed. "I wasn't very good either—at first. My sister Hope taught me how to get better."

This brought Faith's head back up, and she smiled and kept hopping. "I wish I had a sister. Mama said maybe the baby would be a girl. I hope it is."

"I bet your papa would like a boy."

Faith did a little spin. She seemed to have a hard time staying still. "Yes, he says a boy would be just fine, but he'll take another girl. He just wants Mama to get well and for the baby to be well too."

"And so do I. I've brought some medicines with me that

63

should help your mama get well. Now, you go work on your quilt, and I'll go speak with your mother."

Mercy smiled as Faith hurried to her bedroom. It was hard to imagine the child getting much quilting done when she didn't seem to be able to sit or stand still for more than a minute.

Chapter
6

Eletta's door was open, so Mercy peeked inside. "Are you still awake?"

"I am. Please come in." Eletta sat up and reached for the pillow beside her.

Mercy quickly stepped forward and helped her position the pillow behind her. "How's that?"

"Perfect." Eletta smiled. "Oh, Mercy, I can't tell you how glad I am to have you here. It wasn't my idea to bring in help, but once Isaac started talking about it, I knew it was as if the Lord Himself had proposed it. We both almost immediately thought of you."

"I'm glad you asked me."

"Please pull up the chair and sit. We have so much we need to discuss."

Mercy did as she asked. "I'm sure you'll have plenty of time to teach me what I need to know. I don't want to over tire you." She didn't bother to mention that her own exhaustion was getting the better of her.

"I know I look a fright." Eletta put a hand to her hair, which had been plaited into a single braid. Its sandy color looked dull. "I haven't been able to wash my hair for so long."

"You don't look a fright, and as soon as you feel like it, I'll wash your hair for you," Mercy assured. "Tell me about the day-to-day running of your house and what you need me to do."

"Well, the Tututni women have been so good to help me. Of course, they have families of their own to worry about, but the wealthier have slaves."

"Slaves? Truly?" Mercy had never heard of such a thing.

Eletta nodded. "Many of the tribes embrace slavery. The more prosperous families take on poorer members of the tribe to work for them. Sometimes poorer members indenture themselves. They're treated well and given food and lodging. In many ways it's no different than employing servants in any other household. There are always those who treat everyone badly— slave or free—but the people here are very kind."

"I see." Mercy considered this for a moment. "So who is in charge of the tribe?"

"There are many chiefs. Any man with wealth can take on the title. The more prosperous he is, the more importance and power he has." Eletta smiled. "You'll see how it all works once you're out among the people. This group has received the gospel message quite well."

"That's wonderful to hear."

"And like I said, the women have been very helpful. They've washed clothes and brought up water and wood. Adam usually chops wood in his spare time. Sometimes it seems we can never have enough, especially now with the cooler temperatures."

Mercy thought it might be a good time to bring up Adam. "I'm sure Adam has plenty to do, and I'm pretty fair at chopping myself. If he doesn't have time, I can help with that as well."

"Isaac helps too, but he's usually busy. Sometimes just keeping the peace between the tribes gives him more than enough to manage. Nevertheless, I'm sure that compared to all you must have had to do at home, my small household will seem easy."

"I can easily handle cooking and cleaning, as well as sewing and washing clothes." Mercy hid her disappointment that the conversation had moved in a direction that didn't include Adam. She smiled and saw Eletta relax. "What about the school? Faith tells me there are ten children and two adults who attend. What level are they?"

"The children learn quickly and are eager to share their knowledge. Most read at a beginner's level, however. I'm so excited that your sister sent the McGuffeys. I also try to incorporate comparisons between their culture and ours, which will be harder for you, since you don't know their ways."

"I'm happy to learn." Mercy leaned back and felt the tension in her shoulders begin to fade. "Do you also teach them about America and our history?"

"I've shared a little, and now that Adam is teaching, I'm sure they're learning even more."

Mercy saw her opportunity. "Faith said Adam makes up games to help them learn. She said he's quite loved by the Tututni."

"It's hard not to love Adam. He's got such a generous and kind heart. I've never seen anyone save Isaac who held such sincere kindness for others. I doubt there's a person in the world Adam wouldn't befriend."

Except me. Mercy kept the thought to herself. "He seemed, well . . . very serious tonight at supper."

"Probably just tired." Eletta put her hand to her stomach and smiled. "The baby just moved."

Mercy had seen the delight of this moment on the faces of her sisters. She let go of her concern about Adam. Her conclusion about them both being tired was no doubt the reason he'd seemed so distant.

Eletta beamed. "I've waited for this for so long. We weren't sure it was even possible." She fell silent and looked momentarily uncomfortable. "I'm just glad to bring another child into our family."

"My sisters have been doing their part to populate the territory. There are four little ones back in Oregon City and a fifth on the way. Grace is due in late March."

"This babe should come near the first of the month."

"Faith hopes it's a girl, but I told her it might be nice for Isaac if it were a boy."

Eletta gave a light laugh. "You can probably tell that Faith keeps us busy. She's an amazing child—so very smart. Maybe too smart for her own good."

"She told me you taught her to read at the age of two!"

"She was speaking full sentences before her first birthday. She's always been well ahead of other children her age. Perhaps it's because she was constantly surrounded by adults. Perhaps it's just because God has endowed her with a special gift." Eletta shifted in the bed. "She reads anything she can get her hands on. Isaac always tries to bring her books when he goes to Gold Beach and Port Orford."

"I look forward to getting to know her better."

Mercy glanced around the room. It wasn't much larger than Faith's room. There was a single window—or at least a space for a window. It had been boarded up.

Eletta's gaze followed Mercy's. "In the summer we leave it open. Glass is too expensive and would be terribly hard to get this far upriver, so when the weather starts to chill, we put a blanket up. When it's colder like it is now, we board it shut. Isaac put in some bent nails in such a way, however, that we can easily remove the wood and let in fresh air."

"That's ingenious." Mercy noticed a square slot in the overhead logs that comprised the base of the roof. "What is that?"

Eletta looked up. "Now it's access to the roof. It used to be for the smoke from our fire. When we first came here, we didn't have a fireplace or stove. Oh my, you should have seen us trying to get a cookstove up here from the river. Much heavier than the small heating stoves."

Mercy grinned. "But how nice to have such a luxury."

"It is. When we first came, we had to do like the Tututni and make a hole in the roof for our fire smoke. This was our entire house then. We've added the other rooms on over the years. We also added wood planks for the floors. For the longest time we only had packed dirt. Once we got the stove, Isaac went up on the roof and put a little trap door over the hole. You can push it open from inside, but you'll need something to stand on to reach it."

Mercy could no longer fight back a yawn. "I'm so sorry. I'm afraid the day and the excitement has left me worn."

"I'm the one who should apologize. You must be exhausted, and here I am rambling on about the roof and stove." Eletta smiled. "We can talk tomorrow. You go on to bed."

"First I have this to give you." Mercy pulled a letter from Grace and a small bottle out of her skirt pocket. "Grace swears by this tonic to battle the nausea. Take a teaspoon each time you feel particularly bad and one about a half hour before eating. She said it will allow you to eat and not be sick."

Eletta took the bottle and letter. "Thank you. How thoughtful."

"I have some other tonics to put in tea, but they can wait until tomorrow. Grace said the important thing is to get you eating and back on your feet."

The older woman smiled and nodded. "I trust her to know. She saved me once before."

Mercy got up and returned the chair to where it had been beside the wall. "Will Isaac be back soon?"

Eletta nodded. "He's speaking to the men. They need to

know about the wars and what the government is doing." She sighed. "I hope that things calm down and the militia and army stop with this idea of extermination. It's horrible. They have no regard for any Indian life."

"Isaac told me as much. I suppose it's far easier to kill than to learn to live together."

Eletta nodded. "It always has been."

Faith was still awake by the time Mercy was ready for bed. The young girl's sewing lay in a small wooden box beside her bed, and she was settled under the covers.

"I figured you'd be asleep," Mercy said.

"I waited for you. You might need something. There's a pot under your bed if you need to go in the night." She leaned over the side of her mattress and pointed to the end of Mercy's bed.

Mercy made a point to check for it. "Yes, I see it. Thank you."

"Papa made an outhouse, but it's not wise to go out at night. If you need anything else, I can help you." Faith reached down and pushed the box of sewing under her bed, then settled back under the covers. She held her doll close. "If you hear some barking or howling, that's just the Tututni's dogs. They sometimes hear animals in the forest, and Mama says their barking scares off intruders."

"I'm sure she's right. We have a couple dogs back at my home on the farm. We have a herd of sheep, and the dogs help us keep them safe." Mercy snuggled down under the heavy quilt and sighed as her muscles began to relax. "I can tell you all about it tomorrow. It's been a very long day."

"Mama said you had to sail on a ship to get here."

"I did." Mercy tried to suppress her yawn. "I enjoyed it. Ocean travel is amazing. All you see for miles and miles is water. It makes you realize just how small you are and how big the world is."

"Were you ever afraid?" Faith asked.

Mercy closed her eyes. "Only when a storm blew up. It rocked the ship terribly, and knowing we were so far from land frightened me. But I prayed, and my fears went away."

"That's what I do," Faith replied and yawned.

"And what are you afraid of?"

"Angry people."

Mercy opened her eyes and looked at Faith. "Have there been a lot of angry people here?"

Faith nodded and curled up on her side, the doll tucked under her chin. "There's lots of them. They scare me because I know they scare Papa and Mama. I keep praying God will make those people stop being angry, but so far they're still mad, and when they're mad, they kill people. They kill the Indians especially."

"I'm so sorry about that, Faith. I know it isn't easy to hear about such things. I'll pray that God makes them stop being angry too."

Faith nodded ever so slightly. "Pray God hurries, 'cause I don't want them to kill my friends."

Mercy had a momentary memory of the Whitman Massacre and the friends she'd lost. "I will pray for that, Faith. I don't want your friends to die either. I don't want anyone to die."

Adam fought off exhaustion the next morning. He'd hardly been able to close his eyes the night before without seeing Mercy Flanagan's image. He thought of her as he dressed for the day and again when he retrieved water from the creek. She was all he could think about, and it grieved him to no end.

He entered the house, where the inviting aroma of coffee and bacon filled the air. The table was set for breakfast, and bowls of oatmeal awaited. Mercy wasn't in the room, so Adam quickly deposited the water and decided to escape before her return. He didn't like the idea of missing out on a hot breakfast, but he wasn't sure he could endure Mercy's company without saying the wrong thing. He knew he could make some excuse to join one of the Tututni families for breakfast. He turned to go, but he was too late. Faith and Mercy came into the house, caught up in conversation about the chickens and eggs.

"We have to keep them safe from the Indian dogs as well as other animals," Faith was telling Mercy. "That's why we don't let them just roam around."

Mercy glanced up and caught sight of him. Her beautiful eyes grew wide, and she smiled. "Why, good morning." She motioned to her gathered apron. "We were collecting eggs."

Faith dashed across the room to Adam, threw her arms around his waist, and hugged him. "Good morning and God bless you!"

"Good morning and God bless you!" Adam couldn't help but smile. This was their standard greeting at school. He looked over Faith's head and found Mercy watching them. "God bless you too, Miss Flanagan." He felt silly adding that and knew it was only nerves that made him do it. Not that he wouldn't have wanted God to bless her. After all, she'd given up her easier life in Oregon City to come here.

Faith pulled back. "Well, are you?"

Adam shook his head. "I'm sorry. Am I what?"

His niece giggled. "Miss Mercy asked if you were hungry."

He realized his thoughts had overridden his hearing. He looked up at Mercy and nodded. "I am hungry, and it smells wonderful in here."

"Well, have a seat. I've already seen to Eletta, and Isaac has come and gone. He said he had some business to attend to with one of the leaders."

Adam glanced toward the door. "Perhaps I should see if he needs me."

"He doesn't," Faith interjected. "He said to tell you to stay here and explain to Miss Mercy how to handle school so that Mama can sleep."

Adam swallowed the lump in his throat. "I . . . uh . . . very well. That shouldn't be too hard." He let Faith lead him to the table. He helped her with her chair and then took his own.

Mercy deposited the eggs she'd had in her apron on the counter, then brought the coffeepot to the table. "Would you like some?"

He held out his cup. "Yes, please. I find it one of the best ways to warm up."

"I agree." Mercy poured his coffee and then her own. "I've never been much of a coffee drinker. It's so bitter that unless I can sweeten it considerably, I don't drink it. I really prefer tea."

"I'm sure Eletta has some."

She returned the pot to the stove and came back to the table with a plate of bacon. "I brought some of my own, but it seemed silly to brew it up with the pot of coffee hot and ready." She put the plate on the table, then took her chair before Adam could offer to assist her. "Would you ask the blessing?"

Adam nodded and bowed his head. "For what we are about to receive may we be truly thankful. Bless this food and day, we pray, amen."

"Amen." Mercy met his gaze with her infectious smile. "I thought perhaps, if you don't mind, we could discuss the school while we ate. For instance, what time do we start?"

"Eight." Adam helped himself to the bacon. "We have class until noon, then break for lunch. On Tuesdays and Thursdays, we come back at one o'clock and have class for another two hours. Usually I teach some science and history."

"And on Monday, Wednesday, and Friday?"

He shook his head. "The children go to one of the village houses to work on their own crafts and skills."

She nodded. "I understand most of the students read at a beginner's level."

He stirred his oatmeal. "Yes. It's hard for them, but they try. Eletta was using cards with pictures and the word written out. It seemed to really help."

"The McGuffey Readers will also be of tremendous help."

He nodded but kept his eyes on his oatmeal. "Eletta has wanted some for a very long time."

"Perhaps you could teach this morning, and I could watch you," Mercy suggested. "That way you can introduce me to the children and put them at ease, and I can see how you manage the class."

Adam didn't want to spend any more time with Mercy than was necessary, but he knew her suggestion was the best way to manage the situation.

"Very well."

His tone sounded less than enthusiastic, and when he glanced up, he found Mercy frowning. No doubt he'd hurt her feelings or offended her sense of propriety. He started to apologize, then stopped himself. She would just have to get used to the way he was and realize they would not be close friends. He'd tried to be friends with a young woman before, and it had led to him falling in love and making a fool of himself. He wasn't about to do that again. Even for a woman as beautiful and kind as Mercy Flanagan.

Chapter

7

On her first day of school, Mercy observed Adam and his style of teaching. He was fun, despite her concerns that he'd be a strict taskmaster. The children, mostly girls, were giggly and sweet and adored him. More surprising was that he adored them. Mercy hadn't been certain Adam had feelings for anyone other than Faith. After class, some older boys came to visit Adam. Mercy learned that they were usually busy with their fathers, learning to be men of the tribe, but on occasion they were allowed to meet with Adam for classes.

"We can meet tonight after supper," Adam assured them while Mercy watched. The boys looked between the ages of thirteen and fifteen and obviously held Adam in high esteem.

The following day, Adam left Mercy to manage on her own. The class was far more subdued, and Mercy prayed she might somehow draw out the same joyful spirit she'd witnessed the day before.

Hoping to ease the tension, she allowed Faith to reintroduce her to everyone. She knew it would take time to learn all their names. She was grateful they had been given English names that reflected their Tututni names, which were much harder to pronounce.

As the day wore on, the children began to warm to her, and by the time they ended for lunch, Mercy had managed to win them over. The two women who joined them were more shy. The one called Red Deer looked about Eletta's age and was more comfortable than the older woman named Bright Star. Red Deer, in fact, came with a gift for her new teacher. It was a small basket.

"Red Deer, this is beautiful," Mercy said. "Thank you."

The Tututni woman smiled and said something in her native language.

Faith jumped in before Mercy could ask for a translation. "She said you're pretty. She especially likes your eyes."

Mercy looked at the buckskin-clad woman and smiled. Red Deer was shorter than Mercy and wore her hair in two sections tied on either side of her face. "Thank you again. I shall cherish this gift."

"You can use it for almost anything," Red Deer said, surprising Mercy. "It can even hold water."

Mercy looked again at the basket. "I can imagine that. The weave is so tight. You have made me feel most welcome."

"You have come to help us—to help Sister Eletta. We thank you for that. She is . . . she is. . . ." Red Deer looked to Faith and spoke in Tututni.

"Precious," Faith replied.

Red Deer nodded. "She is precious to us."

"She's precious to me as well."

Red Deer didn't waste any more time. She excused herself and made her way out of the school. Faith headed back to the house for lunch, leaving Mercy to take an account of the day. She felt that things had gone well overall. Adam and Eletta had set things up in such a way that it wasn't at all difficult for Mercy to step in. She knew it would take time before the Tututni trusted her as they did the Brownings, but she was determined to win them over. She was determined to win Adam over as well. She wasn't sure why he treated her with such discomfort, but she would find a way to change his mind. It would hardly suit either of them to go on with such a wall between them.

She put away her things, then headed back to the house for lunch. She was nearly to the door when it opened, and Adam stepped out.

"Hello," she offered with a smile.

"Ah . . . hello." His gaze didn't quite meet hers.

"Did you have something to eat? I left a stew on the stove."

He nodded. "I had some." He started to move past her.

"Have I offended you?" Mercy hadn't meant to just blurt out the words, but now that they were said, she was glad.

Adam stopped and looked at her with a frown. "No. Why would you think that?"

She shrugged. "It just seems that you're all smiles and openness with everyone else. I realize I'm a stranger, but I hope we can be friends."

He nodded, but his expression remained sober. "Of course we're friends." He offered nothing more before making a hasty departure.

Mercy frowned and shook her head. He was possibly the most vexing man she'd ever met.

The next day, she felt more confident of her teaching position. She greeted the class warmly and shared a little bit about herself before beginning their devotions.

"I'm very happy to be here with you. I've wanted to teach school for a long time, and I think our class here is just the right size." She smiled at the students and continued. "I've known Brother Isaac and Sister Eletta since coming to this territory. We came west with hundreds of other people. I traveled with my sisters, Grace and Hope." One of the girls raised her hand, and Mercy nodded. "Yes, you have a question?"

The little one nodded. "Did your mother and father come too?"

Mercy shook her head. "No. My mother and father died, leaving just us three girls."

Another hand shot up. "Didn't you have anybody else?" another girl asked.

"Our uncle lived out here. That's why we wanted to come here." She went to the small teacher's desk. It was handmade by Isaac but served its purpose. "You can ask me more questions later. Time is getting away from us, and we should start our day."

She offered a prayer and then opened her Bible. "Today I'm going to read from the one hundredth Psalm." She looked up at the captive crowd and smiled. "'Make a joyful noise unto the Lord, all ye lands.'"

The next two weeks were spent learning all she could. Mercy set up her own routine, and at Eletta's suggestion, taught the children in the morning and left Adam to teach on Tuesday and Thursday afternoon. She liked this schedule because then she had the rest of the day to tend to the household chores.

Eletta grew stronger and was eating regularly. Seeing her doing so well, Mercy decided she could get up and sit rather than just stay in bed. Eletta didn't protest the change at all.

"I'm glad to be feeling better. I knew your sister's cures would help. I firmly believe God has given her a special talent."

"I agree." Mercy was peeling potatoes and reached for the final spud. "I've learned so much from Grace. Hope too. Hope taught me to spin." She paused and looked up. "You taught her to spin when she was staying with you, right?"

"I did." Eletta looked away, as if uncomfortable.

"Are you having pain?" Mercy asked.

"No. I'm fine." Eletta glanced back and smiled.

"Then I'm going to put these potatoes on to boil and give these peelings to the chickens. I'm sure they'll be delighted for the treat."

"I'm sure you're right." Eletta picked up her knitting. "I'm going to work on this baby bonnet. March can be cold around here, and I'll need to ensure my child stays warm."

Mercy put the potatoes into a pot of water on the stove. Since the water was already boiling, she didn't figure it would take long for them to cook. She pulled on her coat and picked up the bowl of peelings. "I'll be back soon. Will you be all right?"

"I'm fine. Please don't worry."

Mercy headed outside and surveyed her world. The sun shone bright overhead, and the sky was a brilliant blue. The weather seemed so changeable, but Eletta had assured her it was generally temperate.

The village itself was unlike anything she'd ever known. It was nestled among the trees, whereas the Whitman Mission had been far more open, and if she climbed the hill not far from the Emigrant House where she had lived, she could see for miles. Here the trees shrouded everything with long limbs that stretched like protective arms. It made things much cooler in their shadow, and no doubt that helped a lot during the summer months.

"Mercy!" Red Deer called and waved. She crossed the yard and joined Mercy at the chicken coop. "You come to make baskets with us today?"

"Not today. I promised I'd watch the boys play shinny ball. I was promised a very entertaining time." Mercy smiled as she tossed the potato skins to the grateful hens. They hadn't been laying well, but with the return of the sunlight, Mercy hoped that might change.

She surveyed Red Deer's buckskin dress and woven basket hat. "You do such beautiful work. That dress is lovely with its fringe and shells." Winter dress for the natives included a generous portion of animal skins. Eletta had told her that in the summer the Tututni wore very little, but in the damp cold of winter, everyone dressed for warmth. Even their moccasins were fur-lined.

Red Deer smiled and lowered her head shyly. "I can teach you how to make one."

Mercy nodded. "I'd like that. There's a great deal I need to learn."

The Tututni woman nodded. "I will teach you soon."

Mercy longed to ask Red Deer about the significance of the three tattooed lines on her chin as well as the piercings in her ears. Perhaps it would be better, however, to ask Eletta. She certainly didn't want to offend Red Deer when she was just getting to know her.

They walked back toward the center of the mission clearing. Mercy looked toward the far side, where the Tututni houses were located. She hadn't yet ventured inside one of the lodges.

"Are your houses warm?"

Red Deer nodded. "They are. You should come see. The earth keeps us warm in the winter and cool in the summer."

"I would like to visit sometime."

"Come today after you finish your work. I will show you how we live."

"If time allows, I'd like that very much."

Red Deer headed back to her house, and Mercy gazed after her. When she passed the building where school and church were held, Red Deer turned and waved. Mercy waved back.

After making sure the chickens had water, Mercy started back to the house. Again her gaze went to the school. In the days since her arrival, she'd seen very little of Adam. He sometimes took his meals with them, but other times he ate with the Tututni. Mercy wondered if he was avoiding her. He didn't even want to discuss the students, and she found that very puzzling.

Perhaps he thought Mercy was beneath his concern. Maybe he didn't like having her help with the school—after all, she wasn't college educated. This thought brought a frown. Would he be so petty as to snub her for her lack of education? It wasn't as if she hadn't wanted to go to college, but it would have required money, especially if she'd returned east.

Mercy decided to leave off further contemplation. She could easily work herself up into taking offense where none was needed. She hurried into the house, eager to put her mind on something other than Adam Browning.

Adam had done his best to keep clear of Mercy Flanagan, just as he had every young woman since leaving Boston, but in the small mission village it was nearly impossible. Especially since they were sharing teaching responsibilities.

He knew he couldn't keep avoiding her. She was sure to realize what he was doing and be offended. If she wasn't already. He had considered talking to Eletta and asking her to explain his past to Mercy, but then changed his mind. It was too painful, and there was no sense in sharing something so private with a stranger who would leave once the baby was born in the spring.

Still, at times like this he just didn't seem able to shake loose from the past and Lizzy. Elizabeth Price, the beautiful blue-eyed, blond-haired daughter of the wealthy and very pious Oliver Price. Price was delighted to have his daughter marry a man of the cloth, especially one he admired as much as he did Adam.

Adam had met Lizzy through his classmate Marcus Price, her brother. When Marcus and Adam hadn't been busy with their studies, they included Lizzy in their outings. The three-some were inseparable for the last two years of Adam's time at Harvard, and despite his intention to remain simply friends with Lizzy, it seemed only natural that they should fall in love. Much to the frustration of other suitors who fancied an alliance with Lizzy's wealthy father. Just before graduation, Adam asked Lizzy's father for her hand in marriage, and he had quickly consented. Mr. Price even had a friend in Boston who headed up one of the larger churches prepared to offer Adam a position. Adam's life seemed clearly mapped out.

But then it all fell apart. One of Lizzy's former suitors took his jealousy a bit further by hiring a man to look into Adam's past. He wanted any information that might discredit Adam and in turn put an end to the engagement. And the detective had found a very big, very unacceptable piece of information. Adam's mother was half Cherokee Indian. The news had spread like wildfire, and the scandal was enormous.

Adam had never intended to be deceptive about his lineage, but he knew how difficult it could prove for him if it were common knowledge. He'd chosen to say nothing, given his mother had already passed away. He knew his black hair and hazel eyes could be seen as stemming from any number of ethnic origins, so he remained silent. He had always meant to discuss the matter with Lizzy, but the right time never seemed to come.

When the truth came out in the most damaging way possible— implying that Adam had been working to deceive everyone— Adam didn't even get a chance to say good-bye or explain himself to Lizzy. Marcus and his father had come to Adam's residence and told him in no uncertain terms that the engagement was over. He had misrepresented himself as a white man and shamed Lizzy, who at that moment was being whisked off to rest at some secluded spa. People he had thought of as good friends turned away. Adam could still remember the accusing looks in their eyes. Thankfully he'd already graduated from university, because otherwise he might have been thrown out of those hallowed halls just as he had been every proper Boston parlor.

Even the church position had been withdrawn. It seemed Boston was not yet ready to hear the gospel preached by an Indian. Adam had reminded himself that it wasn't all that many years earlier that white men of God argued heartily about whether or not a man of red skin could even be saved.

Adam closed the book of mathematics he'd been using to teach the older children and leaned his chin against the top of it. How could people be so heartless—so narrow-minded? His mother had suffered greatly. His father too. No one understood a man taking a heathen for a wife when there were so many available white women of virtue.

He and Isaac and their sisters had lived with ridicule and alienation all of their youth, but God had been good. His sisters had eventually married upstanding, successful men who didn't care about their quarter Cherokee blood. Isaac, too, had married a woman not so different from Lizzy. Eletta had blue eyes and blond hair, and yet the fact that her husband's mother was a half-breed never caused her affection to waver.

Tossing the book aside, Adam got to his feet. It was nearly time for the game he'd promised the older boys. There was no sense in brooding. It wouldn't change a thing about the past, but it did strengthen his resolve toward the future. He wasn't going to lose his heart to another white woman. Not even one with eyes the color of an early morning sky.

"Adam!" five boys called out in unison when he emerged from the school.

He smiled, forcing the painful thoughts from his mind. "Are you ready for our game?"

"Yes. We set the goals," the tallest of the boys declared.

"Very good, Samuel."

Adam looked toward the open area where they often played

rousing games of shinny. Two sticks had been driven into the ground on either end of the clearing.

"Here's your stick," eleven-year-old John said.

Adam took the slightly curved stick. "Which team am I on?"

"Ours," John quickly replied. "You're with me and David."

Adam nodded and followed the boys to the center of the field. The goal was to work a ball made of deerskin down the field and past the goal post of the other team.

Standing opposite twelve-year-old Samuel, Adam gave a nod. "Ready—set—go!"

The ball flew into play, and the game was afoot. They raced back and forth from one side of the clearing to the other—each team doing their best to either make a goal or prevent one.

The physical exertion was just the thing to take Adam's mind off his trouble. Not only that, but he enjoyed the camaraderie he had with the boys. Here he wasn't their teacher, just another player.

The ball shot across the clearing from John to Adam. Without hesitation, Adam worked his way down the field, scooting the ball back and forth with his stick. He was nearly in line to make a goal when Samuel charged in and stole the ball away, and everyone whirled around to head in the opposite direction.

To one side of the field, Adam spied Mercy taking a seat on a log. She wore not only her wool coat, but also a heavy blanket wrapped around her in Indian fashion. He smiled to himself. She had surprised him with her ease toward the native people. Isaac had told him about her ordeal at the Whitman Mission, and he'd been stunned to hear she was one of the victims. It was even more amazing that she would come to an Indian village after what she'd endured.

Despite his resolve to have nothing to do with her, Adam couldn't help but admire her fortitude. He would have liked to ask her about her life among the Cayuse, but to do so would require an intimacy he wasn't yet ready to give.

The game continued down one side of the clearing and up the other. Adam's team got the first goal, and then Samuel's team got the next two. They would play until one team reached five goals.

"Come on, Adam!" David yelled as the ball once again passed to him.

Adam quickly glanced at Mercy, who seemed to be daydreaming. He found himself wishing she would watch him, then chided himself for such thinking. Even so, his heart reminded him that he was still a man who liked capturing the attention of a pretty girl.

He made a goal, much to David and John's delight. "Now we're tied," John declared.

Adam was curious what Mercy thought of the game. Had she ever seen shinny played before? He knew the boys had invited her to watch, but he wondered if she realized he'd be playing too. The women had their own version of the game, so perhaps Mercy would learn to play it with the girls.

Samuel shot past him, and Adam realized he hadn't been paying attention. When Samuel made a third goal for his team, John and David chided Adam for not stopping the ball. He resolved to put Mercy from his mind and focus on the game, but it wasn't easy.

It was when they were tied at four goals apiece that the boys grew intense in their focus. Competitions were encouraged in the tribe. The boys were always trying to best each other. They would soon become men and take on the responsibility of becoming leaders, husbands, and fathers. Of course, with the government determined to move the Indians away from their land, Adam wondered what it would mean for these precious young men.

Again he was lost in his thoughts when he saw the ball go flying in the direction of Mercy. She wasn't paying attention to the game, apparently finding something on the ground of interest. If she had been watching, she would have seen the collection of boys charging her way.

Adam had to act fast. With long strides, he flanked the boys and reached her just moments before they did. Without thinking, Adam threw himself across Mercy, pulling her backwards off the log and to safety.

When they stopped rolling, she lay atop him, staring down at him wide-eyed and open-mouthed. For a moment neither of them moved. They might have stayed that way in stunned silence, but the group of boys were shouting and laughing at what had just happened.

Mercy bit her lower lip and lay motionless with her head lifted and her hands on Alex's shoulders. Then all at once she seemed to realize what had happened, and a look of horror crossed her face. She attempted to jump up, but her foot caught in her blanket, and she plunged back down onto Adam, nearly knocking the wind out of him.

"Oh! Oh my!" she declared, pressing into his abdomen to boost herself up.

"Oof." Adam couldn't contain the groan that came from her pressure on his midsection. The moan made Mercy stop as she reclaimed her feet. She looked down at him.

"I'm—I'm sorry." She cast a quick glance around her. Looking back at Adam, she frowned. "Why did you do that?"

Adam sat up, shaking his head. "You weren't paying attention, and I didn't want the boys to crash into you." He got up and tried to wipe the mud and dirt from his pants.

By now the younger children who'd been watching the game from across the field had joined them and were laughing at their teachers' antics.

Mercy's face flushed red. She looked from the children back to Adam. Her mouth opened and closed several times, but not a single sound came from her. Adam could see that she was embarrassed. He smiled, hoping to ease the tension. "No need to thank me."

This seemed to snap her out of it. "I wasn't going to," she declared and whirled around to leave.

For some reason, her response caused Adam to laugh out loud. She turned back and looked at him as if he'd lost his mind. The children joined in his laughter, which only made the matter worse.

Without another word, Mercy stomped off toward the house.

Chapter 8

Mercy hurried into the house, mortified by what had just happened. She hadn't been paying attention, just as Adam had said. One minute she was lost in thought about how happy and carefree he looked out there with his students—wondering why he never looked that way around her. Then, without warning, the next instant she was in his arms, rolling across the ground.

She entered the house and slammed the door behind her without meaning to.

Eletta looked up from her sewing with a puzzled expression. Cocking her head to one side, she asked, "Are you all right? Is something wrong?"

Mercy glanced down at the muddy blanket still wrapped around her. "I . . . ah, there was a little accident."

"What happened?"

Faith came dancing into the house, giggling. "Oh, Mama, you should have seen what happened to Uncle Adam and Mercy. The boys were running at her, and Uncle Adam saved her life!"

Eletta shook her head and fixed her gaze on Mercy. "What?"

Mercy swallowed the lump in her throat. "I was watching the shinny game, and I got lost in my thoughts and wasn't paying attention. The boys sent the ball my way, and I was nearly overrun by them. Instead, I was knocked out of the way by Adam, who was gallantly trying to save me." Why did his first act of kindness toward her have to be such an embarrassing one?

Hearing herself tell the story, Mercy began to feel bad for the way she'd acted toward Adam. He had probably saved her from being hit by one of the sticks, and the way those boys could swing, she might have truly been hurt.

"It was so funny, Mama. They were rolling and rolling on the ground."

Mercy shook her head. "There wasn't that much rolling, Faith." She looked at Eletta, who was smiling. "It was just enough to be humiliating."

"Oh, nonsense. Things like that are bound to happen. I'm just glad no one got hurt."

"I hope no one did." Mercy frowned as she remembered Adam's groan. "I wasn't too gentle in trying to get to my feet."

"Faith, why don't you get out the washtub so Mercy can put her dress in to soak after she changes?"

The little girl nodded and skipped off to collect the tub.

Mercy looked down at her skirt. It was wet and muddy. The blanket was no better.

Eletta smiled. "Go get out of those wet, dirty clothes. Hang up your coat and blanket, and we'll brush them clean after they dry. You'll feel less embarrassed once that's settled."

Mercy did as Eletta instructed and hung her coat and blanket on hooks by the door. She then went to the room she shared with Faith and began to unbutton her dress. She couldn't help but think of Adam's arms around her. Her heartbeat picked up speed, leaving her feeling flushed all over again. A tingle ran down her spine. It was like a strange sort of madness that she couldn't shake. What in the world was wrong with her?

That evening, Eletta retired early, and Mercy made her way to Red Deer's lodge. Isaac, Adam, and the Tututni men were meeting in the sweathouse, and it seemed like the perfect opportunity to see the inside of a Tututni house.

Since the houses were built partially underground, Red Deer gave Mercy instructions when she arrived. "There is a pole with steps carved into it just inside the door. Climb down with care." She slid back the wooden door.

Mercy had to duck to crawl through the opening and into the plank house. Just as Red Deer had said, a notched pole took her down several feet to the floor of the house. She paused at the bottom and waited for Red Deer to join her.

"Mercy!" Faith declared from where she played with Red Deer's daughter Mary. "Were you looking for me?"

"No, I've come to see how the Tututni live." Mercy turned to Red Deer. "It's quite snug in here."

She glanced around the large open room. The floors were hard-packed dirt, and the roof was slightly peaked. There was a fire pit in the center of the room with a pot sitting right on the burning logs. In the ceiling overhead was a hole for the smoke to exit, but the room still held a bit of haze. Eletta had told Mercy that the pieces of the rafters could be removed to allow in more light and air during pleasant days.

Tule mats were rolled and stowed atop a long bench that ran the entire length of the rectangular house. Opposite this was another long bench.

"We have places inside the seats where we can store food and our . . ." Red Deer paused to ponder the right word. "Property. We put our property there." She lifted up one of the top boards of the bench. Inside were several articles of clothing neatly stacked. It looked very efficient.

Red Deer replaced the board and led Mercy to the far side of the room. Hanging from the ceiling in the corner of the house were bunches of dried herbs, most of which Mercy recognized. There were also baskets hanging from the walls.

"We keep some of our food stores in these baskets. This one has dried meal made from acorns," Red Deer said, pointing. "We hang herbs to dry and sometimes hang other things here as well. In the other corner is a storage pit that will keep things cold. Some of the salmon is kept there, but most of it is smoked and stored in the baskets."

"It's all so neat and orderly. I think it's a very fine house." Mercy looked around and noted that in several areas, deerskins acted as rugs. "It would seem you're well set for the winter."

Red Deer bent over and opened one of the basket lids. "You can try this." She took a piece of something from the basket and handed it to Mercy.

Mercy wasn't at all sure what it was. The rounded ball was slightly sticky and a sort of purplish gray. She held it to her nose and sniffed it. It smelled of berries.

"Taste it," Red Deer encouraged. "It's sweet."

Without further hesitation, Mercy sampled the treat. It wasn't all that appealing, but she forced a smile and nodded. "Thank you."

Red Deer smiled. "It is made with deer fat and dried berries and acorn. My children want to eat it all the time, but we save it for special occasions."

Mercy nodded and slipped the rest of the berry ball into her pocket. She remembered the shortbread she'd made with Mrs. Hull and wondered if the Tututni might like it.

"Come see over here," Faith said. "This is where we make baskets." She took Mercy by the hand and led her to an area where several sizes of baskets were in various stages of creation.

Mats were stretched out on the ground for whoever might gather to work.

"This one is for collecting food," Faith said, holding up a medium-sized basket of woven hazel branches and dried grass. She quickly set it aside and picked up a much smaller piece. "And this one is going to be for my own hat."

The bowl-shaped creation had a long way to go before it was finished, but the tight weave impressed Mercy.

"They're beautiful. I can't imagine how much work must go into each one."

Faith smiled. "You can come and learn. Red Deer's very good at teaching us."

Mercy nodded and reached out to touch the crown of the hat. "I'd like that."

Red Deer joined them and lifted one of the planks from the bench. She reached inside and drew out a piece of finely tanned deer skin. "This is going to be a dress for Mary."

"It's so soft." Mercy rubbed her fingers along the leather. "I'm sure it will make a beautiful dress."

Red Deer smiled proudly. "I will teach you to make one."

"I have so much to learn, but I'm a good student." Knowing the hour was probably getting late, Mercy decided to excuse herself. "I should go. Thank you so much for showing me your house."

Red Deer beamed. "You will come back and let me teach you to make baskets?"

"I will." Mercy looked at Faith. Tomorrow was Saturday, and Eletta had mentioned that Faith often liked to sleep over with Mary. "Are you staying here tonight, Faith?"

Faith shook her head. "No. Papa told me to come home. I'll go with you." She gave Mary a hug and jumped to her feet, stopping to give Red Deer a hug as well before taking Mercy's hand. "I'm ready."

Mercy smiled and followed Faith to the notched pole leading to the door. The child scooted up the pole as if she'd been doing it all her life. It dawned on Mercy that she probably had.

Such a lifestyle wasn't designed with long dresses in mind, however, and Mercy went much slower. She gathered her skirts in one hand and held on to the pole with the other. She crawled awkwardly out the door and was surprised to find Adam there waiting. He helped her to her feet then quickly let her go.

"Isaac sent me to bring you both home," he explained.

Faith wrapped herself around Adam, and Mercy smiled when he lifted the girl into the air and tossed her. Faith squealed in delight and cried for more. Adam tossed her up and down several times before finally putting her back on the ground.

"You're getting too big for this," he said, rubbing his arms.

Faith giggled. "You're strong, Uncle Adam. You're so strong that you could throw Mercy in the air and catch her too."

Mercy felt her face grow hot and was grateful for the twilight and shadows. She longed to change the subject. "Faith, you need to help me brush out the blanket before we go to bed. The mud should have dried by now." She started walking toward the house, and Faith shot past her.

"I'll get the cleaning brush!" Faith ran across the clearing, heading for the house.

Mercy started after her, hoping Adam would say nothing more. She'd only managed a few steps, however, before he called after her.

"I want to apologize if I offended you."

She stopped and did her best to ignore her guilt. Drawing a deep breath, she turned. "You didn't. I'm afraid I was less than grateful, and for that I apologize."

Adam gave her a rare smile. "It was quite an ordeal."

"And one I find unpleasant to remember, so if we could just forget about it, I'd be even more grateful."

His forehead wrinkled as his brows knit together for a moment. It looked for all the world as if he were hurt or upset by her comment, but Mercy saw no reason for that. Men were such strange creatures. Their way of reasoning through matters always seemed the complete opposite of a woman's.

Mercy squared her shoulders. "If you'll excuse me, I have some work to do before I can retire."

She continued toward the house and breathed a sigh of relief when Adam offered no further comment. Hopefully the entire matter could be swept under the rug and forgotten. But even as Mercy hoped for that, she remembered the feeling of Adam's arms around her. His face just inches from her own.

On the first Sunday in December, after leading their little village in church services, Adam and Isaac took off for another Tututni village some miles upriver. Adam knew Isaac was concerned about the people of that gathering. The men there were far more given to conflict, and he wanted to speak to them about keeping the peace. Perhaps even moving closer to the mission. At the meeting in the sweathouse, Isaac had learned from some of the Tututni men that there was trouble building. The Tututni warriors were tired of the whites falsely accusing them of everything from thievery to murder.

As they paddled their small canoe against the current, Adam thought about the conflict going on all around them. They wouldn't be able to keep it out of their own village much longer. The men there were related to many of the Tututni living elsewhere. They had sisters and children who married into other villages and were concerned they were in danger.

"I think Mercy is fitting in nicely, don't you?" Isaac said after they'd traveled in silence most of the trip.

The memory of Mercy in his arms flashed through Adam's

mind. She'd told him it was an unpleasant experience, but it certainly hadn't been for him. "She seems to be. I have to admit she's far less concerned about her surroundings than most white women."

"Eletta is doing so much better that I would be happy to have ten of Mercy living with us if it kept my sweet wife feeling good."

Adam laughed. "I don't know that we could manage ten of her. Mercy has a feisty streak."

"Noticed that, did you?" Isaac looked over his shoulder at Adam. "I'm betting you noticed how pretty she is too."

Adam looked away, which only made Isaac laugh.

"She's very pretty," Isaac said. "No need to deny that."

"I wasn't going to." But neither did he intend to admit it.

"She and her sisters are all beauties. I was surprised to hear that Mercy hadn't married. Happy for it, since it allowed her to come here, but surprised all the same. She had more than her fair share of attention on our trip down from Port Orford. The soldiers treated her like royalty. Billy Caxton had more than a passing interest in her. I did what I could to nip that in the bud, but he's a persistent sort. I'm surprised he hasn't come around."

Adam knew only too well how persistent Billy could be. When he set his mind to something, he usually saw it to completion no matter the cost. Adam had seen him in action in trade and also in matters of revenge.

"But I was less worried once Mercy put him on his backside."

"What?" Adam asked, then wished he hadn't when Isaac chuckled.

"Thought that would get your attention. He was trying to woo her and said something that she didn't like. She gave him a push, and he landed smack on the ground. That'll teach him to be more cautious. She isn't a woman to be trifled with."

Adam smiled at the thought. If anyone deserved to be knocked down a peg, it was Billy. And he had no doubt that Mercy was more than capable of defending herself. She showed no signs of being a dainty, spoiled girl who expected others to look after her.

"What's that in the water?" Isaac asked.

Adam strained to look around him. "Where?"

"Up ahead. It looks like clothing."

They paddled a little faster, and as they neared, they could see that it wasn't just clothing, but a body. Isaac and Adam worked together to pull the body of a young Tututni man into the canoe. He was hardly more than a boy.

"It's Red Sun. He's been shot." Isaac pushed back the young man's shirt. "Several times, from the look of it."

Adam glanced upriver toward the bank. The village wasn't far. The silence filled him with dread. Even on Sundays, the sound of children playing and other activities would fill the air.

"The village has been attacked."

Isaac picked up his paddle. "Let's go."

They fought the current to regain the ground they'd lost. It wasn't long before they were dragging the boat onto the shore. They raced up the bank, and only when they reached the top did Adam realize that the attackers might still be in the area.

But he needn't have worried. Dead bodies were strewn across the open ground, and most of the houses had been burned and were still smoldering. There wasn't a single sign of life.

"They weren't attacked by another tribe," Isaac said as they began to inspect closer.

"No. I'm sure it was the volunteers or the army." Adam had been certain of that when he'd first seen Red Sun's wounds. "Probably Billy's group, since they aren't all that far from here."

They moved in the cold, eerie silence, checking each body. All had been shot, and some were even mutilated.

"This was senseless," Isaac said. "There's no sign the Tututni knew an attack was imminent."

"Perhaps they were duped." Adam doubted they had been taken by surprise. The Indians were much better at being aware of their surroundings and the threats of attack than the whites. But he could imagine some of the militiamen coming in the pretense of peace and then opening fire on everyone. It wouldn't take very many men or guns to cut down defenseless people.

"I don't see . . ." Isaac fell silent and raised his hand, signaling Adam to do the same.

Both men listened for a moment. The muted sound of a baby's whimper could be heard across the clearing. Isaac headed toward one of the few unburned houses, and Adam followed. They made their way inside. The whimper had been silenced, but Adam was certain it had come from this lodge.

Isaac called out in Tututni. "We're here to help. Please come out. It's Brother Isaac."

A woman peeked around a stack of tule mats and baskets. "Brother Isaac?" She barely whispered the words.

Isaac and Adam moved quickly to her side and pulled the baskets away to reveal the injured woman and her baby. Adam lifted the young woman in his arms and carried her outside, while Isaac followed with the baby.

Adam placed her on the ground. "What happened?"

"Men came. White men—in the night," she explained. "They hit me with the end of their gun."

Isaac assessed her injury. He handed the baby to the frightened woman and then took out his handkerchief and canteen. He dampened the cloth as he bent to clean the gash across her forehead.

"This cut isn't too bad," Isaac told her in Tututni. "And the baby looks unharmed. The blood on the infant is yours."

She winced as Isaac continued cleaning. "There was no warning. The men keeping watch gave no alarm."

"No doubt they were killed first," Isaac replied, glancing up at Adam.

Adam looked around. "Do you suppose any of the attackers are still around?"

Isaac shook his head. "I doubt it. Even though they'd get no chastisement from the government for this heinous act, they'd still be concerned about other Indians."

The woman looked around and for the first time began to weep. "My family is dead. My husband and mother. My children except for this one." She hugged the baby close, but motioned with her head. "My husband tried to save them."

A man lay over the bodies of two young boys. He'd been shot twice in the back, and his head had been bashed in. Anger coursed through Adam's blood. How could men be so heartless?

Adam realized most of the men who lay dead were old. "Where are the other men—the younger ones?" he asked the woman.

"There was much fighting in the trees." She pointed in the direction of the forested area behind them. "Our men tried to lure the white men away from the village. My husband was trying to get our boys to safety." She shook her head. "I tried to help, but a man hit me, and I fell. After that I ran to hide with my baby." She looked around at the bodies and sobbed. "They are all dead."

Isaac put an arm around her shoulders, and the baby began to cry in earnest. "Adam, get her down to the canoe. I'm going to check the trees and see if anyone else is still alive."

Adam took the woman's arm and led her down the path to the river. She continued crying even while trying to soothe her child.

Without speaking a word, Adam helped her down the bank and into the canoe. He pulled a blanket from his pack and carefully wrapped it around her and the baby to ward off the cold. He glanced skyward. Thick rain clouds had moved in to blot out the sun. They'd be lucky if it didn't pour rain before they made it back to the mission.

He glanced down at the woman and her baby. "You're safe now." The Tututni woman looked up at him with an expression of gratitude and fear. Adam smiled. "We'll take you to the mission, and the Tututni there will care for you." She seemed comforted by him speaking her language and nodded.

It wasn't long before Isaac returned. "They're all dead. The attackers left them where they lay, but since I found no whites, I presume they took their own injured and dead back with them when they left."

Adam nodded. "We should bury them."

Isaac glanced wearily up the bank. "I think it'd be better to get back to our own camp. I don't trust the militia not to attack the mission. We'll tell the men there what happened. I'm sure they'll arrange for burial."

Adam hadn't even considered the possibility of the militia attacking the mission village. Images of Billy Caxton and his companions came to mind. Adam felt certain he was responsible for this extermination. Billy had no respect for life. Especially not Indian lives. The very thought of him attacking again caused a chill to run up Adam's spine.

He picked up his paddle. "I think you're right."

Chapter

9

It wasn't long after learning what had happened at the upriver village that Eletta began spotting blood. Grace had tried to prepare Mercy for every possibility, including this one, so it didn't come as too much of a surprise. Just a disappointment. Since Eletta had been doing so well, Mercy had hoped the worst was behind her. Of course, no one had expected the attack so close to the mission.

"It's probably best that you stay in bed except to relieve yourself." Mercy tried to sound encouraging. "It's just a precaution."

Eletta's eyes filled with tears. "I'm so frightened. I try to pray, but my grief gets in the way."

Mercy sat on the edge of the bed and took Eletta's hand. "I know." They had talked quite a bit about what happened at the other village. It was a grave concern to Mercy as well, but she couldn't let on.

"I keep thinking about those poor people, and then I think about this baby and how I still might lose it."

"But you mustn't dwell on those things. It isn't healthy for you or the baby." Mercy squeezed her hand. "Think on lovely things, as the Bible says. Let's talk about Faith. Did she really learn to read at the age of two?"

Eletta drew in a deep breath and nodded. "She's so smart. I've taught her many things, and she's good at the ones that strike her fancy. If she doesn't like something, however, I'm hard-pressed to get her to work on it."

Mercy laughed. "I asked her about spinning, but she wasn't all that interested."

"No, and she isn't fond of crocheting or knitting either, but I keep reminding her that a proper wife will need to know all of those things in order to clothe her family."

"I'm very impressed with her writing. She's quite the storyteller. She's written pages and pages about her life here with the Tututni."

"I've encouraged her to keep a journal, as I do."

"I know. She let me read some of it. She's very observant. Keen on the details."

Eletta relaxed a bit and smiled. "She is. She always sees things that I don't. From the time she was little, she seemed to have an understanding that went beyond the normal expectations of a child."

"I'm amazed that she speaks English and Tututni with equal ease. I still stumble over the Tututni words, and I'm not sure I'll ever be able to master them."

"Writing them is even harder," Eletta admitted. "In English, we sound things out phonetically, but the Tututni language isn't that way. Some of the sounds are nothing like the written form. They use marks and symbols that we don't use in our alphabet."

Mercy nodded and let go of Eletta's hand. It was good to see her thinking about something else. "I've seen some of it. I had the children write their Tututni name and then their English name side by side. It was an interesting exercise."

"Mama?" Faith bounded into the room. "See what I made?"

She held up her Tututni hat. It was a tightly woven pattern of various colors.

"It's beautiful," Eletta said. "Come closer so I can inspect it."

"I'll get on with my chores." Mercy got to her feet and smiled at Faith. "I'll count on you to be here for your mama while I get the laundry off the line and tend to a few other things. Later you can help me iron the clothes."

Faith jumped up on the bed next to her mother and gave Mercy a smile. "I like to iron when it's cold."

"Me too."

"Take your time, Mercy. I want to speak to Faith about a few things." Eletta looked at her daughter and smiled. "It seems there's never enough time."

Her comment cast a bit of melancholy over the moment. Mercy nodded and did her best not to frown. "If you need anything, just have Faith get it or have her fetch me. You are not to get out of that bed."

She didn't wait for Eletta's response. She made her way into the kitchen and checked the sourdough bread in the oven. It was golden brown. She pulled out all four loaves and placed them on the counter. By the time she returned from the clothesline with the laundry, they hopefully would have cooled enough to cut.

Mercy pulled on her coat, then picked up the laundry basket. It was another Tututni creation, with thin, pliable branches woven to create a circular container. The weave on this basket wasn't very tight, but for laundry there was no need.

The clothesline was just behind the house and consisted of nothing more than a string tied between two small trees. It wasn't as nice as the ones Alex and Lance had built for them at the farm, but it did the job.

Mercy placed the basket on the ground and felt one of Isaac's shirts. The damp weather hadn't allowed the clothes to dry completely, but that was to be expected. She took them down nevertheless. She would hang them up in the cabin and then iron them dry. She looked around as she tended to the laundry. There was hardly anyone to be seen. Everyone was subdued by last week's news of the attack. Many of the people there had been related to people in the mission village, and the sorrow was overwhelming.

Mercy had done her best to avoid discussing the attack. The details she'd heard from Isaac and Adam were enough to give her nightmares. She couldn't help but recall her days at the Whitman Mission and the massacre.

She spied the young mother who had survived and come back to the village with Adam and Isaac. She was a distant relative to Bright Star, and as such, Bright Star's son had taken her into his house and married her. In the Tututni tribe, if a man had wealth, he could take more than one wife. Mercy wondered if that met with the woman's approval, since she'd just lost her husband and sons. How terrible it would be to have no time for mourning your husband, but instead have to go right into an intimate relationship with another man. Mercy couldn't bear the idea. But she wasn't sure the Tututni women had much say in such things.

Leaving the basket of clothes by the cabin, Mercy decided to take a short walk to clear her mind and pray. Eletta wanted some time alone with Faith anyway, and a few moments of quiet would do Mercy good. She'd been so worried about Eletta and the possibility of an attack on the village that she hadn't had much time to herself.

She walked across the open grounds and past the field where the boys had played shinny. Adam came to mind. In some ways she'd been much too hard on him. It wasn't right to punish him just because he wasn't given to sharing his thoughts with her. And his apprehensive attitude toward her abilities had proven unfounded, so he had been a little friendlier lately. Not much, but a little, and that was a move in the right direction.

When she'd first come here, Mercy had been more concerned with being able to care for Eletta's needs than befriending her brother-in-law. When Eletta improved, Mercy had been confident that all would be well and Grace's cures would do the trick. Now, with this new round of problems, Mercy was more than a little worried. Bleeding during a pregnancy was never good.

She sat on the same log Adam had knocked her off of and smiled. It wasn't such an embarrassing memory now, and she wished she'd handled the entire matter differently.

The tall pines and oaks at her back rustled as the breeze picked up, and Mercy hugged her arms to her body. Glancing heavenward, she began to pray in silence. She could feel God all around her, and it seemed only right to praise Him.

Thank You for Your kindness, Lord. Thank You for Your fairness, generosity, and righteousness. You alone are worthy of such praise.

She closed her eyes and let the stillness of the moment wash over her. God had been so good to her. He had always been there for her in the best and worst of times. When she'd lost her father, the pain had been intense, but losing her mother had been devastating. She had tried to find comfort in her sisters, but they were too overwhelmed with their own grief to be much help. Mercy had turned to God and found His presence so notable that it was almost as if she could feel His embrace. The same had been true at the Whitman Mission.

During and after the attack, prayer had been her refuge. Prayer was vital to all the women there. God was their hope—He was all they had. Now Mercy found the world around her at war and the killing continuing. This time it was at the hands of her own people.

"You awake?"

Mercy's eyes snapped open at the sound of Adam's question. She looked up and found him standing in front of her.

"I am. I was just reflecting and praying." She smiled, determined to break down some of the barriers between them. "Would you like to join me?"

He looked surprised for a moment, then nodded and sat beside her. He sat as far from her as possible—whether for his own comfort or hers, Mercy didn't know.

"What were you reflecting on?" he asked, his voice still reserved.

"My life. I was just thankful that I've always known who God is—that I've never had to question if He's real or not. Mama and Da saw to that, even though I lost both of them at a young age."

Adam nodded. "My mother and father also raised us with a fear of the Lord."

"I can't imagine how folks deal with the despairs of life without Him. The times in my life when I was hurting most, God always seemed present."

"People without Him usually try to deal with life in their own strength, and it never works for long," Adam replied.

"We always had the Bible to go to if we needed answers." She looked at the village houses across the field. "How do you share the gospel with a people who don't know anything about the Bible? It's nothing more than a book of English words to them. How do you instill respect and faith in it?"

Her question appeared to ease Adam's discomfort. He stretched out his legs and followed her gaze to the Indian houses. "You can't just rush in and wave the Bible and tell them they must believe. I've seen preachers who tried that, and it never works. Isaac has always maintained that you have to be a living example. That you live your faith in front of them and invite them to share your life and ask them to share theirs. You don't impose upon them and demand they do things only your way, but rather work with them to show that you are open to learning about them and what they believe.

"Little by little, trust is formed, and of course they see us reading the Scriptures and want to know what we're doing. We always start the children reading with Bible verses, and that allows us to explain them. And then we teach them to memorize Scripture and use it to practice writing. As time goes by, they see and hear for themselves what our faith means to us, and they gradually form a respect, whether they believe it for themselves or not. At least most do."

"That makes sense. I was never sure how Dr. Whitman went about his work with the Cayuse. I think his heart was good. He certainly loved God and did his best to be a righteous man. But he imposed on the Cayuse and Nez Perce. He demanded change from them."

"In what way?" Adam asked.

"He told them they had to settle in one place and farm instead of being nomadic and following the food. He told them they needed to learn English and to put aside their customs and superstitions." Mercy shrugged. "I suppose I understand what he was trying to accomplish, but even then it seemed the wrong way to treat such a proud people."

"Isaac said he was here nearly a year before the people started to accept his presence and work with him. This wasn't a village then. Isaac and Eletta came here and built their cabin, and every day they ventured out to try to meet the native peoples. Some had already had bad encounters with the whites and distrusted them. Others were more open and invited Isaac and Eletta to sit at their fires and share food. They were fascinated by Faith. Many had never seen a white baby." He shifted his weight, and the log rocked. He reached out to steady Mercy. "Sorry about that." He quickly dropped his hold and looked away.

"Isaac started inviting them to his house so that he and Eletta could reciprocate, but the Tututni were very skeptical. It took nearly another year before they would come. By then, Isaac was trying to add on to the cabin, and some of the Indians even lent a hand. When the time came to build the church, he had made good friends and received all the help he needed. It was while they were building that the families came and set up camp here. It was summer, so they mostly lived outside. Isaac said it was the most amazing thing. They allowed Isaac to preach and Eletta to teach their children. All the while, they worked on the church, and more Tututni arrived to join in. By the time it turned cold, Isaac and Eletta had integrated themselves into the lives of these people, and they in turn decided to remain here. They dug houses, and Isaac helped. He told me the leaders were surprised that a white man would lend a hand to help Indians."

"I wonder how different things might have been if it were that way with the Whitmans. On the other hand, the Cayuse were a different people. They were known for being aggressive, warring people."

"What was life like there?" Adam asked.

"Nothing like this. We came to the mission from the wagon train just as a measles epidemic started. There were wide-open fields that had been planted and harvested, as well as hills and valleys. It was pretty and unseasonably warm."

"Why did you and your sisters travel west?"

"That's a long story." Mercy smiled. "Our uncle invited us to come live with him in Oregon City after our parents died. We sold everything and prepared for the trip, but none of the trail masters wanted to take on women traveling alone. My sister devised a plan with a man who wanted to come west as a missionary. The mission board wouldn't allow him to go without a wife. So they married."

"Just like that?" Adam sounded surprised.

"Yes. We told Grace it was ridiculous to marry someone she didn't love, but she honestly couldn't see another way, and our time was running out. The house had been sold, and we had no place else to go. So we joined the wagon train west and arrived at the mission. The Whitmans invited us to stay through the winter, as they often did with travelers, and since we weren't sure our uncle was even in Oregon City anymore, we accepted their offer."

"What was the mission like?"

"There was a large T-shaped mission house where several families lived with the Whitmans. In the longer part of the T, there was a school, which also doubled as our church. There was an entirely different house called the Emigrant House positioned on the other side of the acreage. Half a dozen families lived in it, and that was where my sisters and I stayed. It wasn't much, to be sure, but better than being out in the elements." She smiled and continued.

"Everyone had jobs to do. I fell ill with measles, however, and was of little use to anyone. So many were sick, and my sister Grace did her best to help. She even went to the Cayuse village despite Dr. Whitman saying that none of us should ever go there. Alex, her husband now, told her how great the need was, and they went to the village with Sam Two Moons, his Nez Perce friend, when Dr. Whitman wasn't around. Grace said the conditions were horrible."

Mercy found herself going back in time. Instead of the Tututni village before her, it became the Whitman Mission grounds with Cayuse teepees in the background.

"The Cayuse didn't live like the Tututni. They had lodges like the prairie Indian teepees. But instead of hides, the lodges were covered with mats of tule grass. I never saw the inside of one, so I can't tell you much about them. The people dressed in buckskin and whatever else they could trade for. The women seemed to love trading things for our dresses and skirts, and the men often wanted shirts." She looked at Adam and shrugged. "I suppose they thought them more comfortable."

"Maybe it was a prestige thing," Adam suggested. "Having possessions that once belonged to whites might have been a way of suggesting they'd conquered the whites."

Mercy shrugged. "Could be. Anyway, the measles spread fast, and things didn't improve for the Cayuse. Many of their children died—adults too. They became convinced that Dr. Whitman was poisoning them. One of the half-breeds was a troublemaker, and he told the Cayuse chiefs that this was true. The day before the attack, my sister Grace went north to find your brother's place. Eletta was quite sick, and Isaac was worried about her. Hope and I stayed behind because I had just gotten over the measles and Hope was in love."

The cries and screams of those who were killed during the massacre filled her head. "I was in school when the attack started. Our teacher, Mr. Saunders, had gone for water or something. I don't recall. He was attacked on his way back while two of the chiefs were in the mission house killing Dr. Whitman. Everything went crazy after that. We children tried to hide in the loft, but it didn't work. The Cayuse found us and forced us to come down. They made us line up. I was sure they were going to kill us right there and then. One of the children was the daughter of another minister. She had learned the language, so she tried to talk to the Indians, but they didn't listen. They forced us outside and made us watch as they continued to kill the men. It was terrifying. We were held hostage for a month after that. Death was a constant threat, and we were treated abominably."

She shuddered and looked at Adam. "When you came back and told us what had happened at the other village, it was like I could see it in my mind. I've seen death like that up close, and it never leaves your memory."

Adam's expression was grave. "I'm sorry you had to go through that. It would be hard enough as an adult, but as a child, it must have seemed like the end of the world."

"Being a child was to my benefit in the long run. The older girls and women were forced to . . ." She shook her head. "I'm sure you understand." She briefly allowed her gaze to meet Adam's. When he nodded, Mercy looked away and continued.

"It was the end of my world as I knew it. I'd never experienced such fear until then. The Indians we'd encountered on the trail had been helpful, and although they were pestering at times, wanting to trade or expecting us to give them things, they weren't at all threatening." She shook her head. "My sisters didn't want me to come here because of the fighting. They're afraid I'll find myself right back in the same situation."

"I understand that. I don't know that I would want one of my sisters here. I can't lie to you and say I think this is a safe place anymore. The fact is, I've been trying to talk Isaac into sending you and Eletta and Faith away."

Mercy knew the circumstances were more dangerous than before, but she'd assumed that since the whites were doing most of the killing, they would still be safe.

"Do you know something I don't?"

Adam looked almost apologetic. He turned his face away and nodded. "There have been signs of people nosing around the village. Boot prints, not moccasins. The Tututni are taking turns watching through the night."

Mercy felt a tingle run down her back. Without thinking, she scooted a little closer to Adam. "But the militia knows that this is a mission with white men and women. Surely that makes a difference."

"I don't know. From what I'm hearing, the tolerance and patience of the government is waning. Word came that the Indians all along the Rogue River were joining together to kill the whites. Some of the natives at the Table Rock Reservation left without permission and are considered to be on the warpath. And some of the people here were related to the people killed upriver. It's questionable how long the peace will hold."

Visions of the death and destruction she'd witnessed at the Whitman Mission flooded her thoughts. Mercy looked out across the village and imagined it happening here. She could see Red Deer and her children running for their lives only to be shot down. She could imagine Faith running into the middle of things to save her friends.

Something moved in the brush behind them, and Mercy let out a cry and threw herself against Adam. When a deer darted out and raced across the forest edge and finally back into the woods, Mercy let out the breath she'd been holding. She could feel Adam's arms around her—holding her safe.

She slowly lifted her face. His dark eyes bore into her—his expression one of desire but also conflict.

For a moment, neither moved, but then Adam lifted her chin and lowered his mouth to hers.

Chapter
10

The kiss sent a lightning streak through Adam, and he jumped up as if he'd been burned. He stared down at Mercy, who was trying to right herself on the log. He felt bad for nearly knocking her off of it again, but his actions couldn't be helped.

"I'm sorry. That should never have happened, and it won't happen again. I never intended to do that." He knew he was rambling. "I think we should get back to the house. It's not safe to be out this far anymore." He turned to leave, glancing over his shoulder to make sure Mercy was following. She wasn't.

He stopped and pulled her to her feet. "Did you hear me? We need to get back. That deer wouldn't just bound out of the woods without a reason. Something must have spooked it, so we should go."

"I heard you." Mercy frowned and pulled away from him.

He readied himself for some protest or downright defiance, but instead Mercy gathered her skirts and marched back to the cabin. He followed, and when she stopped to pick up the laundry basket, he reached out to take it from her. Again he expected her to reject his offer, but she let him have the basket.

"Mercy, wait." He hurried to catch up with her. "I'm truly sorry. I know what I did was wrong. I never meant it to happen."

"So you keep telling me," she said angrily. Without another word, she headed through the open front door of the house.

Isaac stood just inside. "I was coming to look for you. Faith said you were gathering clothes, and I found the laundry but no sign of you."

Mercy looked back at Adam. She grabbed the basket from him and pushed past Isaac. "I went for a walk and met with a skunk."

"A skunk?"

Adam looked at Isaac. "I'll explain later." His voice was barely a whisper.

He watched as Mercy all but threw the basket down near the fireplace. She didn't say anything, but he could almost hear her muttering. Perhaps it was just the onslaught of regrets echoing in his own mind.

Isaac shook his head. "One of the men spotted Billy and some of his militia downstream. Their camp isn't but five miles away. I figure I should go down there and try to talk some sense into them."

Adam frowned. "Do you think that's wise, since I'm leaving tomorrow?"

"I'd forgotten you were going." Isaac considered this for a moment. "I think you still need to go. It's only right that we try to warn the other tribes and help them figure out how to negotiate with the government. I want the killings to stop, and if we don't both do what we can, I'm afraid it will just continue."

Mercy had stretched a clothesline from one wall to the other in order to hang the damp laundry in front of the fire. Adam could see she was calming down as her mind focused on the work at hand. He hated that he'd upset her so much.

"It's most likely going to continue anyway." Adam turned back to Isaac, who was watching him in a curious fashion. "I'll leave at first light." He said it loudly enough that he hoped Mercy heard him.

Isaac stood without a word of reply for several moments. Adam wondered if his brother was trying to figure out the conflict with the Indians, or the obvious issue between Adam and Mercy. With a shake of his head, Isaac grabbed his hat. "I'll go after I speak with the men. I'm also going to see Tunchi about getting Eletta to Ellensburg."

Tunchi, whose name translated to the number four, was Red Deer's brother-in-law. He was not only the fourth son born to his family, but was born in a village where four roads converged. His full name translated to "Four Roads Come Together," but everyone called him Tunchi. Adam knew Isaac had chosen him because he had a large, long canoe that could manage the ocean if need be.

Adam lowered his voice. "Do you think you can get her to go?"

"She's not well, and it would give me peace of mind to have her near a doctor or hospital. I'd also like to have our girls where there are soldiers to protect them. From just talking with the other men, I believe the peace is sure to pass from us soon enough."

"Maybe I should stay here then."

Isaac shook his head. "No, you must get to the other tribes— the ones away from the river in the higher elevations. They may not realize how quickly things are deteriorating. We need to encourage them to come down peacefully and give themselves up for transportation to the reservation. As much as I hate it, I think it's now the only way. Perhaps if they show cooperation, the government will organize a reserve down here and allow them to return."

Three days later, Mercy still felt mixed emotions when thinking about Adam. She couldn't deny that what she felt for him was stronger than it had been just days before. That kiss had changed everything. The kiss and the way he'd held her in his arms when she'd been frightened.

Perhaps it was foolish to put so much stock in that moment, but she couldn't help it. Nothing like that had ever happened to her before, yet Adam treated the entire matter as distasteful and something to be forgotten.

"But I can't forget." Mercy touched her lips. It was the first time she'd ever kissed a man. Many a fellow had tried, but Mercy had managed to avoid their attempts. With Adam, she had welcomed it.

Faith murmured softly, rolling over in her sleep. Sometime in the night she had grown cold and had climbed in bed with Mercy. It was becoming a habit.

It was nearly dawn, and Mercy figured it was better to get up and get to work than to lie sleepless in bed, wondering about her heart.

She inched her body down the mattress and managed to separate herself from Faith. The child rolled over and curled into a ball. Once out of bed, Mercy hurried to dress in her warm wool skirt and stockings. She topped this with a flannel camisole and long-sleeved cotton blouse before exiting the bedroom. There was no sign of anyone else being awake, so she went about her business as quietly as possible.

After donning her boots, Mercy stoked up the fire in the stove and then added more wood to the fireplace. They were getting low on wood, but it would have to wait. She lit a lamp and again thought of Adam. Where was he now? Had he encountered any danger? Did he think about their kiss?

"Stop it!" she commanded herself.

She pulled on her apron and did her best to focus on breakfast. As she worked, the fire in the hearth caught and began a cheery blaze. It wasn't long before Isaac appeared. He yawned and rubbed his eyes.

"Thanks for starting the fire. Feels colder this morning," he said, reaching for his boots.

"I thought so too. We're going to need more wood." Mercy turned with the coffeepot in hand. "I was just making coffee."

Isaac nodded. "I sure could use a cup. Make it strong, and I'll fetch the wood."

He didn't bother to put on his coat but quickly exited the house, leaving the front door open. Mercy turned back to the water she'd boiled the night before. She poured half the normal amount into the pot, then put it on the stove to heat. Next she took out a portion of coffee beans and put them in the grinder. By the time she'd finished grinding them, Isaac was back with his first load of wood.

Isaac was just bringing in his third armload of split logs when Faith appeared in her nightclothes. She crossed to the table and plopped down without so much as a word. It wasn't like her, and Mercy feared she was sick.

She went to Faith and put a hand to her head. "Do you feel all right?"

Faith shook her head. "I had a bad dream."

Mercy knelt beside her. "Sometimes talking about it helps."

Faith glanced at her father as he stacked wood near the stove. "No. I don't want to talk about it."

It was a strange response for the little girl who always seemed keen to share her thoughts. "Well, anytime you want to talk about it, I'm here." Mercy rose. "Is Eletta awake?" she asked Isaac.

"No. At least not when I got up."

117

"Good. She needs her rest. I'm going to whip up some flapjacks, so breakfast will be ready shortly." She went back to the counter, where she'd left a large mixing bowl. "Faith, why don't you get dressed, and then you can help me."

Mercy heard the chair scoot across the floor. She glanced up to see Faith lumber back to the bedroom. The little girl was definitely not herself.

By the time breakfast was ready, Eletta had awakened. Mercy fixed her a cup of raspberry leaf tea and brought it to her with a single flapjack. She'd smeared the top with some berry jam, hoping it would entice Eletta to eat.

"How are you feeling today?"

Eletta smiled. "Stronger, I think."

Mercy knew she was trying to be positive. Isaac had told them the night before that if Eletta was stable enough, he planned to go downriver and see if he could find Billy and his confederates. He'd planned to go the day Adam left, but Eletta hadn't been well, so he'd delayed.

"Well, I think eating will prove that to all of us."

Eletta looked at the plate and nodded. "It looks good, and the tea smells wonderful."

Mercy smiled. "I'll be back to check on you in a few minutes."

"Tell Isaac that I'm doing just fine. Please."

The two women exchanged a knowing look. Mercy felt conflicted about telling Isaac that all was well, but at the same time, she knew it was urgent that he speak with the volunteer militiamen. Rumors abounded up and down the river, and it seemed that war was coming ever closer to the mission. If someone didn't make an effort to encourage peace, Mercy feared full-on war.

In the kitchen, Faith was finishing the flapjacks, and Isaac stood at the stove, pouring himself a cup of coffee. He turned to study Mercy for a moment, and she beamed a smile.

"Eletta's eating and feeling much better."

A look of relief washed over Isaac's face. "That's good." He took his coffee and sat at the small table. "I'll plan to leave just after breakfast."

"Do you want me to pack you something to eat?"

He shook his head. "I'll just take some dried salmon with me. It'll see me through."

Mercy nodded and brought him a stack of flapjacks. Going back to the stove, she smiled down at Faith. "Take your seat, and I'll bring our plates."

Faith handed her the spatula and did as she was told. Mercy worried about what was troubling the child. Perhaps after her father left, Faith would feel more like talking.

They ate in silence. It seemed the worries of the situation held them all captive. Isaac was no doubt concerned about convincing the militia to hold off on any more attacks, as well as worried about Eletta. Faith was troubled by her bad dream and perhaps was coming down sick. Mercy, on the other hand, was trying to figure out what in the world she was going to do about Adam.

Isaac made it clear that he wasn't sure when he'd be back. He hoped it would be by nightfall, but there was a chance it might not be until the following day.

"I can't be sure where they're camped. They were just a few miles downstream, and hopefully that's where they still are," he told Mercy as they stood at the riverbank. "If they've gone closer to Gold Beach, I might go on in to town and speak with the army doctor about Eletta."

Mercy looked across the gray water and then to the equally gray skies. "It looks like rain." She knew his mind wasn't at all on the weather.

He nodded. "Try to keep Eletta calm. Hopefully when I get back, I'll have a plan for getting all of you out of here. I think it'd be best if you stayed with the Hulls in Port Orford, but I don't know if Eletta can travel that far. You might have to remain in Gold Beach."

"Just come back safe, and don't worry about us. We'll be ready for whatever you decide."

He glanced back at the cabin. "I fear for her. I know she's not as well as she lets on."

Mercy nodded. "But she's determined. Try not to worry. I think she'll be fine."

She wasn't certain about that, but it seemed to give him comfort to hear the words. Mercy watched as he climbed down the narrow path to the river and threw his gear into one of the canoes. One of the Tututni men stood by. They exchanged a few words, and then Isaac climbed into the canoe while the Indian pushed him out into the river.

The current caught the canoe just as Isaac began to paddle. Before long, he was around the bend and out of sight, and Mercy was staring down at empty river. She didn't like knowing that both Adam and Isaac were gone.

As she walked back to the cabin, she heaved a sigh. She was scared, but she didn't want to let on for Eletta and Faith's sakes. Still, she couldn't shake a deep sense of dread.

~~~

Isaac returned the following afternoon. Mercy and Eletta had just started to grow concerned when he bounded into his bedroom with a scowl on his face.

"What is it? Did you talk to the militia?" Eletta asked. Mercy began to gather the remains of the tea she'd served Eletta.

"I didn't have a chance. I couldn't locate them. Traces of their camp were there just as I figured, but they were nowhere to be found. I saw neither them nor any Indians. It was as if everyone had fallen off the face of the earth. It started pouring rain, and I figured it best to just come home rather than continue searching for them in bad weather."

Eletta frowned and sat up. "What will you do?"

"I'm going to talk with the men here and encourage them to speak to some of the nearby villages. If I can't reason with the militia, then I'll reason with the Tututni. They've a more level head on the matter than the whites have shown, anyway. Then, in a day or two, I'm going to go upriver to where the army is camped. I'll have to be gone for a week or more, but I think it's important that I speak with whoever is in charge. If it's the captain who came with us from Port Orford, I think I can reason with him."

Mercy nodded and clutched the tea tray as though it were a lifeline. "He did seem reasonable."

Isaac looked at Eletta and shook his head. "I don't like the idea of leaving you two alone for that long. I just don't know if you'll be safe."

Eletta eased back against the pillows. "The people here would protect us with their lives, and we'd do the same for them. Besides, like you told me long ago, we didn't come here to be safe."

She forced a smile that Mercy knew she didn't feel. The fact was that Eletta was weakening by the day. It didn't seem to matter what Mercy fed her or what herbal tea she concocted, Eletta was fading fast. She had once heard Grace mention a situation where a woman could actually be poisoned by the baby inside her. If that were the case, there was very little Mercy could do. She could hardly cause the unborn child to be expelled. That would be murder. No, it was all in God's hands now.

"I'll be out in the kitchen." Mercy walked to the door. "Isaac, would you like some coffee?"

"Yes. I'll come get it in a minute."

She nodded and reached for the door to close it behind her.

No doubt the privacy would do them good. Maybe Eletta could cheer her husband.

Since Faith was playing with Mary, Mercy took the opportunity to bake a pie. She made enough dough for two double-crusted pies, then put it in a lidded tin and set it outside to chill. After that, she collected some jars of preserved berries for the filling. It wasn't long before Isaac appeared for his coffee.

"Mercy, I want you to know that I wouldn't go if I didn't think it was necessary. I didn't want to say anything in front of Eletta, but I did meet up with a couple soldiers. They were heading downriver for supplies. They said they're planning to attack the area villages unless the Indians surrender without a fight."

"We'll be all right. If anything goes amiss—if Billy and his men show up—they won't do anything to us. Hopefully they'll leave the Tututni alone, but the men are keeping watch. If we come under attack, they should have time enough to flee."

"I'm sure you're right." Isaac sighed. "I just wish there were another way. I know Eletta isn't well."

"No. She isn't." Mercy put her hand on his arm. "I won't leave her even for a moment. I'll be here all day, since we're not having classes, and I'll keep Faith close." They'd concluded, with Adam's departure and the growing danger, that it would be best to suspend school.

He sat down at the table. "I just wish there were another way. I wish Adam hadn't gone, but it's just as vital that he speak with the Indians. They'll listen to him, even if they choose not to heed his advice."

Mercy could see the turmoil within Isaac. She moved to the table and sat opposite him. "Why don't we pray?"

Chapter 11

In the days that followed Isaac's departure, Mercy felt the full weight of responsibility for Eletta and Faith. The growing concern within the village was evident in the way women and children stayed close to their homes, while the men were alert and on guard. Mercy kept Faith with her most of the time, unwilling to let her roam even as far as one of the Tututni houses. If an attack came, she didn't want Faith to be separated from her mother. Not only that, but given the child's brown-black hair, it would be easy enough for a militiaman to mistake her for an Indian, especially if she wore her Tututni hat.

"It's probably best if you don't wear it," Mercy told Faith one evening. The child looked at her oddly. "The militia aren't expecting white children to be wearing Tututni clothes. I fear the way they're acting toward the Indians, they might hurt you, not realizing you're white."

Faith was fearless. "I don't care. If they come to hurt my friends, they're hurting me too." In the end, however, Eletta had asked her to do as Mercy suggested. The look Mercy exchanged with Eletta left little doubt that both women were concerned about the potential trouble.

Prayer became their mainstay. At night, the three of them gathered in Eletta's room and prayed for the safety of everyone and for understanding and calm to guide the people in charge. Mercy could sense the tension all around her, but amazingly enough, she felt at peace. God had always seen her through, and if it was her time to die, then she would do so knowing that her eternal reward was greater than life on earth. Even so, she knew Eletta was terrified for her husband and unborn child, as well as for Mercy and Faith, and it wasn't doing her health a bit of good. Try as she might, Mercy couldn't convince her that all would be well when they both knew otherwise.

When Isaac didn't return after a week, Mercy tried not to worry. It had been raining, even snowing a bit. With the weather so foul, it might have been necessary for him to wait before returning home.

To keep everyone occupied, Mercy suggested they work on baby clothes. Sitting together in Eletta's room, they crafted little gowns, and Mercy helped Faith make diapers from flannel Eletta had saved.

"Christmas will soon be here." Eletta looked at Faith. "I'm afraid I have no presents for you."

Faith bounced on her knees, material in one hand, needle and thread in the other. "Christmas isn't about getting presents. It's about Jesus being our gift from God."

Mercy smiled. "That's right. We can always bake some cookies. I think there's enough flour and sugar to spare."

Faith grinned. "We could make cookies into shapes like stars and angels."

Eletta smiled. "I can just imagine them."

They talked about the cookies and what kind of Christmas

meal they might serve. Eletta suggested they gather everyone in the village together and have a shared celebration.

But two weeks later, when Christmas arrived and Isaac had still not returned, nobody felt much like celebrating, and even the cookies went unmade.

December spilled into January with no word from Adam or Isaac. Mercy couldn't help but fear the worst. She tried to keep up a positive spirit for the sake of Eletta and Faith, but she could see how the absence of their men caused both to sink into despair.

As the weeks went by, Faith continued to have nightmares that often caused her to cry out and wake Mercy. Mercy did all she could to soothe the little girl, but it was hard to encourage her when she saw her mother growing sicker.

Mercy felt it was very likely Eletta would die, but she didn't want to say as much. Not even to Eletta, whom Mercy was certain already knew the truth. Besides, miracles did happen. God could save Eletta and the baby and bring Adam and Isaac home safe. He could cause peace to fall upon the tribes and the militia. He could—but would He?

The morning of Sunday, January twentieth began normally. While Faith ate breakfast, Mercy read from the Bible.

"Psalm forty-six starts, 'God is our refuge and strength, a very present help in trouble. Therefore, will not we fear, though the earth be removed, and though the mountains be carried into the midst of the sea.'"

Mercy paused at the sound of a woman's scream. She looked at Faith. "Go stay with your mother. Don't come out of the house. Do you understand?"

Faith nodded, her eyes wide. She got up from the table and ran to the bedroom. Mercy headed outside to see what the trouble was. One of the Tututni women called out to summon others. Mercy couldn't understand everything that she was saying, but she knew enough of the language to realize there was danger.

Tututni men gathered around the woman, and she pointed toward the river. There was a brief exchange of words, and then the Tututni headed to their houses. Mercy decided to walk to the top of the riverbank and see what was going on. Perhaps the army had come. If that were the case, it would no doubt alarm the Indians. Still, if it was the army, then Isaac would be with them.

She didn't even reach the edge of the bank, however, before Billy Caxton and another man popped up over the ridge. They carried something between them wrapped in a blanket. Mercy felt her heart in her throat. It looked like a body.

"Sorry to break the bad news to you, Miss Flanagan," Billy began, "but I'm afraid the Indians killed the pastor."

Mercy looked at Billy and then to his friend. "Which pastor?"

They set the body on the ground, and Billy folded back the blanket. It was Isaac.

A gasp escaped Mercy, and she knelt beside Isaac to assure herself he was really dead. The body was cold and stiff. She looked back up at Billy for an explanation.

"I'm real sorry. We found him upriver. There's no telling how long ago it happened. When we came upon him, he was dead. He had three arrows in his back."

Billy gave her a look of sympathy. He reached down to help her up, but Mercy ignored his hand and stood.

"What tribe were the arrows from?" She knew the tribes marked their arrows, and it might help to know who was responsible.

"Tututni. They probably saw a white man and didn't wait to ask questions or see who it was. Or it could have been someone from this bunch who just wanted him dead." Billy motioned behind Mercy to the Tututni village.

"These people are peaceful." She turned and found several

of the Tututni men watching her from a distance. "Bring Isaac to the church."

Billy nodded to his companion, and together they lifted the blanket. Eletta and Faith appeared at the door to the house.

"What's happened?" Eletta asked, coming forward. It seemed she already knew.

Mercy ran to her side. "Eletta, you're far too weak to be up. Go back to bed."

She fixed Mercy with an emotionless expression. "It's Isaac, isn't it?"

Billy and his friend stopped and put the body down once again. With the blanket still pulled back, there was no hiding Isaac's identity.

Eletta leaned against the doorjamb. "What happened?"

"Sorry, ma'am." Billy took off his hat. "Indians—probably the ones you call friends—they killed him."

She shook her head and started to collapse. Mercy barely caught her. "Mr. Caxton, please help me."

He dropped his hat and came immediately to her side. He lifted Eletta in his arms and followed Mercy into the house. She led him to the bedroom. "Put her on the bed."

He did as instructed, then stood back as if to receive his next command.

"Thank you. Now please take Isaac's body to the church and go. Just go, before there's any trouble," Mercy said.

"There won't be trouble unless the Indians start it," Billy countered. "I don't know why you care so much about them, especially now. Those heathens don't care nothing about you and yours. You need to understand that we're at war, 'cause the Tututni sure enough know it."

Mercy had forgotten about Faith. The little girl stood with wide eyes, biting her lower lip. "Faith, go stay with your mother. I'll be back in a minute."

She pushed Billy toward the open door and outside. Once they were out of the house, Mercy turned on him. "That child has just lost her father, and my friend has lost her husband. I don't need your commentary on how bad the Indians are or a reminder of the fighting going on. What I need is for you to go before you create some sort of conflict where one doesn't exist. These people are peaceful, although they might cease to be if they think you had anything to do with killing their friend."

Billy's eyes widened before he bent to pick his hat up off the ground. When he looked back up, he was scowling. "I do a good deed and get accused of causing trouble. How's that for a thank-you?"

"I do thank you for your help, but we both know it won't help for you to remain here accusing the Tututni of killing Isaac. Please just go."

Billy shrugged. "Fine. We'll put him in the church and go."

Mercy watched as they carried Isaac away. She remained fixed to her spot until Billy and his friend returned, blanket in hand. They said nothing, and she offered nothing in return. It was senseless to prolong their departure. She needed to tend Eletta and Faith and somehow arrange for Isaac's burial.

When Billy and his friend disappeared down the riverbank, Mercy turned to go back into the house. The man she knew as Tunchi and several other Tututni dispersed from the trees. No doubt they had been there the entire time.

"We will prepare the body and bury him," Tunchi said.

Mercy looked at his sad face, and then her gaze traveled down his buckskin-clad chest to the knife he wore in his belt. Could he or one of the villagers have killed Isaac?

"Do you really think Tututni killed him?" she asked, not sure she should even pose the question. If they were responsible, she doubted Tunchi would ever admit it.

"Brother Isaac was a good man, and the Tututni would do

him no harm. Most of the tribes around here accepted him and would not have harmed him." Tunchi looked toward the river. "That one I do not trust to say the truth."

Mercy nodded. She glanced across the grounds to find the rest of the Tututni people coming toward them. She looked at Tunchi. "I have to care for Eletta. She's not well."

"You go now," he said, nodding. There were tears in his eyes.

Mercy hurried back to the cabin and reached Eletta's side just as she started to come to. She looked at Mercy as if hoping she might tell her it was all just a bad dream. Mercy could only shake her head.

"He can't be dead. He can't be," Eletta said, trying to sit up. She moaned and clutched her swollen abdomen. "No. No. It just can't be true."

Mercy sat on the edge of the bed and forced Eletta to lie back. "You've had a tremendous shock. You need to stay in bed." Glancing to where Faith sat on the floor in the corner, rocking back and forth, Mercy called to her. She took Faith in her arms. "I'm so sorry about your papa."

There were tears in the little girl's eyes. "The Indians wouldn't hurt him. He loved them. He loved everybody."

Mercy nodded. "I know he did."

Faith buried her face against Mercy's neck. She didn't cry, just clung to her. What could Mercy say to make her feel better? Nothing could undo the horror of what had happened. She remembered how Grace would handle similar matters. She always got people busy doing other things. Then, once the shock was past, she would get them to talk.

Mercy pulled back and lifted Faith's chin. "I need you to bring your mother a cup of the tea I made this morning."

For a moment she wasn't sure Faith had heard her, but then the child nodded and walked from the room. Mercy took that opportunity to tell Eletta about her talk with Tunchi.

"He says they'll prepare the body and bury him. I know nothing of their customs, but I presume that's all right with you."

Eletta nodded. "They're good people. They didn't do this."

"I know." Mercy sat on the bed beside her. "Eletta, as soon as Isaac is buried, I must get you out of here. I'll take you to Oregon City, and you can stay with Grace and Alex. There's plenty of room, and I know she'd want it that way."

"I don't think that would work."

Mercy's eyes narrowed. "Why not?"

"I . . . well . . . because of Faith. I mean, it's not that . . ." She shook her head.

Leaning close, Mercy whispered, "I know all about Faith. I know she's Hope's daughter."

"How? I was sure Grace said she never told you."

"She didn't. I overheard her and Hope talking about it when Grace had her first baby. I was just outside the door. I don't think anyone will refuse you a home because of that."

Faith returned, walking with deliberate steps to keep from spilling the tea. When she reached the bed, she stopped and extended the cup. She was so stoic that it worried Mercy.

"Thank you, sweetheart." Mercy took the tea and helped Eletta sit up. "You need to drink this now." She handed her the mug.

"When is Uncle Adam coming home?" Faith asked.

Adam. Mercy hadn't even thought of him. He would return to find his brother dead and family gone. She frowned. "I don't know. I'll speak to Tunchi and see about having someone go find him." She looked at Eletta. "Do you think someone could go after him? Someone from the tribe?" She couldn't imagine there would be any other choice.

Eletta took a little more tea, then pushed the cup back toward Mercy. "You can trust them, Mercy. They're good people, and they know the routes he would have taken. Someone is sure to go."

Isaac was laid to rest in Tututni fashion. His body was wrapped in a fine deerskin and then placed in a plank-lined hole. His head faced north, but the significance of this wasn't known to Mercy. She doubted Isaac would care.

Eletta was too sick to attend, but Faith and Mercy stood with the Tututni while Tunchi spoke of how Isaac had led him to the Lord a year earlier.

"I was made in the Lord when Brother Isaac told me how much he loved Jesus. Brother Isaac was a good man. He came to be with us and became like one of us in work and love for our people. We will bear great sorrow with him gone."

Mercy could see that most of the people were moved by Isaac's passing. The women wept, and the men stood fixed with fierce scowls. When Tunchi finished speaking, he looked to Mercy. She stepped forward with Isaac's Bible and read from John.

"'I am the resurrection, and the life: he that believeth in me, though he were dead, yet shall he live: And whosoever liveth and believeth in me shall never die.'" She raised her gaze to the Tututni people. "'Believest thou this?'" She had only intended to read the Scripture and then pray, but something nudged her to stress the meaning of the verse. "Jesus gives life beyond death. Isaac and Eletta believed this. I believe this. Some of you believe it also. Jesus tells us that if we believe in Him and die—we will live. Isaac came here because of his deep love of God, and his desire to share the good news of salvation in Jesus with you. He came to love you all and told me so."

She smiled and looked from face to face. "I have come to care for you as he did. As Eletta and Adam and Faith do. You are a good and kind people, but that isn't enough. Being good cannot save you. Only Jesus can do that. Jesus came to this earth to save all people who would come to Him. It doesn't matter the color of your skin or the language you speak. Jesus calls us to repent and turn away from wrongdoing. He cleans our hearts and wipes away our sins when we ask for His forgiveness. You must put your faith in Him—believe in Him. Then, when life ends in this world—as it must—you will live forever with Him in eternity."

Mercy closed the Bible. "I'm no preacher, but I know Isaac would have wanted me to share this with you. Let us pray." She waited until the people had bowed their heads. "Father, we know that You have received Isaac into Your care. He loved You so very much, and he wanted only to bring others to an understanding of the love You have for them. If anyone here today desires that love—let them seek You. Let them put their trust in You—repenting of their sins. Let them believe in You that they might never die.

"I ask for Your hand to be upon these people. This is a difficult time of pain and death. Not just Isaac's death, but the deaths of Indians and whites alike as they war against each other. Father, we call upon You, pleading for peace. Guide the people who make decisions for their people. Let all act in wisdom and unselfish consideration. Let them seek You. In Jesus' name, Amen."

She looked up and tucked the Bible to her breast. Faith slipped her hand in Mercy's. It was icy cold, which matched the day. Tunchi gave her a nod, and Mercy took this as a sign that she and Faith should leave.

"Are you ready?"

Faith nodded, still clinging to Mercy.

They made the walk back to the house in silence. Mercy knew there would be other times for talk, and this solemn event seemed to beg stillness. It wasn't going to be easy for Faith and Eletta without Isaac, and Mercy could only hope and pray that Adam returned soon.

When they entered the cabin, Mercy led Faith to the fire. "Don't worry about taking off your coat just yet. Warm up a bit, and I'll go check on your mama."

Faith pulled up a little stool and sat right in front of the blaze with her hands extended. Mercy drew a deep breath and went to see Eletta.

She was ashen-faced but awake—awaiting Mercy's return. "Is it finished?" she asked, her voice barely audible.

Mercy nodded and sat beside her. "It was a fine funeral. The people were clearly moved. They loved Isaac a great deal."

Eletta nodded. Tears streamed down her face. "They did. They would never have hurt him."

"I know. I don't know who did this, but I know it wasn't any of our people."

Eletta gave a hint of a smile. "Our people? It's good to hear that you've taken them to your heart as well."

Mercy hadn't realized just how precious the Tututni were to her until that moment. "I've come to love them as you do."

"In spite of what happened at Whitman's?"

"Maybe even because of what happened there." Mercy pushed back her long dark hair. She'd been so busy that day that she'd only taken the time to pull it back and tie it with a ribbon. Somewhere along the way, her ribbon had come loose and been lost.

Eletta said nothing, as if expecting Mercy to continue, so she did.

"I saw that hatred did nothing to resolve the problems between the Cayuse and the whites. Both sides acted out of fear, just as they do now. I wish the men running this campaign of hate could see that. Maybe if they understood that, things could become peaceful again."

"It's also happening because of greed," Eletta countered. "The white man has come west and found the land plentiful and fertile. He wants it for himself, and rather than live in harmony with those already here, he deems it better to rid himself of those people altogether."

Mercy nodded. "I don't see it changing anytime soon."

Eletta gave a weak shake of her head. "No."

Adam felt a growing sense of dread. He had trudged all over the mountain paths to speak to the various tribes still in the area. Snow had made travel difficult, but so too had the growing anger among the Indian people. Often they avoided him altogether, while other times they approached him in a threatening manner. He felt as though he'd failed on his mission—failed Isaac and God.

He sat by his small fire and stared at the flames. As usual, Mercy was at the forefront of his thoughts.

"I mustn't care for her. It will only end in sorrow as it did in Boston. I can't expect her to overlook who I am—can I?" he said as if expecting some sort of reply. "Lizzy couldn't overlook it. Her family was appalled and treated me no better than . . ."

He looked around and thought of the various tribes he'd tried to speak with. The tall firs and pines created an arbor overhead, but still the snow managed to slip through the branches to dust the ground.

Expecting Mercy to overlook his heritage, after all she'd endured at the hands of the Cayuse, seemed to hope for too much. She had come to care for the Tututni people, but that didn't mean she would ever consent to marry a man of native blood.

"What do I do now?"

It was time to head home. He knew that, but he didn't know how to deal with his feelings for Mercy. She was beautiful—kind and gentle. She worked with the Tututni children as if she'd been born to it.

He remembered his earlier fears that Mercy would be flirty and silly. She was anything but. Nor was she one to shrink from hard work. There had been absolutely no basis for his worries at all. She was the most remarkable woman he'd ever known.

"And I love her."

Speaking the words aloud only darkened his mood. The situation was impossible.

The sound of something or someone moving in the woods drew his attention. Adam got up slowly and looked around. He had a rifle in order to ward off animals or show his ability to protect himself should thieves or worse approach.

"You might as well join me at the fire," he called out.

A reply came back in Tututni. "You have good ears for a white man."

Adam smiled and sat back down as one of the men from the mission emerged from the trees. He crossed to where Adam sat and joined him.

"Were you trying to find me, Joseph?"

The Tututni man nodded. "There's been great sorrow in the village."

Adam steeled himself for the worst. Eletta had been quite ill. Had she died? Had the village been attacked by the militia? Was Mercy all right?

"Tell me."

"Brother Isaac—your brother was killed."

"What!" Adam hadn't meant to shout. "That can't be." He couldn't believe that he'd heard correctly. "Isaac?"

Joseph nodded. "He was shot three times in the back with arrows. A couple white men brought him back to the village."

"Where had he gone?"

"To make peace with the soldiers for our village. There's

been much trouble along the river. Brother Isaac talked with some soldiers, and they said war was coming. He wanted to talk to the chiefs in the army."

Adam felt as if someone had punched him in the stomach. He could scarcely draw breath at the thought of his brother being slain.

"And what of the others? Sister Eletta and Sister Mercy? Faith?"

"They are well but filled with sorrow and fear. Sister Mercy asked that someone come to find you. She said Sister Eletta is sick and needs to be taken away."

Adam nodded. "We'll leave at first light."

Chapter 12

"When is Adam coming home?" Faith asked as Mercy added logs to the fireplace.

It was a question Mercy had been asking herself for days. "I wish I knew."

It had been weeks since she'd sent one of the Tututni men to search for Adam, and so far there had been no word. Worse yet, the militia and army had been up and down the river, making threats and causing the local tribes to panic. There had been reports of mass murder and entire villages burned to the ground, and Mercy had no doubt they were true.

The Tututni were planning to leave the mission and head high into the mountains, where the government would have a harder time reaching them. Isaac's death had left the leaders certain that it was no longer safe for their people. Already most of the families had departed. The people remaining were the elderly and a few women with young children. Two younger men remained behind to act as guards, but their presence was far from a guarantee of safety.

The fire in the hearth caught and began to grow, warding off the damp cold. Mercy held her hands toward the flames, and Faith came alongside her to do likewise. She leaned her body against Mercy's.

"Do you think Adam will come back before all the Tututni leave?" Faith looked up at Mercy as if she knew all the answers.

"I hope so." Her thoughts had been overwhelmed with concerns about what they would do if the Indians deserted them altogether.

"I hate that my friends have gone. Except Mary, of course," Faith said as she wrapped her arm around Mercy's waist. "Everything is different now. Papa is gone, and Mama is so sick."

Mercy gave her shoulder a squeeze. "I know, and I'm no happier about it than you are. Still, we need to trust that Adam will return soon and that God will guide us in whatever way He wants to take us."

Faith sighed but said nothing more. There was nothing more to be said.

Mercy tried to sort through her thoughts, allowing for all the possibilities that might occur. If Adam didn't return and the Tututni departed, she would have to ask the volunteer militiamen or the army regulars to get her, Eletta, and Faith to Gold Beach. Since most of the Indians had headed into the mountains on foot, there were canoes available, but Mercy wasn't sure she could command one of the boats by herself. But if the army wouldn't help her, she had already decided she would take Eletta and Faith downriver anyway. Her prayer was that it wouldn't become necessary.

"What say we get some oatmeal cooking for breakfast?" Mercy forced a smile and tried to focus on the present rather than worry about the future. "Maybe Adam will come home today."

Faith followed her to the kitchen. She had shadowed Mercy constantly since her father's death. She plopped down at the table as Mercy added wood to the stove and poked at the dying embers.

"My mama is going to die, isn't she?"

Mercy was so startled by the comment that she dropped the poker. Turning to look at Faith, she knew she couldn't lie. "I honestly don't know. She's very sick."

Faith nodded. "I know she's going to die. I dreamed about it. I dreamed that she and papa were both dead. I keep dreaming about it."

Moving to stand next to Faith, Mercy wondered how to handle the situation. "Well, you know you don't have to be afraid for her. She loves God, and you'll see her again in heaven—if she dies."

"I know."

Mercy could tell there was something more. She looked at the child, and a thought came to mind. When her mother was dying, Mercy had been terrified of who would provide for her and where she would live.

"Faith, if you're afraid that you'll be left alone, then put that thought aside. I'll see to it that you're taken care of. I know Adam feels the same way. We both love you very much."

Faith's stoic expression seemed out of place on the once carefree child. Mercy knelt beside her and covered Faith's hand with her own.

"No matter what, you'll be with people who love you."

"Where will we live?" Faith looked at Mercy. "We can't stay here."

Mercy was surprised at how astute the child was. They had discussed the ongoing problems, and Faith knew her mother needed medical care elsewhere, but Mercy hadn't expected this comment.

"No. We can't. The Tututni are leaving, and that will make us very vulnerable. Besides, we won't have anyone to bring us game or fish, and I'm not very good at hunting or fishing." She smiled and squeezed Faith's hand. "But don't you fear. We'll get by. We have plenty of food stores, thanks to your mother and the Tututni women. We'll be just fine for a while, and when Adam gets back, then we'll figure out what to do."

Mercy rose and returned to the stove. She filled a small pot with water and put it on to boil. Next she went to the cupboard and pulled down a small sack of oats. She was about to measure out a portion when she heard a scream in the distance, followed by gunfire.

Faith jumped up, but Mercy beat her to the door. Opening it, Mercy couldn't figure out what was happening. Although it was dawn, the heavy clouds overhead subdued the light, and the figures of people running across the clearing were more like shadows.

More screams and gunshots sounded. It seemed to come from the direction of the creek. At this hour, the Tututni women and children would be gathering water. Mercy felt her skin crawl.

"Faith, go stay in your mama's room and bar the door."

"Where are you going?" The child looked terrified.

"I think the militia is attacking. I'm going to get all the Tututni to come here, and we'll try to keep them from being killed." Mercy pulled on her coat. "Go now. Tell your mother what's happening."

No doubt Eletta had already heard the gunfire, but Mercy figured it would give Faith a purpose. Before stepping outside, Mercy hurried to the fireplace mantel where she kept Hope's revolver. She didn't know if she'd be able to use it, but it couldn't hurt to have it.

She reached for the front door just as someone began to pound on it from the other side. Opening it, Mercy found Red Deer. She was bleeding from a wound on her arm.

"The men are killing us," she said, collapsing against the doorjamb.

Mercy pulled her into the house. "Stay here. I'm going to get as many people as I can."

"My children are in the house. I'll get them."

Mercy nodded. There was no time to argue. "Tell everyone to come here and keep the door barred unless it's one of us."

She stepped outside. Guns were being fired from what seemed like all around them. She spied several Tututni children and pointed toward the house. "Go hide in the house. Red Deer will soon be there." They ran toward the refuge, crying and screaming as if the Devil himself were on their heels.

Mercy sprinted to the nearest Tututni dwelling and knelt down to call into the house. An old woman and her daughter came to the opening. "Go now to the mission house. Wait there. You'll be safe." At least she prayed they might be.

She hurried to the next dwelling. She knew most of the remaining Tututni would have been about their morning chores, so the houses were probably empty. Even so, she did her best amidst the chaos and confusion. When a bullet whizzed past her head, Mercy knew it was time to seek shelter.

Red Deer and her children led another woman and her family to the mission house. Mercy was thankful that most of the village had already departed. At least they would be safe—for the time being.

With Red Deer and the others, Mercy ran for the safety of the house. She pushed everyone inside and directed them to the far wall. "Keep down in case they shoot into the house." She couldn't imagine the militia would do that, given this was the house of a white family, but in the midst of war, people seldom paused to consider such things.

Mercy waited at the door for a moment to see if anyone else might join them, but she saw no one through the river mist and gun smoke. She closed the door and secured the bar. Turning, she looked at the small collection of people. There were three women and ten children. Of the twenty-two people who had remained in the village, a little over half had managed to get to safety. But for how long?

When the gunfire grew less frequent, Mercy realized that the militia had probably killed all the others. It sickened her. She could easily remember the Whitman Massacre and shuddered as an occasional round was fired. No doubt to finish off the injured.

She looked around the room, wondering how in the world she could keep these people safe from further harm. Even if the militia left without another word, they wouldn't be safe here for long.

"Mercy Flanagan, I know you're in there!"

She stiffened at the sound of Billy Caxton calling her name. Frowning, she moved closer to the back of the room. Faith had opened the bedroom door and was staring wide-eyed at Mercy.

"Everyone go into the bedroom." She motioned them to the door where Faith stood. "Faith, get everyone settled in your mother's room. There won't be much space, but it'll be the safest room for now. Bar the door."

"But what about you?" Faith asked.

"I'll join you shortly. I'll knock and tell you it's me. Now go."

Faith nodded while Red Deer spoke to the others and herded the children into the room. Mercy returned to the door just as Billy began to pound on it.

"Let me in, Mercy! I know you've got heathens in there, and we're going to kill them."

His callous words sent a shiver down her spine. "Not unless you kill me first. Are you killing white women now? There are three of us in here, and we'll each fight to the death for our friends."

The pounding stopped. "Look, Mercy, this is the way it's

got to be. Nobody wants to shoot you or Mrs. Browning or her little girl. We've got a job to do, and we're going to do it."

"You've already done plenty. I think you and your men should go."

"Not without the others. Our orders are to kill every single Indian."

She thought of Faith. The poor girl didn't even know she was half Cayuse. Would they see her dark hair and high cheekbones and realize her heritage?

A thud sounded against the door, and Mercy realized Billy was trying to force his way into the house. Mercy gathered her strength. "Mr. Caxton, I have a gun, and I will use it if you or any of your men attempt to come into this house. If I can only shoot one man, I assure you—it will be you."

Silence fell. Mercy waited for Billy to offer some sort of response. Finally, he spoke.

"We can wait you out. We can even burn the place down around you. You can't stay in there forever, and no one is coming to your rescue."

"That's where you're wrong, Mr. Caxton. The Lord has already provided us with protection and rescue. You might have little regard for killing the native people, but once word gets out that you set fire to the home of white citizens, you will face murder charges. Everyone knows how much you hate the Indians, and there would be little doubt as to who killed us, so you might as well leave and wreak your havoc elsewhere. God is my defender and He will not allow you to harm me."

She felt her courage build at the thought of God's protection. He had never failed her, and she knew He never would.

When Billy didn't reply, Mercy used the opportunity to check the room. She assessed the furniture and the shuttered windows. The door and windows would have to be reinforced. There was no telling what Billy and his cohorts might do to gain entry.

Mercy went in search of Isaac's tools. She knew he kept them in a box by the fireplace, but she had no idea what she might find. Assessing the contents, she found a hammer and box of nails, a saw, and several clamps. There were also several chisels, a wedge, and a hand drill. Only the hammer and nails seemed promising at that point. Without wasting time, Mercy rid herself of her coat, careful to keep the revolver with her. She tied on an apron, then placed the revolver in the deep pocket. The weight gave her a sense of assurance.

Next she went to check on the women. She knocked on the bedroom door. "Faith, it's me. Open up."

She waited as the bar was slid out place and Faith pulled the door open. Mercy stepped into the room to see fifteen frightened faces turned toward her. Someone had lit the bedside lamp, but it was smoking badly and made the situation seem all the more sinister.

Eletta looked up from her bed, shaking her head. "Is this all of us?" she asked.

"Yes. I'm afraid so." Mercy looked to the Tututni women. Red Deer had a piece of cloth tied around her wounded arm. "I need your help. I don't trust Mr. Caxton and his men. I fear they'll try to break in to the house, so we need to reinforce the boarded windows and the front door."

Faith interpreted to make sure all the women understood. They nodded and got to their feet, setting aside their frightened children. Even Red Deer was determined to do whatever she could.

"Eletta, we have to tear up some of the furniture and cup-boards." She looked to the sick woman for permission. Eletta said nothing but gave a slight nod. Mercy coughed from the smoke. "Faith, trim that wick so the lamp will stop smoking." Faith moved immediately to comply.

Mercy led the Tututni women into the front room. "Here's

what we need to do. First take the mattresses and bedding from this room and put it in Eletta's room." She pointed to Faith's room. "Then we'll tear the beds apart." She knew the long framing pieces would work well to secure the front door and windows. All she needed to do was nail them in place. The boards that composed the counter in the kitchen would also serve well. They would cover most of the window except for a small space at the top and bottom. Since the windows were already shuttered due to the cold, Mercy felt confident they would hold.

The women went to work, and in two hours they had reinforced the windows and front door. Standing back to survey the results, Mercy knew they'd done all they could. Their last task was to strengthen the boards that covered Eletta's bedroom window.

Mercy was certain Billy and his men would have heard the hammering. They would know she had reinforced the house, and hopefully that would discourage them from further attack. Nevertheless, she moved food and water into the bedroom in case the men somehow managed to break in to the house and the women and children were forced to remain in Eletta's bedroom for safety.

Of course, none of that would matter if Billy and his men decided to burn them out. In fact, if he did that, they would have a difficult time escaping the cabin. She could only pray the men wouldn't go to such extremes, given there were white women who would also be injured or killed.

By the clock on the fireplace mantel, Mercy knew it would soon be dark. She had no idea what Billy might try once he thought them all to be sleeping. It made her even more determined to keep watch. Hopefully between her and the Indian women, they could take turns.

Oh, Adam, where are you? Have you been killed as well?

The questions would not be silenced. She had no way of knowing if Adam knew of their plight, and if he did, she had no idea how he might rescue them. She wished there was some way to sneak everyone out under the cover of darkness, but that would be impossible. Eletta could barely sit up and would never be able to walk.

It was Faith who helped lighten the situation. She suggested they sing hymns and started them in a series of songs. The words of encouragement seemed to comfort each of the hostages. Mercy wondered what Billy and his cohorts thought of the singing. She hadn't heard anything from them since earlier in the day and had begun to wonder if they were even out there.

They're out there. I know they are. Billy isn't the type to give up.

With that thought, Mercy rechecked the revolver. Another hour passed, and when the group grew tired of singing, Mercy suggested they eat something. She handed out smoked salmon and bread, then offered a prayer.

"Father, we ask Your blessing on this meal. We ask for a miracle as well. Please send Adam back to us so that we might be rescued from harm. And if not Adam, then send someone worthy of trust who will deal honorably with us. Amen." She looked up and found all eyes watching her. She smiled. "Let's eat."

After another few hours, the children, including Faith, had fallen asleep. Wrapped up together with their mothers, Mercy knew they'd be warm enough. She didn't want to build up the fire in the hearth. It would be just like Billy to cover the chimney and smoke them out.

Faith was in bed with Eletta, who had long been asleep. Mercy wondered how much longer Eletta had. Without the help of a doctor, Mercy knew she and the baby would die. The baby might already be dead. A feeling of gloom settled over her. She looked at the sleeping children again and wondered if they would ever grow up to become adults. Did any of them have a future?

Seeing there was nothing else to do, Mercy blew out the lamp and settled in.

Snug in her coat and leaning against the barred bedroom door, Mercy thought only of how to keep these people safe. She thought it ironic that she was being held hostage for the second time in her life. Although this time it was by her own hand, both situations were life-threatening.

She spent a good deal of the night hours praying. She intended to keep watch until two, and then one of the other women had promised to take a turn. Even so, Mercy doubted she'd be able to sleep, knowing Billy was just on the other side of the cabin wall.

Chapter 13

Something was very wrong, but Adam couldn't say exactly what. He felt it more than heard it. Squinting against the darkness, he tried to see any sign of life in the mission village. Turning to Joseph, he shook his head. "It's too quiet."

The Tututni man leaned closer. "I check the river. You stay."

Adam nodded, although he wasn't sure Joseph even saw him. Their journey back to the mission had been fraught with problems. At the higher elevations, snow slowed them down, and then there were warring tribes to avoid. It seemed the Indians of the Rogue River were preparing to make a final stand against the white soldiers. From the few people they'd allowed themselves to encounter, Adam had learned that the army was moving downriver toward the mission. They had one goal: move the Indians out . . . or kill them.

It seemed forever before Joseph returned. Adam barely heard him approach as he squatted down beside Adam.

"There are white men camped at the top of the bank behind the sweat lodge."

"Soldiers?"

"I think it's those men Brother Isaac didn't like."

"Billy Caxton and his militia?"

"Yes."

Adam felt his blood go cold. "Did you see anything else?"

"No. There was no light from the houses or people. No guards either. I think they must have attacked the village. My people are gone. Maybe dead."

Despair flooded through Adam. "But why would they still be there?" he asked, although he didn't expect an answer.

"Maybe they wait for you."

Adam shook his head. Billy Caxton wouldn't care where he was. "Look, I don't know what's going on, but I intend to find out." He knew it would soon be light, so acting now was of the utmost importance. "Follow me."

He moved back, away from the village. When he felt they were far enough away, Adam took off his pack, keeping his rifle slung over his shoulder. "I'm going to write a letter to the captain of the soldiers. I need you to take it as quickly as you can. I don't think they'll harm you. The captain is an even-tempered man and seems to have good control of his men. Give him this letter and cooperate with him in any way he demands." Adam took out his journal and tore a page free from the back. Next he dug around for his pencil.

"The white soldiers will take me to the reservation." Joseph's statement was matter-of-fact.

Adam nodded. "Most likely. But they're going to do that anyway. You might as well turn yourself in. I'll give you my white shirt. When you approach, wave it in the air. That will signal your surrender. I'll tell them in this letter that you can act as their guide. Hopefully they'll allow you to come back to the mission, and we can speak to them about getting my family out of here."

He knew it didn't meet with the young man's approval, but

there was no time for argument. "I know this isn't right. I know you will be making a great sacrifice." He frowned. "I just don't know another way to ensure the safety of my sister-in-law and niece."

"And Miss Mercy," Joseph added.

Adam had done his best not to think of Mercy, but he gave a reluctant nod. "Yes."

"I do this for you and for them." Joseph smiled. "I'm smarter than the white man, and I can always escape later."

Adam couldn't help but smile back. "I've no doubt you could."

Once the letter was written, Adam handed it over. "I'm going to the village. I'll sneak into the mission house and see what's happened. Try to get the soldiers here as soon as possible. I don't think Billy and his men are very patient, whatever their plans might be."

With Joseph off and running for the soldiers' camp, Adam made his way back to the edge of the village. He knew the lay of the land like the back of his hand. He would come in from the far eastern edge by the chicken coops. From there, he would slip along the tree line and come up behind the outhouse. Then it was only about twenty feet to the back of the house.

He crept into position, careful to keep himself hidden in the trees. The cold permeated his bones as rain began to fall. There was nothing to be done about it, however. At least the rain helped muffle any noise he made.

He hurried from the trees and flattened himself up against the chicken coop. His boots sank into the mud, putting him off balance. He quickly regained control, however, and listened for any sound that might suggest the militia had noticed him.

There was still no sign of life, but he suspected Billy probably had at least one man on guard. His fear was that Caxton and his men had already killed everyone—including Eletta, Faith, and Mercy. The militia wouldn't set out to kill white women, but Adam knew Mercy would never let him harm the others unchallenged. She would stand up to the militia, and in turn they would have no choice but to get her out of the way.

Barely controlled rage raced through him at the thought. He was a man of the cloth, but injustice and evil still riled him until all he could think about was righting the wrong. If Billy had hurt Mercy or the others, Adam didn't know what he would do. In his heart he knew that without God's calming grace, he was capable of doing almost anything.

He took a deep breath and prayed. *Lord, You know my heart better than I do. You know how helpless I feel in this situation. Please, Lord, give me wisdom and calm my spirit.*

With that prayer, Adam crept forward, keeping close to the small coop. He would have to cross ten or so feet without anything to hide behind in order to reach the privy. Crouching low, he hurried to close the distance and straightened only after he could use the outhouse for cover. Still there wasn't a single sound to suggest his presence was known.

The house was only a short distance away. He felt confident he could reach it without anyone being the wiser. Adam waited just in case Billy or his men were patrolling the grounds. The minutes ticked by, and the quiet remained. It was now or never.

The ground between the house and privy was covered in puddles from the rain, but planks had been put down to create a walkway to the house. He could go that route, which would be the quieter one, but it would also leave him the most exposed. Still, if he tried to race across the muddy yard, he would make a lot of noise and perhaps even trip on something.

He drew a long breath. He'd take his chances with the walkway.

Easing out from behind the outhouse, Adam moved with the grace of a wildcat stalking its prey. He had learned quite a few tricks from the Tututni that allowed him to sneak up on deer or other game. He would never be as good as they were, but he had been successful numerous times. Those skills came in handy now.

Twenty feet seemed like miles, but Adam reached the cabin wall. He gave it a cursory study. The back wall of the cabin was solid except for the window in Isaac and Eletta's room. He knew that had been boarded up for winter, so there was no chance of getting inside that way without creating a lot of noise.

He could knock on the boards. If anyone happened to be inside, they might respond. Of course, they might also think they were being attacked. Then there was the possibility that the women and Faith had already been moved from the area. Maybe some of the militia had taken up residence in the house.

Then an idea came to him.

There was the roof access. He hadn't been here when it was used to draw smoke from the house, but he had utilized it with Isaac when the roof had been damaged by a fallen tree branch. After they'd repaired the roof, they'd cut down all the nearest trees and used the lumber to enlarge the church.

Adam gazed upward. If he could get on the roof, he could get into the house by way of the trapdoor Isaac had made. But how would he get on the roof? And after he was there, how would he move without being seen?

Again he surveyed his surroundings. He knew there was a rain barrel alongside the house as well as a couple wooden crates. It might be possible to use them to build a makeshift ladder and hoist himself onto the roof. It was a risk, but there seemed to be no other way. Already the skies were starting to lighten with a predawn glow.

Mercy tossed and turned in a restless sleep. In her dreams she was searching for something but had no idea what it was. She ran from place to place, and still didn't know what she was after. As she started to move again, she stepped on a twig, and it snapped. The sound was so loud that Mercy came fully awake. She sat up and looked around the dark room.

"Someone is on the roof," Red Deer whispered.

Mercy stood and let her blanket drop to the ground. She felt in her coat pocket for the revolver. "Everyone keep quiet," she whispered for the sake of anyone awake.

The sound of the rain was mingled with a scraping sound as someone crawled across the roof. No doubt the trapdoor was their goal. She was glad she'd had everyone lay down on the far side of the bed. The space below the roof access was clear.

Whoever it was reached the door and began to pull at it. It appeared to be stuck, however, and Mercy found herself praying it would hold. It didn't. A moment later, the door opened slowly.

She drew a deep breath and raised her revolver. "Whoever you are, I've got a gun pointed right at you. If you try to come into this house, I will shoot you."

"Mercy, it's me. Adam," the whispered reply came.

She almost cried aloud with joy. "Adam. Oh, thanks be to God." She lowered the gun. "The floor is clear beneath you."

That was the only encouragement he needed. In a matter of seconds, Adam came through the opening and landed only a foot or so away from Mercy. The trapdoor fell back into place with a thud.

Without any shame, Mercy threw herself at him and hugged him close. Her heart felt as though it might beat out of her chest. She'd been so frightened.

"Are you hurt?" he asked.

"No, but I'm so glad you're here. Billy Caxton and his men are trying to kill us."

"I figured as much." He held her tight. "Who else is in the house?"

"Thirteen of the Tututni—ten are children. We're all here

in the bedroom. Oh, Adam, I'm sure they've killed everyone else." She felt his hold tighten. "And Isaac . . ."

"I know. How is Eletta doing?"

"She's very weak. She and Faith are asleep on the bed."

"No, I'm awake," Faith interjected.

"Well, pretend you're still asleep," Adam countered. "We need to keep still. They no doubt heard the trapdoor, but hopefully they have no idea what it was." Still he held on to Mercy as if she were as much his lifeline as he was hers.

"We managed to nail up more boards over the window shutters, as well as reinforce the door."

Adam began stroking her hair. "You did well. I'm sorry I wasn't here to see this never happened."

"You couldn't have known. No one expected Isaac to be murdered." She calmed under his touch. "Billy said it was the Tututni, but I don't believe him. No one believes him."

For several long silent moments, Mercy let Adam hold her. She wanted only the safety of his embrace and the warmth of his breath against her ear.

"It's cold in here," he said.

"We didn't dare light a fire. I was afraid Billy would try to smoke us out. I'm sure come light he'll continue his threats to set fire to the cabin."

Adam pulled away and took her face in his hands. Mercy couldn't see much more than his outline. "Listen, I sent word to the army. I gave Joseph a letter to take to them. They aren't far from here and should arrive soon. We just have to keep Billy and his men at bay until they get here."

She nodded but didn't otherwise reply because Adam's thumb was stroking her jaw. She couldn't explain what was happening to her, but it felt like everything inside her body was melting. Mercy marveled at the sensation, and her breath quickened as she remembered his kiss.

"Come with me to the front room. I want to make some holes in the wood over the windows so I can see what Billy and his men are doing once it's light."

He dropped his hands from her face, and for a moment Mercy couldn't seem to make her legs work. She shook her head to clear the fog, but still that feeling of wonder remained.

"I . . . ah . . ." She stammered for a moment then went silent.

Adam was already at the bedroom door, lifting the bar. Mercy forced herself to move. "Red Deer, I'll be just outside. Keep everyone in here."

"I will," the woman whispered.

Mercy stepped through the open door. She could hear Adam moving around the room and thought of the tools she'd used earlier. "What do you need to make a hole?"

"Well, I thought maybe I could tear away a bit of the board on the window. We don't want to remove so much that it weakens our defense, but it would be good to see what the enemy is up to."

"There are tools in the box beside the fireplace."

"Of course."

He went to the box, and Mercy could hear him rummaging through its contents. The clock on the mantel chimed, nearly causing her to shriek. She barely got her hand over her mouth in time.

"It'll be full light within half an hour. It was already starting to dawn when I was still outside," Adam said.

Mercy slowly lowered her hands. "It's still raining, so maybe the militia will want to stay in their tents."

"I wouldn't count on it. I'm going to try drilling a hole instead of tearing away the wood. A hole won't weaken the barrier."

"And we can easily stuff something into it to keep them from looking in."

"Exactly."

Adam went to the window, but Mercy couldn't see what he was doing. She realized she could help him by lighting a candle. Feeling her way around, she found the small supply of matches Isaac kept in a jar. She then quickly found a candle and lit it.

The glow allowed her to see Adam for the first time in many weeks. He glanced back at her. He looked tired and unkempt, and his pack and rifle had been slung into a corner of the room. He wore the beginning growth of a beard, and his hair was still wet from the rain. Even so, Mercy had never known a handsomer man.

He smiled as if he could read her thoughts. "Bring it here."

She watched as he drilled into the board. It was slow work to get through the thick oak plank she'd nailed in place. By the time he finally managed to make a hole big enough to see through, it was nearly eight o'clock, and everyone was awake and curious about what was happening.

Unfortunately, Billy and his men were also awake. Adam remained crouched by the window and motioned Mercy to his side. He looked out of the peephole. "He's coming this way. Say nothing about me."

"Of course not." Mercy frowned. "I'm not stupid."

Adam looked up with a grin. "So you've managed to pull yourself together then?"

Mercy felt her face grow hot and looked away. "If you're referring to when you first arrived, then . . . well . . . yes. You nearly scared the wits out of me."

She stomped off to check on the others.

"Red Deer, Billy is heading this way. Keep everyone in the bedroom." Faith frowned, and Mercy knew she was about to protest. "Faith, I need you to stay with your mother and take care of her for me. I have to help your Uncle Adam."

"Mercy Flanagan!" Billy yelled.

Mercy bit her lip and squared her shoulders. She would conduct herself in a manner befitting a proper young woman. She moved to the front room and put her hands on her hips to steady herself. "What is it that you want now, Mr. Caxton?"

"You know full well what I want. I want you to open this door and send out those heathens."

"Do you still plan to murder them?"

"I plan to do my duty, if that's what you mean."

"Then I can't help you. I will not turn helpless women and children over to you to be slaughtered."

"Then you're going to die with them, because we're going to set the place on fire in exactly five minutes."

"You'll kill an expectant mother—a white woman too weak to leave her bed? You'd let her seven-year-old daughter die at her side?"

"It's not the way we want it, Mercy, but we have our orders. I told you we'd see you and Mrs. Browning and her child to safety."

Mercy felt her resolve weaken. She looked at Adam as tears came to her eyes. By refusing to give up the Tututni, she was signing everyone's death warrant. Even Faith's.

Adam came to her and took her in his arms. He whispered against her ear. "Don't be afraid. The soldiers will be here soon."

Then, as if speaking the words had made it so, Mercy heard the shouting of other men.

"Billy—the regulars are here!" someone yelled.

She gasped and looked at Adam. His face was just an inch away from hers, and suddenly all she could think about was his kiss. She pushed him back, shaking from head to toe.

"We . . . we're . . ." She shook her head. "The army is here." She went to the door. "The army is here, Mr. Caxton, and you can no longer threaten our lives."

Billy didn't respond, but Mercy could hear him cursing and calling out to his compatriots to break camp. Hugging her arms to her body, Mercy leaned back against the door. For just a moment, she thought she might faint and closed her eyes.

"Are you all right?" Adam asked.

She opened her eyes again. He hadn't moved from where she'd left him. His dark eyes bored into her, and Mercy couldn't look away. She knew without him saying a word that things had changed between them. What she couldn't figure out was whether that was a good thing . . . or a bad one.

Chapter
14

After insisting they bury the dead, Mercy was relieved
to leave the village. Her only regret was the insistence
of the army that the surviving Tututni remain with
them. They were to be sent to join a larger group of Indians
being marched north to the reservation.

The tearful good-bye left Mercy with an enormous sense
of loss. Would they be all right? Would the soldiers treat them
fairly? There was no way to be certain they would even survive
the brutal march north.

With the help of three soldiers and the use of two large
Tututni canoes, Mercy and Adam managed to get Eletta and
Faith to Gold Beach without further problems. Mercy had taken
what they could pack of clothes and personal articles, as well
as a crate that Adam stuffed with food. There was no way of
knowing what the situation in Gold Beach might be, he had told
her. She was glad he was thinking of such things. Her thoughts
were a terrible scramble of worry over Eletta and Faith and
acceptance of her feelings for Adam. Thankfully, she hadn't

been forced to deal with Billy Caxton, although he and his men were still somewhere nearby.

Gold Beach was much the same as she remembered it. The small fort being built was further along, with a much higher wall of dirt mounded around two small buildings. There were several families in residence, as well as soldiers and other single men.

The army physician arranged for Mercy, Eletta, Adam, and Faith to have a small house normally shared by some soldiers who were off fighting Indians. It was hardly more than an unpainted plank shack, but Mercy was grateful for a roof over her head and a floor, albeit a very rough one, beneath her feet. So many of the others were living in tents.

It would normally have been inappropriate for a single woman to share a house with a single man to whom she wasn't related, but these were difficult and dangerous times. Mercy wasn't about to be left alone to watch over Eletta and Faith without Adam to watch over all of them.

Mopping Eletta's brow with a damp cloth, Mercy continued to pray, thanking God for their safe arrival and pleading for the life of her friend. When Mercy went to wet the cloth again, she was surprised to find Eletta awake.

"How are you feeling?"

"I'm. . . ." Eletta said nothing more about herself. "How's Faith? Is she bearing up all right?" Her voice was hardly more than a whisper.

"She's doing well. She's just outside in the main room. Would you like to see her?"

Eletta shook her head. "Not just yet. I want to talk to you alone."

"What is it?"

"I know I'm dying. I believe the child inside me has already passed."

Mercy bit her lower lip to keep from contradicting Eletta in empty encouragement. The army physician had already told Mercy that he believed the unborn baby to be dead. He had told Mercy and Adam that he could operate and remove the baby in the hope of saving Eletta's life, but he felt the chances of her survival were extremely low. Neither she nor Adam wanted to put Eletta through such misery only to see her die anyway. More importantly, Eletta wanted no part of it.

Mercy took Eletta's hand. "I'm so sorry. We've done all we could."

"I don't fear death," Eletta continued. "My life was over with Isaac's passing, although I've tried to hang on in case I could bear his child. And for Faith." She closed her eyes and shook her head. "But I'm too weak, and I know I will die soon."

"What can I do?"

Eletta opened her eyes again and gave a weak smile. "Take care of Faith for me."

"Of course. She will always have a home with me."

"I wrote a journal for her." Eletta pointed to the bag that held her things.

Mercy knew exactly where the journal was, since she'd packed these things for Eletta. "I know."

"I wanted to keep a record from when she was born. I wanted her to know about Hope one day . . . and even Tomahas." She paused for a long moment, then began again. "I thought it important that she know the truth about her origins. I would want to know if it were me, and while it might be difficult for Hope—I think it's only fair."

Again, Eletta fell silent. Her eyes opened and closed several times, as if she were trying to clear her vision. "Mercy?"

"I'm here." Mercy squeezed Eletta's hand.

"I want you to read the journal . . . then keep it for her. One day when you think she's ready—share it with her. Help her understand."

"I will. I promise." Mercy fought back tears. "What else can I do?"

"I'd like to write in the journal one more time."

"I'll get it." Mercy went to the bag and found the journal and pencil Eletta had tied to it. She brought it to the bed and placed it in Eletta's hands. "Here you are."

"I don't think I have the strength to write, and I'm not seeing well. Will you do it for me?" she asked.

Mercy nodded and quickly took the journal back. She untied the pencil and opened to the last entry Eletta had made. "Do you want to know what you wrote last?"

"No. I remember well enough."

Mercy turned to a blank page. "All right. I'm ready."

Eletta drew a ragged breath and closed her eyes. "Faith, as I lie here, knowing my time is very short, you are my only thought." Her words were barely audible and slow. "You have been such a joy to me. I could never have known such completion . . . such joy without you. I'm so sorry to leave you, and sorry too that I could not fill this book with all . . . manner of wisdom and thought. It was always my intention to do so and leave it for you as a legacy."

She paused, and for a moment Mercy thought she'd fallen asleep. She rechecked the words she'd just written and had started to close the book when Eletta opened her eyes and continued.

"Your papa and I loved you very much, even though you were not flesh of our flesh, and we will continue to love you in glory. God gave you to us. Despite the past and the difficulties that accompanied your birth, I want you to always remember that you are . . . a gift from God."

Eletta seemed to gather strength, and her voice grew steady. "He alone can create life—or take it. Please remember this and do not abandon Him in anger at my passing or your papa's.

My only regret in having you as my daughter is that I won't get to see you grow up—marry and perhaps have children of your own. But that is my only regret where you are concerned. You have been a wonderful daughter. I pray you will be a godly woman—one who continues to love all and not judge men by the color of their skin. Given your own mixed heritage, I'm certain you will be generous with your consideration and kindness."

Mercy finished writing. Eletta remained silent, causing Mercy to look up. "Is there anything else?"

"Yes . . . just a bit more." She drew another ragged breath and then continued. "Mercy is your aunt by blood and Adam is your uncle by . . . because of love. They will care for you and see that you are always provided for. I know this, because they love you even as your papa and I have loved you. They are good and loving people, and I have faith in them to make you a good home. Always remember, you are loved."

Mercy couldn't help the tears that came to her eyes. She closed the journal and again took hold of Eletta's hand. "I will see to her upbringing in whatever way I can. I do make you that promise."

"I know you will care for her as if she were your own." Eletta smiled. "I could not rest half so easy if it were not for knowing you and Adam will always be there for her."

Mercy smiled. "I know he will do whatever he can."

"I'm glad you found each other."

Mercy looked at her oddly. "Faith and I?"

Eletta shook her head. "You and Adam. I know you've come to care for each other. I hoped for that from the moment you first arrived. Before . . . actually. Grace used to write of her concerns about you finding a proper husband who loved God. We've long prayed for you."

"For me?" Mercy could imagine the content of the letters that had passed between Eletta and Grace. She smiled. "I suppose that shouldn't come as any surprise. Grace has mentioned on many occasions praying for me to find the right man to marry."

"We prayed for more than just that, but a woman alone is so vulnerable to the evils of the world, and we both wanted you and Hope to be safe. When Hope found her husband, we both rejoiced. I cried when I read of Lance's love for her. She so needed that love."

Mercy couldn't agree more. "Well, I know we all appreciated your prayers." She patted Eletta's hand. She could see by the woman's eyes that she was in pain. "Why don't I fix you some tea?"

"No." Eletta shook her head. "I'm beyond it helping."

Biting her lip to keep from crying, Mercy tucked Eletta's journal in her pocket. She had come to care so much for this woman—had hoped to keep her and the baby alive. It was so hard to accept that she could do nothing more.

"Adam went through some very painful rejections in his past," Eletta whispered. "I'm sure he'll tell you about it one day, but for now . . . just love him."

Mercy swallowed the lump in her throat. "I . . . I will."

Eletta nodded. "Would you ask Faith to come be with me? I want to hold her and say good-bye."

Mercy could barely speak for the sorrow in her heart. "Yes."

She stepped out into the main living area where Faith sat with her doll by the crudely fashioned woodstove. "Faith, your mama wants you to come see her."

She abandoned the doll and got to her feet. "Is Mama much worse?"

"I don't think she has much time." Mercy brushed back Faith's bangs and kissed her forehead. "I know you'll bring her comfort. Be strong—for her sake."

Faith nodded and went into the small room where she and her mother, as well as Mercy, had slept since their arrival in Gold Beach.

Mercy tried to busy herself with daily duties, but her mind was on what Eletta had said about loving Adam. She did love him. There was no doubt in her mind. The only problem was whether she could convince him to return her love.

She thought of Grace and Hope and how they had managed to fall in love and secure their men. Grace had never been one to give her heart easily, but Alex had completely won her over. They hadn't come together without difficulties, to be certain, but their love had been too strong to let them be separated for long. With Hope, it had been the opposite. Hope had given her heart away quite freely as a young woman. Mercy couldn't remember how many times Hope had declared herself to be "in love." Even at the Whitman Mission, she had fallen in love with young John Sager. When he was killed in the massacre, everything changed for Hope. She lost her carefree spirit and her ability to love. At least until Lieutenant Lance Kenner came into her life.

With a sigh, Mercy picked up one of Adam's shirts, which she'd promised to mend for him. She brushed the edge of the sleeve against her lips. She hardly knew this man, and yet she'd lost her heart to him.

She settled onto the wooden bench they'd positioned near the stove and took a needle and thread from her small sewing basket. With each stitch, Mercy thought of her future. At this point she had no real choice but to return to Grace and Alex's home. However, Faith would be with her—perhaps Adam too. But while Adam wouldn't cause any upset, Faith was another story. How could Mercy just show up with Faith and demand Hope accept her? It would be cruel.

"But what other choice do I have?"

She finished the shirt and decided to work on a pair of Faith's stockings that needed darning. Going to the bedroom, Mercy peered in to see Faith tucked in bed alongside Eletta. Both were asleep. It made for a tender picture—one Mercy knew she'd not soon forget. She remembered doing something similar when her mother was dying. She'd hoped to give her mother strength and health through their embrace. She had wanted to will Mama to live—just as she was sure that Faith wanted to will Eletta to live.

"But it wasn't enough," she whispered to herself.

Tears begin to fall, and Mercy quickly wiped them away and forced herself to be strong. Crying wouldn't help anything. It wouldn't bring the dead back or keep the dying alive.

Picking up Faith's clean stockings, Mercy hurried back to the front room and focused on her work.

~

By eight o'clock that night, Mercy knew Eletta was going to die. She no longer woke, and her breathing had grown shallow. Sometimes she even stopped breathing for several seconds.

When the front door to their house opened to admit Adam and the army doctor, Mercy felt a sense of relief. She needed someone else to be in charge. Even for a few minutes. She went to the far corner of the room where a small table stood with two empty crates for chairs. Faith sat on one of the crates, reading one of Mercy's books.

"Are you enjoying learning about the kings and queens of England?"

Faith looked up and nodded. "I never knew about all the trouble folks had with church."

Mercy was glad for something to discuss other than Eletta's condition. "Yes. We have freedom of religion here in America because of what happened in Europe. When folks came here, they were determined to worship in whatever way they felt was right. It's a very important freedom we've been given, and we should never take it for granted."

"I don't know why God let there be so much trouble over it,"

Faith replied, closing the book. "A lot of people got killed for what they believed. King Henry the Eighth had people killed who didn't think he was in charge of the church. Then his daughter Mary killed people who didn't worship like she did. So many people died for wanting to worship God in their way."

Mercy nodded. "People still do." She thought of the Indians and the missionaries who'd come west to minister to them. That had started so many of the problems they were dealing with today, and yet God admonished His believers to go into the world and share the gospel.

"Belonging to God isn't an easy thing to do, is it?"

Faith's question made Mercy smile. "Belonging to Him is easy enough, but serving Him can cost a man his life. But we must be ready to lay down our lives for Him."

"Like Mama and Papa?"

"Yes. Like your mama and papa."

Adam stepped out of the bedroom. The look on his face said it all.

"Is she gone?" Mercy asked, getting to her feet.

Adam crossed the room to Faith and lifted her into his arms. "Yes. Your mama and papa are both with God now."

Mercy forced her sorrow down deep and remained composed. She looked at Faith, who also wore a stoic expression.

"Can I see her?" Faith asked.

Adam nodded. "If that's what you want."

"I just want to see her one more time, and then they can bury her."

Adam carried her to the bedroom door, then set her down. Mercy followed them. She had said good-bye to her dead mother in a similar fashion. It had been important to see her one more time—to assure herself that death was nothing to fear.

She and Adam watched Faith as she moved to the side of the bed. The doctor was putting away his things. He gave Faith a nod, then picked up his bag and came to where Mercy and Adam stood.

He spoke in a whisper. "I'll have a grave dug. We can bury her tomorrow."

Adam nodded. "Thank you. Thank you for all you've done."

The doctor shrugged. "I wish it could have ended differently."

"So do I," Adam replied.

The doctor left, and Mercy turned her attention back to Faith. The little girl was tenderly stroking her mother's face and speaking in whispers too low to hear.

"I'm going to see about making a coffin," Adam said. He started to leave, then turned back to Mercy. "Will you be all right?"

She nodded. "Yes. When Faith is done saying good-bye, I'll put her to bed and then prepare Eletta for burial."

Adam gave her arm a gentle squeeze and then left. Mercy had felt a sense of comfort in his presence that was now gone. She prayed she could stay strong for Faith's sake, but already she could feel her emotions getting the best of her. She gathered bedding from the floor of Eletta's room where she and Faith had been sleeping and made a place for them in the open front room. She positioned them on the opposite side of the wood-stove from where Adam had made his pallet.

She'd no sooner finished that task than Faith appeared at her side. The small girl looked up at Mercy, then took hold of her hand. Tears began to stream down the child's cheeks. Mercy gathered Faith into her arms and carried her to the bench in front of the stove, where she cradled Faith like a babe.

For a long time, Faith cried in Mercy's arms. Mercy could only hold her and let her sorrow play itself out. There were no words that could make this better. Sometimes the quiet could be more comforting.

Mercy lost track of how long they sat there, but after a time,

Faith fell asleep. Her face was still wet with tears, and from time to time she gave a little sob in her sleep. Mercy stared at the child for several minutes. She could see her sister's features in Faith's face. She hadn't thought much about it, but Faith looked very much like Hope. Maybe once Hope saw that, she would be able to let Faith back in her life.

She put Faith to bed and whispered a prayer for God's strength and guidance. It wasn't that she was afraid of the future, but she felt ill-equipped for it. She had promised to take on the responsibility of a child, and even though she had it in the back of her mind that Hope might want to raise Faith herself, Mercy had made a promise. It was a daunting thought.

Mercy found her bag of herbs and vinegar and set it aside. Next she filled a bowl with hot water. She added vinegar and lavender to the water and took it to the bedroom to prepare Eletta's body for burial. She washed Eletta first, then dressed her in her best gown. It was nothing fancy, just a simple plaid wool of blue and green. Mercy combed out Eletta's long blond hair and then braided it into a single plait to coil around the top of her head like a crown. Last of all, she gathered sage and lavender from her herb bag and bound them together, then lay them in the bowl of her clay mortar. Then she lit them on fire.

For a moment she let them burn as the smoke filled the air with the scent of the herbs, then she blew out the flame and left them to smolder and put off their heady aroma. It was a ritual she'd seen her mother and grandmother use each time death came to a house. Her mother said it kept the odor of death at bay.

Her work done, Mercy left Eletta and closed the bedroom door.

She had managed to keep her thoughts on the tasks at hand, but now that she was finished, Mercy could no longer keep back her tears. She didn't want to wake up Faith with her sobs, so she went to the table and buried her face in her hands.

The events of the last month had taken their toll, and Mercy wept softly for all those they'd lost. She wondered what had happened to Red Deer and the others. So many had been killed, and she knew the Tututni were mourning their losses as well. It was heartbreaking to imagine the death of some of the children she and Adam had taught. How could men be so cruel as to cut down children?

She didn't notice Adam's return until he pulled her up and into his arms. Mercy wrapped her arms around him and felt her tears ebb. She buried her face against his coat and let him comfort her. Time seemed to stand still.

"I don't understand why God has allowed any of this to happen," Adam whispered against her ear, "but I know He is good, and I trust that He has a plan even in this."

Mercy nodded and slowly lifted her face. "I can't believe Eletta is gone. I never thought this would happen. I thought we could save her."

"I know. I thought so too."

"Maybe we could have if not for the militia's attack. I don't know how a person could live with themselves after such slaughter."

"Nor do I." His expression was angry. "I hate what I've seen happen and would gladly avenge those who were killed. It wasn't right. None of this has been handled honorably."

"No, it hasn't, and I can't help but be more afraid than I've ever been before."

At this, his expression softened. He reached up and laid his hand against her cheek. "Don't be afraid, Mercy. I'll take care of you and Faith. You don't have to worry about that. I'll get you out of here and away from all this madness."

He held her gaze for a moment longer, then lowered his lips

as if to kiss her. Mercy pushed back against his chest, remembering the last time they'd kissed. She wanted this to happen, but not at the expense of being rejected again.

"As I recall," she said, "the last time we kissed, you hated it. In fact, you were quite vocal about it never happening again."

"I never said I hated it." His husky voice made Mercy tremble. "In fact, I liked it very much. Too much."

He bent his head again and kissed her with such passion that Mercy could scarcely draw breath.

Chapter 15

On the twenty-second of February, Gold Beach residents held a grand celebration of George Washington's birthday. There was to be a party and a dance, but given it was just a few days since they had buried Eletta, Mercy didn't feel like attending. Adam, however, had other ideas.

"I think we should go. There will be other children there, and it would do Faith good to get her mind on something other than losing both parents inside of a month."

Mercy immediately felt guilty. "Of course. I hadn't thought of it that way."

Adam's dark-eyed gaze held her with a look that caused Mercy's breath to catch. Everything was happening so fast, and she could hardly sort through her feelings. They'd said nothing about the kiss the night Eletta died, but Mercy knew Adam had been equally affected by it. She wanted to say something—declare her love or at least talk about the future—but surely it was the man's place to bring up such things first.

"We don't have to stay all night," he assured her. "I know they'll be dancing until morning. People who live with the constant threat of death are all the more determined to live life to its fullest."

She nodded and looked across the room to where Faith sat reading. "I'd best get to work fixing something to take. I know everyone is supposed to bring some food."

"I've been talking to the army officials—trying to figure out how to get us out of here. Unfortunately, no one is heading to Port Orford. The captain feels it's far too dangerous. The tribes are warring up and down the coast and river. It's like a wildfire spreading. He tried to get one of the schooners in here, but between the weather and their fear of the Indian uprising, none of the captains are inclined to try it."

"I wish we could just be in Oregon City."

"Why there?"

Mercy smiled. "Because my family is there, and I know they'd take us all in."

A knock sounded on the cabin door, startling both Adam and Mercy. Mercy quickly glanced at Faith, who had paused in her reading to look up.

"I'll get it." Adam crossed to the door and opened it. "Yes?"

A man stood just outside. Mercy couldn't see him, but when he spoke, she hurried to Adam's side.

"Nigel Grierson, as I live and breathe." She looked at the tall, blond-haired man who stood with his hat in his hand.

"I heard you were here, Miss Mercy. I thought I'd stop by to pay my respects."

Adam looked at her oddly, and for a moment Mercy thought she saw a jealous possessiveness in his expression.

She reached out to take hold of Nigel's arm. "Well, come in. Mr. Grierson, this is Adam Browning, and across the room is his niece, Faith. Faith's mother . . . passed away just a few days ago. You remember Eletta and Isaac Browning, don't you?"

"Yes, and I heard about their deaths." Nigel stepped inside the house but remained near the door. "I'm sure sorry, Miss Mercy."

"Thank you." She smiled and decided to put Adam out of his obvious discomfort. "Adam is Mr. Browning's brother. Isaac was killed a few weeks ago." The days had blurred one into the other, and Mercy wasn't even sure how long ago it had been. She looked at Adam. "Mr. Grierson was once engaged to my sister Grace. He was on the wagon train that came west with us to Oregon." She didn't miss the relief that passed over his expression. "I was just a young girl, but I remember Mr. Grierson's kindness to us." She turned back to Nigel. "What brings you here?"

"I'm fighting with the militia."

Mercy didn't try to hide her frown. "Why would you want to do that?"

"It pays better than the gold fields. I'm afraid that selling my farm wasn't the best decision. Gold fever's a terrible thing to catch, and there's not much that satisfies it."

She nodded. "I can't imagine you wanting to kill women and children. You never seemed like that kind of a man."

"It's kill or be killed. The Indians have declared all-out war, and we mean to put an end to it. I'm surprised you would defend them after what you went through."

"Maybe it's because of what happened at the Whitman Mission that I have a better understanding. I know what it is to be the helpless victim." Her frown deepened. "I just came from a mission where Billy Caxton and his confederates cut down the elderly and children who had no intention or means of harming anyone. It was murder, Mr. Grierson. Plain and simple."

"I don't know about that. I haven't been at this all that long. My brothers and I weren't having any luck mining for gold so we had to make some kind of a living. I hear the attack at Whitman's often mentioned as a reason to fight here, however."

"It's wrong. Not all Indians are to be blamed for the acts of a few. And as I recall, those deemed guilty for the massacre were hanged. The Rogue River Indians had nothing to do with that attack, yet they're being killed." She shook her head. "Nigel, you'd be better off going back to raising dairy cows. I find it appalling that a godly man such as yourself would do something so heinous."

Nigel had grown visibly uncomfortable. "I . . . well . . . I just wanted to pay my respects. Will you be at the party?"

"We're planning on it."

"Perhaps we might talk about better times, and you can tell me how your sisters are doing." He moved to the door and gave Adam a nod. "Nice meeting you, Mr. Browning."

Once he'd gone, Mercy went to the small area of the cabin that served as a kitchen. "I have some preserved apples and oats. I'll make a crumble if you can find me some butter and a little flour." She looked at Adam and smiled. "If you don't mind."

He was staring at her with something that seemed almost like awe, and Mercy felt herself flushing. She supposed she had been rather forceful with Nigel.

But then Adam's expression shifted, and he looked strangely uncomfortable, unable to meet her eyes. With a curt nod, he turned and left the house.

Mercy sighed. If his emotions were even a tenth as confused as hers, then she knew he would go on suffering until he sorted out what to do about his feelings.

⁓

Adam didn't feel like being at the party any more than Mercy did, but when he saw Faith playing happily with two other little girls, he knew they'd done the right thing. At least where she was concerned. Mercy, on the other hand, was receiving far more male attention than Adam cared to see. That Grierson fellow made a pest of himself by cornering Mercy to talk. He'd seen some of the other men attempt the same, and it irritated him to no end.

Mercy didn't seem to mind, and in truth she could handle herself. But there was also the truth that Adam was in love with her and didn't want to see her with other men.

He reminded himself that the behavior of the other men was appropriate, given the social setting, but it didn't stop him from wanting to push through the crowd and claim Mercy for his own. She consumed his thoughts day and night, and their kiss had nearly been his undoing. Still, the past kept him from feeling free to do anything about it. He remembered the condemnation of people he'd thought were his friends once the news of his Cherokee blood became a well-known fact. It was strange that a man could be perfectly accepted, even lauded, but then thought to be completely unworthy once news of his family heritage became known.

There was no reason to expect anything different with Mercy. She had shown a great deal of compassion for the Tututni, perhaps even love, but that wasn't the same as marrying a man considered subhuman because of his Indian blood. Even if she could look past that, Adam wasn't sure her family would. More than once he had almost told her everything, but the thought of having to endure her scorn until they reached Oregon City kept him from speaking.

He spied her being cornered by Billy Caxton and felt his blood begin to heat. Caxton was a fool to think she'd have anything to do with him now. Nevertheless, Adam felt it only right to support Mercy. As he joined them, Mercy rolled her eyes at him while Billy continued ranting about something. It was clear she wasn't happy to be talking to the militiaman.

"But you've got to understand," Billy insisted. "They killed my best friend. Several good friends, in fact. I wouldn't have gone off like I did, and I never would have threatened you if I hadn't been half out of my mind."

"Well, I'm certain you're right in saying you were half out of your mind." Mercy looked at Adam. "Mr. Caxton was just apologizing for attacking our mission and killing so many helpless women and children."

"I'm sure that's a comfort to them, Caxton." Adam's sarcastic tone hung in the air between them.

Billy narrowed his eyes. "I'm just doing my job. If the Indians attack here, you'll be glad enough for our presence."

"I doubt that. If not for you and your men, I don't think the Indians around here would be attacking at all. Frankly, you've pushed them so far that they have to retaliate." Adam narrowed his eyes as well. "And wasn't that the plan?"

Someone struck up a fiddle tune, and although Adam had no intention of dancing when they first arrived, now he saw it as a means to get Mercy away from Billy.

He held a hand out to her. "I believe this is our dance."

She only hesitated a moment before placing her hand in his. "Why yes, I believe it is."

"I thought you said you didn't mean to dance," Billy said, staring daggers at Adam.

Mercy glanced back over her shoulder as Adam led her to the dance floor. "No, Mr. Caxton, I only said that I didn't mean to dance with you."

Adam gave a soft chuckle as he swung her into the collection of other couples for the Virginia reel. "I suppose I shouldn't laugh." They separated and came together in curtsy and bow before linking elbows. "But I can't help myself."

"He's a menace. Thank you for rescuing me."

They maneuvered down the line, weaving in and out, performing a do-si-do with other partners, until finally they were back together again.

"It was my pleasure." Adam joined her outstretched hands with his, and they did a sidestepping skip all the way down the line. "I like your company."

"Ah, but do you like it enough?" Mercy asked and then once again was spirited away as they peeled off in either direction and headed for the end of the line.

Adam wondered what she was getting at, but when they came back together, making a tunnel for the other couples to pass under, they had no chance to speak. By the time all the couples had passed, they were once again in motion, and Adam gave up.

When the dance ended, Mercy was immediately set upon to share dances with some of the other men, leaving Adam the odd man out. With women so scarce, Mercy took pity on them, much to Adam's surprise.

He stood back against the wall and watched her for a long while. Her dark brown hair was braided and pinned to the back of her head in a simple fashion. Her dress was nothing more than a dark-colored wool. It certainly was nothing like the majestic gowns Lizzy had worn in Boston, yet as far as he was concerned, Mercy was far more beautiful.

But it wasn't just her appearance that attracted him. Her heart was so genuinely full of love and kindness. He'd seen her working patiently with the Tututni children when she didn't realize he was there. She gave them gentle pats on the back and hugs of affection when they performed well. And she even held the children when they were upset. She gave the same treatment to the adults. Red Deer had told him that sometimes she even forgot Mercy was white. Her comment had made him smile, but it had also endeared her to him.

It was nearly ten o'clock when Mercy finally slipped away from the others. "I'm done in, and if you look over there, you'll see that Faith has fallen asleep. I think it's time we go home."

"I agree." Adam crossed the room to retrieve his niece. He lifted her to his shoulder. "Why don't you collect our coats?"

Mercy went to do just that. As she skirted the edge of the room, she was inundated with offers to dance or just sit and talk. Adam knew just how lonely it could be for some of these men. He'd experienced it for himself and had to admit that Mercy had done much to alleviate his loneliness.

After a few minutes, Mercy returned with their coats. "I'll just put mine around her," Mercy said, covering Faith. "We won't freeze on the short walk home, but the cold might wake her up."

"Good thinking."

Adam moved toward the door, only to be stopped by Billy Caxton. "You aren't leaving already, are you?" Billy asked, looking at Mercy. "This party will go on until dawn."

"Yes, but we won't be going on with it." Adam shifted Faith to cradle her in his arms, causing the coat to slip. He was surprised when Billy helped by pulling it back in place.

"I'm sure sorry you're leaving. I wanted to make things right with both of you. I know I acted terrible back at the mission. I can't excuse myself, except to say I saw the blood haze."

"It seems you're often given to seeing it," Mercy countered.

Billy looked pained. "I don't mean to, but you have to understand. I lost good friends just the day before. We had nearly forty-five men, but now we're down to thirty. I guess I just wanted justice for them."

"No, Mr. Caxton, you wanted revenge—even at the price of threatening innocent lives."

"Those squaws weren't innocent. Some of them killed just like their men."

Mercy put herself between Billy and Faith. "My friends at the mission didn't kill anyone. They had been with me since I first came here. They never went on raids. You killed innocent people. Murdered men and women too old to defend themselves, as well as little children who weren't even old enough to have enemies."

Billy started to reply, but Mercy pushed past him. "No more, Mr. Caxton. No more of your excuses and pretense at caring about my feelings."

She stormed out of the building, leaving Adam to stare after her in admiration. She was quite the woman. He glanced at Billy, who instead of looking contrite was fuming.

"I would suggest steering clear of us, Mr. Caxton. We are sworn to practice Christian charity and God's love, but where you are concerned, I'm not sure we wouldn't all revert to our baser natures."

It was nearly dawn when Mercy woke up. She smiled at the way Faith had curled against her. The child was so precious to her that Mercy even found herself imagining what it might have been like had Hope kept Faith. Would she have taught Faith to love sheep and spinning, instead of teaching her to read at the age of two? Hope had never had much interest in books.

Yawning, Mercy stretched and slid out from under Eletta's quilts. She was so glad they had decided to bring them among their meager belongings. She wanted Faith to always have these reminders of her mother. Mercy had nothing of her mother's. What little she had brought west with her had been stolen by the Cayuse. She missed the pieces of lace her mother had designed and the bookmark she had crocheted and embroidered with Mercy's name.

Adam was already gone, as he was most mornings. Often he went fishing to bring them something for breakfast or gathered wood for the stove. It seemed they couldn't have too much of either thing. Adam took care of her as he might if they'd been husband and wife. She glanced around the small shack and realized anew how inappropriate it was for them to live under one roof. She knew back east a woman would be tainted for doing so, but here, given the circumstances, Mercy felt it wasn't out of line. If she and Faith were alone, less honorable men would no doubt try to take liberties, and she would rather risk her reputation than Faith's safety. Besides, she was already determined that Adam would be her husband one day. She just had to figure out a way to make him propose.

Is that a terrible idea? Is it wrong for me to want to take the initiative?

She had been raised to believe it was for the man to lead in a relationship, but Mercy felt she had every bit as much at stake. Maybe she would just put the idea on the table. She knew Adam cared deeply for her. She could even go so far as to say that he desired her. His kisses had told her that much.

Mercy considered all of this as she filled the basin to wash her face. She had just dipped her hands in the water when Adam burst through the door. His face was ashen.

"Collect our things. We've got to get across the river to Fort Miner."

"What's wrong? It's not even full light."

"The Indians have attacked and burned out everything along the river and coast. They haven't yet reached Gold Beach, but they're headed this way with the intent of killing everyone. Reports are there are over three hundred warriors."

Mercy felt as if her stomach had dropped to her feet. She moved quickly to throw supplies into her medicinal bag. "You take care of gathering your things, and I'll get Faith's. I don't suppose we can take the food, can we?"

"I think we'd best take anything we can carry. Who knows how long we'll have to wait out the attack."

A woman screamed somewhere outside, and Faith stirred and sat up. "Are the bad men coming?"

Mercy went to her. "The Indians are very angry, and they're attacking all around us."

"Not my friends?" Faith said in a questioning tone.

"I don't know." Mercy helped her up. "We have to get across the river right away and take shelter at the fort." She didn't know how much shelter the fort would provide, however. It was only half done, but she supposed something was better than nothing.

"Come on, we have to get to the river," Adam declared.

Mercy helped Faith roll up the quilts and tie them with string so she and Adam could wear them on their backs. Faith put on her boots, while Mercy went to collect the book Faith had been reading as well as Eletta's journal. She stuffed both in her bag, then spotted Hope's revolver. Without hesitation, she slipped it into her coat pocket, then went to get her boots.

Adam gathered his things into his pack, then slung it over his shoulders. He picked up the crate of food. "Let's go."

Mercy helped Faith into her coat and then grabbed her own. She hadn't even had time to tie her boots, much less comb her hair and braid it. No doubt she looked like a wild woman. Thankfully, she still had her scarf. When they were finally at the river, she would tie it over her tangled hair.

The Rogue River was far too wide and deep at its mouth to wade through, even if it hadn't been too cold. Thankfully, there was a ferry, as well as other boats, to get people across the river. Even so, as the panicked citizens of Gold Beach milled along the riverbank, Mercy could see they would have to wait their turn. Women and children were given first priority, however, and it wasn't long before she and Faith were squeezed into one of the boats with ten other people. She worried about leaving Adam on the south bank. No one knew how much time they had. Perhaps even now the Indians were waiting in the forest near the fort. She prayed fervently that despite all the killing, they might still have peace.

Lord, please help us. Please bring peace and let calmer heads prevail.

She thought of Tunchi and some of the other men who'd resided at the mission. Would they really kill her? Adam? Faith? Adam and Faith had lived with them for a long time. Faith even longer than her uncle. Could the men be so heartless when Mercy had done all she could, even risked her life to save their women and children when Caxton's men had attacked?

At times like this, Mercy supposed the deeds of the past didn't weigh heavily enough against the chaos of the moment. She hugged Faith close as they reached the north bank of the river. Would they live out another day?

Chapter

16

This is hardly enough to be considered a fort." Adam looked around in horror. To hear the militia talk, hundreds of Rogue River Indians were about to descend upon them, and all they had for defense was two cabins and an embankment of dirt.

"We have to build up these levees," one of the men said. "Grab every pick and shovel available. The rest of you need to position yourselves with your guns."

Billy Caxton stood only about three feet from Adam. He turned and looked at him with a scowl of displeasure. "I see you have a rifle, Indian lover. You gonna use it?"

"Not to kill other human beings."

"Those heathens ain't human," another man said, passing by. He didn't wait for a response from Adam.

Billy nodded with a smirk. "See, no one but you believes them to have souls. I suppose that's only natural, what with you being a preacher."

This brought the attention of Billy's captain. He joined them and extended his hand to Adam. "They call me Captain

Andrews. I'm not in charge here—not by a long shot—but did I hear Billy say you're a preacher?"

"I am." Adam wasn't at all sure what this meant to the captain. "Why do you ask?"

"Well, men have died and more are soon to follow. We'll need a preacher for hearing their confessions and dying words. And for speakin' over 'em when they get buried."

Adam nodded. "I'd be happy to do that. I'll even dig graves and help with the embankment work. But as I told Billy, I won't be joining in the killing."

The captain frowned as he considered Adam's comment. "Well, truth be told, Preacher, I wouldn't expect you to. Bein' a man of God and all. I know you folks have particular thoughts on how God views such things."

"I'm glad you understand." Adam glanced at Billy. "Some men don't."

"Well, Preacher, I figure you're going to have your hands full. It would be helpful if you were to let someone use your rifle." He nodded to the gun Adam wore slung over his shoulder.

He considered the captain's request for a moment, then nodded. He had hoped to use the gun to hunt game, but obviously that wasn't going to happen anytime soon.

"I understand why we must make this stand." Adam looked at Billy. "Now that the tribes have been incited to war, it's going to be a matter of self-defense. But you have to realize that there may be men out there I know and have broken bread with. I can't kill them."

"No, but I'll bet they can kill you," Billy countered. He looked at Adam, just daring him to deny it.

Instead, Adam gave a slow nod. "They very well may, and if so, then I'll meet my Maker with a guiltless conscience. Can you say the same, Mr. Caxton?"

Billy threw back a stream of expletives and turned to go.

"Just a second there, Billy," his captain called. "I have a particular job for you." He looked at Adam. "If you'll hand over that rifle, Preacher, I'll be on my way."

Adam gave him the weapon and watched as the two soldiers departed. Billy Caxton was a man full of hate, and that made him dangerous.

Going in search of a shovel or pick, Adam tried not to think about the battle to come. Already they could hear gunfire across the river. They couldn't see anything yet, but Adam had a feeling the few folks still on the south side were probably dealing with the forward scouts of the Indian warriors.

He found an old man trying to dig and gave him a smile. "How are you with a rifle?"

The old man looked up and gave a toothless smile. "Not much better than I am at digging. I've spent most of my days on the water. Fell off the mast of a schooner and broke my back a few months ago. They left me here to recover, or so they said. I'm thinking it was more leaving me here to die."

Adam smiled. "Well, I'm better at digging than standing watch, so why don't you give me a turn with that shovel, and you can keep an eye out while I climb the embankment."

The old man frowned at him. "I ain't helpless. I can earn my keep."

Adam nodded and took hold of the shovel but didn't try to pull it away from the man. "I want to do the same, and like I said, you'd probably be better at spotting enemy movement. I don't want to die while I'm helping fortify this sorry excuse for a fort. I need someone to keep watch and tell me when to duck." Adam smiled, hoping to put him at ease.

The old man seemed to consider this for a moment, then let go of the shovel. "I got me a pistol." He opened his coat to reveal the gun tucked into his waistband. "I suppose I could do you some good standing watch."

Adam was relieved the old man's pride could be assuaged. "Thank you. My name is Adam Browning, by the way. I'm a minister of the gospel."

"Well, I'll be tarred and feathered. My pa was a preacher man. Glad to meet you. Just call me Shorty. That's what I'm known by."

"Good enough, Shorty. What say we get to work?"

The old man nodded. "I'll find me a place at the top where I can look out without giving those Injuns too big of a target."

Adam immediately went to work digging in the wet ground. All around him, organized chaos continued. Nearly a hundred people were taking refuge in the fort. A handful of those were women and children. Amazingly enough, some of the women were of Indian blood, but they'd lived with their white husbands for so long that they would never think of leaving to join their relatives in the attack. That didn't stop the occasional fight between a man who figured another man's wife to be a spy, though.

Adam had been at work for nearly three straight hours when one such argument started between the men nearest him.

"I say that squaw will run out in the night and probably take valuable weapons with her," one man declared.

"And I say she won't. She obeys me, and she'll do what she's told," the other countered.

The first man cursed. "Ain't no woman who always does what she's told. Especially no squaw. I say we should kill 'em before they kill us in our sleep."

"I'm not tolerating your threats." The man moved in, his rifle at the ready.

Adam broke in before things got worse. "Fellas, I'm sure this is an argument worth considering, but right now the enemy we know is the one we have to prepare against. We can determine if there are enemies within later." He hoped his words would at least make the men think for a moment.

It appeared to be working. The first man finally said, "I suppose he's right. We ain't gonna have no chance at all if we don't build up this wall."

The other man nodded. "That's a fact."

And with that, the argument was over and the two men went back to working side by side as if nothing had happened.

Adam breathed a sigh of relief and went down the embankment for more dirt. Thankfully, Shorty had made a skid of sorts to haul the earth. It was nothing more than several plank pieces tied together with twine, but it had a rope for a pull and a wooden crate on top. The crate had seen better days, but it served their purpose.

As the day continued, the gunfire grew more frequent, and it wasn't long before an all-out battle raged on the south side of the Rogue. Smoke filled the air as the Indians set fire to the buildings. Nearly twenty men had stayed behind to defend the town and continue ferrying over supplies. Now they were most likely dead or soon would be.

It was a little after midday when Mercy appeared with a canteen of water and a chunk of bread and cheese. "I thought you should eat something."

"I'm more thirsty than anything." He smiled. "But thank you." He took the canteen and drained it of its contents. He handed it back and took the bread and cheese.

"We heard about the town being fired." Mercy glanced in the direction of Gold Beach. "Smoke is still pretty bad."

"Yes. The men here figure the Indians will attack us anytime now. They might wait until night. There are probably more warriors on the south side of the Rogue, so they may use the cover of dark to get across the river unseen and then attack in the morning. Indians have already been spotted on this side, but their main force is on the south side, we think."

"Do you believe that?" Mercy asked.

"Well, I suppose they can see that we're digging in here for a fight, so we're not going anywhere anytime soon. Maybe they don't feel a need to rush us."

Mercy hugged her arms to her chest. "I suppose not."

"How's Faith holding up?"

"She's fine. She's playing with some of the children. They've put the white men with white wives and children in one cabin. That's where we are. You have a place there too. The other cabin is for the white men with Indian wives."

Adam had taken a bite of the bread and cheese and could only nod. He had heard about the arrangement. It saddened him to think that even here they were separating out the races.

"I'll bring you more water," Mercy said after a moment.

Adam shook his head. "Don't risk it. I'd rather you be safe inside. Those logs on the cabin are thick and will protect you. I'm sure one of the men will come around with water. They did once this morning."

She looked at him in such a fearful way that Adam wanted only to take her in his arms. He couldn't deny his love for her, and yet he couldn't bring himself to confess it either.

God, please show me what to do.

He patted her cheek as a father might do to a child. "Go now and tell Faith that I love her."

Mercy lowered her arms. "Is that all you have to say?"

Did she expect him to tell her that he loved her? "I . . . uh . . . in our current situation, I don't know what else I can say."

Mercy's chin jutted upward. "Very well." She whirled on her heel and headed for the cabin.

Adam watched her go for a moment. "I do love you," he whispered.

Mercy had barely entered the cabin before Billy Caxton was at her side. He scowled and looked her up and down.

"You sure give that preacher a lot of your attention." The scowl left his face and was replaced by a lopsided grin. "I could show you a much better time than he does."

"I don't seek his company for a good time." Mercy was determined to keep calm. "Adam is a good, godly man. He doesn't let hatred control his actions, but seeks to do God's will."

"I don't see a man as good who won't protect his loved ones."

"Adam is doing what he thinks is right. And in working to improve the embankment, he is protecting us."

Billy was frowning again. "Ain't nothin' I can say to convince you that I can be just as good?"

"Mr. Caxton, you threatened to kill me." Mercy put her hands on her hips. "What could ever persuade me to desire your company after that?" She started to go, then turned back. Pointing a finger at his chest, she added, "I hold you responsible for the death of Mrs. Browning and her unborn baby. If not for your attack and heartless killing, we might have gotten her to Gold Beach sooner, where a doctor might have saved them."

Billy shook his head and pointed back at Mercy. "Weren't my doin'. You were the one who refused to leave. Once Mr. Browning was dead, it would have only been right to take yourselves back to Gold Beach, but instead you stayed to keep company with the Indians."

"It wasn't just a matter of keeping company with them, Mr. Caxton." Mercy knew arguing with him further was pointless, but she felt the need to say all that had been on her mind since the attack. "I'm sure you know very little of loyalty, but my loyalty had been given to the Brownings and their daughter. By nature of their work, my loyalty also extended to the Tututni. If you would have bothered to get to know those people rather than just killing them, you could have seen how gentle and kind they were. You might have learned how to get along and work together, but instead you let greed and anger guide you."

"Greed? What's that got to do with it?"

"I've heard plenty of talk around here about the amount of money being offered to men to kill the Indians rather than try to bring them in alive. Money was apparently far more important to you than the value of a human life."

He shook his head and spat on the floor. "There ain't a heathen alive who has the soul of a human. They're animals, plain and simple."

Mercy narrowed her eyes. "No, Mr. Caxton. You're the animal."

There were occasional exchanges of gunfire throughout the night that grew into outright battle by first light. Some of the Indians had rifles, but most of their attack consisted of fired volleys of arrows that had little trouble striking inside the embankment. The men were watchful, but it was impossible to avoid injuries completely.

Over the next several days of battle, Adam found himself busier than he could have imagined. When he wasn't helping reinforce the wall, he was tending injured men. If a man was hurt badly enough, Adam took him to one of the cabins for the women to tend. Otherwise, he would just do what he could to patch them up and get them back on the embankment.

It wasn't long before men started dying, and Adam found himself called to speak words of comfort and to dig graves. Throughout the day, there was an ebb and flow to the fighting, but always there seemed to be some threat and little rest for the men. The captains did what they could to give each man a break, but it wasn't for long. Certainly not long enough to make up for their long hours without sleep.

Adam returned to where Shorty stood with the skid. It was full of dirt. Adam gave him a nod and took the skid up the embankment. He had no sooner dumped the load when a bullet whizzed by his ear.

He looked across the embankment to see Billy shrug. "Sorry, Preacher. You were in my line of fire. Sure didn't mean to scare you."

Anger surged at the blatant lie, but Adam managed to push it back down. He said nothing and instead pounded out his aggression on the loose dirt. Once it was secured in place, he went down for another load. He managed to transport three loads, sporadic gunfire going off all around him, before he had another encounter with Billy. This time, however, they were well away from the others, and even Shorty had gone to the cabin for a rest.

"I've had my fill of you, Preacher," Billy said.

Adam looked at Billy for a moment then gathered the rope pull on the skid and headed up the embankment. He wasn't surprised when Billy came bounding after him. "I've got no time to argue with you, Mr. Caxton."

"I ain't here to argue."

"Shouldn't you be firing upon the savages, as you call them?"

"I'll get back to that in my own good time."

They had reached the top of the levee, and Adam dumped his load of dirt and rock, all but ignoring Billy. This only served to anger the young man more. Adam sighed. "I don't suppose you're going to leave until I allow you to speak your mind."

"I didn't come here to speak my mind, but now that you mention it, I do have a few things to say before I do what I came to do."

"And what is that, Mr. Caxton?"

"I'm going to kill you, Preacher." Billy pulled a large knife from the sheath at his side.

Adam froze. This was a turn he hadn't expected. "And how are you going to explain that to your militia friends? The bullet you fired earlier could have easily been explained, but not a knife wound."

"I'll tell them you were a spy. That you were helping the enemy." He climbed to the top of the earthen battlement. "They'll believe me, 'cause they know you've been living with the heathens. They know you're an Indian lover. They don't like it any better than I do."

"Is that a fact?"

"It is." Billy fingered the blade, but his angry gaze never left Adam's face. "I can't figure out why a gal like Miss Flanagan would put store in you, but once you're dead, she ain't gonna have reason to give you another thought. Maybe then I'll be able to get somewhere with her." He grinned, but his eyes still held a look of contempt. "I'll be a comfort to her."

"She'll never find comfort in you. Especially not after you kill me. Mercy will make it her sole purpose to see you punished."

"Well, that ain't the way I see it. She don't need to know that I was the one doing the killin'."

Adam glanced across the open yard. No one seemed to notice them at all. The men who were resting were most likely asleep, and those who were fighting had no thought for other men on the wall. The only chance Adam had was to take a running jump down the hill or to call out for help. Neither seemed promising. By the time anyone got to him, Billy would have already done his best to end Adam's life.

Billy seemed to understand Adam's thoughts and smiled. "It's gonna be as easy to kill you as it was your brother."

Adam's eyes widened and he forgot his fear. "You killed Isaac?"

"Had to. He was going to negotiate a peace—bring the savages in without further fighting. I couldn't let that happen."

"So you shot him with a bow and arrow and blamed it on the Tututni."

Billy laughed. "That's right. That's exactly what I did. When he took to his canoe, I followed him along the bank of the river, just far enough so that I couldn't be blamed for his death. Then I killed him."

Adam's anger returned unchecked. "I'll see you hanged for this." He clenched his fists at his side.

Billy shook his head as gunfire erupted on the embankment across the way. "No, you won't. You'd have to be alive to do that."

He lunged much faster and farther than Adam had expected and was on him in a flash.

There was barely time to dodge Billy's blade, but before Adam could attempt to disarm him, a gunshot rang out, and Billy's eyes widened. He dropped the knife and clutched his side where a crimson stain was starting to spread.

Adam felt as if he were glued to the ground. Billy's eyes rolled into the back of his head, and he fell face-first down the embankment.

Only then could Adam rally his senses. He looked out across the field to the trees where the shot had come from. There, standing just within view, was Tunchi.

He still held his rifle to his shoulder, but when their eyes met, he lowered it. For a moment neither man moved, and then Tunchi gave a nod, pounded his fist over his heart in a gesture of friendship, and disappeared into the trees.

Chapter 17

Mercy found their captivity maddening. There was little food and no way to keep clean or have any real privacy. She busied herself with treating the injured until every herb and tonic in her bag was gone. Even her precious vinegar had been used up, though she was trying to make more from beer. Grace had done it on more than one occasion, so Mercy knew it was possible, but given the cold weather and the chilly temperatures of the cabin, she wasn't sure it would take. Besides, it would be a long time before it would be ready for use.

Every day there were sounds of gunshots and war cries. Just outside the door was a large pile of arrows that had been collected inside the fort. Someone said there were over five hundred. Mercy had no idea if that was accurate, but it was a reminder of the death raining down from the skies. The women and children were told not to leave the cabins for any reason.

Inside, there was a variety of work to be done. Some of the women worked at melting lead, while others were busy making minié balls for the men's guns. Most of the women had given up their underskirts and petticoats for bandages. One woman tried to keep some normalcy by teaching the children. Mercy had made it clear that she would be happy to help in this as well, but her healing skills were far more important to those in the fort.

But with her supplies gone, Mercy wasn't sure she could offer much more than to clean wounds and bandage them. She wondered when it would end. At Whitman's, she'd been hostage for a month. Would it be the same here? They'd only been here a week, and yet it felt like months. It was unnerving, and no matter how hard she tried to just rest in her assurance that God was in control, Mercy felt her faith wavering. She'd never had an issue with her faith in God or His will before. Even when she didn't understand why things happened the way they did, she still held strong to the belief that God had a purpose in it.

She still felt that way, but this time she was starting to be concerned. It wasn't that she feared death. Death came to all, and while she wanted very much to live for a good long time, she knew that death had no power over her. However, she couldn't help worrying about Faith and Adam. She didn't want to lose either of them. She didn't want the Tututni friends she'd made to die in this unjust war.

"Do you think my friends are out there?" Faith asked out of the blue.

Until now, the child's spoken concerns with the ongoing war had been minimal. She still missed her mother and father at night, though. Mercy often heard her crying in her sleep.

"I don't know." She wouldn't lie to Faith. "They might be. Not the children, of course." She smiled and tried to sound more encouraging. "I'm sure the people from our mission are safely in the mountains."

"Not the ones who got killed at the mission."

Mercy saw the grief in Faith's expression. "No. They're with Jesus now."

For a long moment, neither said anything more.

"But the men from our village might be out there," Faith finally said. She pulled at one braided pigtail and then the other. "Mary's father might be there, and Tunchi and the others. What if they get killed?"

"It would be very hard on their families to lose their fathers. You know how sad that is. I lost my father when I was about your age. It's never easy at any age to lose someone you love, but when you're still little, the loss sometimes causes more than just sadness. It can cause fear too."

Faith nodded. "I'm afraid. Aren't you?"

"A little, but I keep reminding myself that the Bible says that when I'm afraid, I can trust God. The Bible has a lot of verses about not being afraid." Mercy knew this very well because she'd been trying to find them all in Adam's Bible.

Faith dropped her hold on her hair and nodded. "Like when the angel told the shepherds about Jesus's birth. They said, 'Fear not!'"

"Exactly." Mercy began tying a cloth over the top of a crock of water. "We don't have to be afraid, even if someone takes our lives, because they can't touch our souls when they belong to Jesus."

"But I don't want to die," Faith said.

Mercy finished with the crock and turned to Faith. "Nor do I." She squared her shoulders, determined not to give in to her fears. "And you know what, I don't think we will. I think we'll be just fine."

Faith wrapped her arms around Mercy. Even though there were other women and children milling about the cabin, it was as if she and Faith were the only ones in the world. For several minutes, Mercy just held Faith and prayed. She let Faith be the one to pull away, and when she did, Mercy was relieved to see her smiling.

"Thank you, Mercy." Faith scampered off in search of her playmates.

Mercy watched her from across the small cabin, marveling at how easily Faith changed her focus. The children seemed capable of forgetting about the affairs going on outside. At least for a little while.

Faith found her friends and joined in a game of some sort. Mercy couldn't tell what the little girls were doing, but they seemed happy, and that was all that mattered. She didn't want Faith to be afraid. She wanted to take Faith away from all of this and see her happily settled in an environment where she could be loved and nurtured, just as she had been. Mercy did wonder, however, how she would manage things once they left Gold Beach and headed to Oregon City. She'd already determined that it wouldn't be fair to just show up at the farm with Faith in tow. Somehow, she needed to get a letter to Hope and Grace and let them know what had happened. Her sisters didn't even realize that Isaac and Eletta were dead. The news would be hard to hear.

Adam came into the cabin and looked around the room until his gaze locked on to Mercy. He motioned her to join him.

She left what she was doing and went to him. "What's wrong?" His expression was grim and there was a sort of wariness about him.

"I need to talk to you—alone."

He opened the cabin door and pulled her outside. He looked toward the embankment and the sky overhead as if expecting a barrage of arrows. They walked a little way from the door, but not so far as to be unable to return quickly should the need arise.

"What is it, Adam?" Mercy searched his face. "What's happened?"

He took hold of her arms. "Billy Caxton is dead. Tunchi shot him."

"How do you know it was Tunchi?"

"I saw him."

Mercy shook her head. "I don't understand."

Adam tightened his grip. "There's so much more. I can hardly sort it out. Billy tried to kill me."

"Kill you?" Mercy fought a wave of fear at the thought. She'd just told Faith they didn't need to be afraid. It wouldn't look good if she gave in to it now. "Why would Billy want to kill you?"

"Probably for the same reasons he killed Isaac."

"What!" She hadn't meant to cry out.

"Shhh, I don't want everyone to know." Adam pulled her a little farther from the front of the cabin, but kept glancing to the skies. "Billy told me he was going to tell everyone I was spying for the Indians. He figured to kill me and then tell them he'd done it to keep everyone safe. Then he told me he killed Isaac because he was going to broker peace."

Mercy listened without interruption. She had always suspected Billy of having something to do with Isaac's death, but hearing the truth was almost too much to bear.

"Isaac never made it to the army. Billy followed him along the riverbank, and when just the right moment came along, he shot three arrows into Isaac's back and killed him."

"And told us that the Tututni had done it." Mercy was so mad she trembled. "How dare he? I'm glad he's dead. I'm glad Tunchi killed him."

"He could have killed me too, but he didn't."

"Tunchi?" Mercy couldn't begin to fathom all that had happened. "How do you know that?"

"Billy and I were on the top of the north embankment. Most of the fighting was taking place on the south and east sides, so there was no one else around. Billy found me and lunged at me with a knife. It happened so fast, I didn't even know what to do. But before he could hurt me, he was shot. I looked in the direction the shot must have come from, and there was Tunchi tucked in the shadows of the trees. He let me see him. I don't know if he knew that Billy killed Isaac or not, but he shot Billy with the rifle Isaac gave him."

"But he didn't try to shoot you?"

"No. He wanted me to know that he could have killed me but chose not to. He put his hand to his heart, assuring me of his friendship. Then he left."

"Oh my!" Mercy's knees felt weak. She didn't know what else to say. It was almost too much to take in.

Adam surprised her by pulling her close. She was grateful for his warmth and strength. In his arms, she felt there was nothing she couldn't face.

"The Tututni are out there—our friends are out there."

Mercy pressed her cheek against his chest. "I wish they would simply run to the mountains and hide. I hate to think of them being killed. They're only defending what is rightfully theirs."

"I'm glad you don't hate them."

She gave a small shake of her head. "I couldn't. I saw how those men loved you and Isaac. I saw how the women loved Eletta and Faith. I loved them in return. I loved those precious children." She thought of the dead they'd left behind. The ones she hadn't been able to save the day Billy attacked. They would always haunt her.

"They were good people. I knew a great many of the Rogue River Indians, and I will miss them when they go north to the reservation."

"Perhaps we could go to the reservation too," Mercy murmured. She wasn't at all sure he'd heard her, but when he pulled away from her, she knew by the look on his face that he had, and that he understood her implication.

Adam said nothing. He stood silently watching her face. Mercy knew it was foolish to deny her feelings anymore.

"Adam, I've never been one to lie about my feelings. I'm an outspoken woman, as you well know, and I'm not afraid to let my thoughts—even my desires—be known."

His brow rose, betraying his curiosity, but still he said nothing.

"I have for some time known that my feelings for you were changing. I think you know that, and furthermore, I think you feel the same way I do." She drew a deep breath to steady her nerves. She might sound bold and be outspoken, but deep inside she was still afraid of his rejection. "I feel things for you that I've never felt for any man. From the first moment I saw you, I knew there was something about you that was important to me. I can't explain it, but I knew you would change my life."

"Mercy, you don't know what you're saying."

"Yes, I do." She nodded and stepped closer. "I love you, and you are absolutely the only man I will ever love."

He took hold of her arms again, but this time to hold her back. "I know you feel that way at the moment, but living under siege with the threat of death makes us think strange things."

"I felt this way before my life was endangered. I've felt this way for a long time."

"You haven't known me for a long time." He looked almost stunned by her declaration.

Still Mercy knew that he felt the same way. "You can say what you want, but I know you have the same feelings for me."

"I . . . I can't deny that I . . . have feelings for you." He stopped and dropped his hold. "But . . . there's something I have to tell you. Something that I think will probably change how you feel about me."

"They've killed Ben Wright!" someone yelled from across the grounds.

Chaos was immediate, and there was no longer any thought of Adam's confession. Mercy had no idea what he'd been about to say, but at least he had admitted to having feelings for her. She started across the yard to hear what had happened, but Adam reached out to pull her back.

"Get inside. I'll bring you news when I know something."

"But—"

He pushed her toward the cabin door. "Please just do as I say. It isn't safe out here."

She considered protesting but instead turned and headed for the cabin. She didn't like the fear she'd seen in Adam's eyes. Not for himself . . . but for her.

The women inside the cabin had heard the commotion and wanted to know what was happening.

"Have we been breached?" one woman asked Mercy.

"Someone said that Ben Wright had been killed," she said.

The woman put her hand to her mouth. Another woman began to cry. "They're going to kill us all."

"Hush!" Mercy spoke in a harsher tone than she'd intended. "You'll scare the children. We're perfectly safe here. As I understand it, Ben was on the south side of the river."

"That's true, Miriam," another woman said, putting her arm around the one who'd spoken.

They waited for what seemed an eternity before one of the men returned. He was the husband of one of the other women, who'd just had a baby not two weeks before the attack.

"The Indians have killed or burned out everyone up and down the coast. They got Ben Wright and others. We're next."

So much for keeping the children calm and unafraid. Mercy looked around for Faith. She stood with the other children, listening with wide eyes.

"What can we do?" one of the women asked.

"We've got to have help. We're going to sneak someone out of here when it's good and dark and send them up to Port Orford to bring the army."

The women nodded and murmured their approval, but one spoke up. "That will take time, and we don't have much of that."

"We're still well enough fixed," the man countered. "We can hold them off for quite some time."

"We haven't got enough food or provisions," the woman called Miriam countered. "How can we keep going on what little we have?"

"We'll have to ration it out."

"We're already doing that, and it's still slipping away much too fast," she answered.

The man looked irritated. "We'll do what we have to do. But for now, all we can do is send the runner and wait."

And wait they did. February turned into March, and still no help came. Neither was there any word of help coming. The man they'd sent to Port Orford hadn't been heard from. He could have been killed on the way; there was no way to know. Mercy felt like they were stranded on an island in the middle of the ocean.

Strangely enough, the Indians hadn't attacked again. Not in full force. In fact, some even thought the Indians had given up on the fort and left the area altogether. Even the sentries had seen no sign of them, and because of this, the men who'd taken charge called everyone together.

"We believe the Indians may have left the area," the leader began. "I think it's safe enough to at least go out and forage for food."

Adam inserted himself into the conversation. "You're fools if you risk leaving the fort. They're still out there. I know they are."

"You're wrong. They would be attacking us if they were still there." The leader clearly didn't like to be contradicted. "We've got to have food. There's no denying that. I want a group of seven men—volunteers—to go retrieve food. There's a potato field about a half mile upriver. Plenty of spuds were left for just such need. We might even catch some game or fish. I'll be one of the seven to go, and I only want single men to volunteer."

"I'll go," Nigel Grierson said, stepping up.

After that, everyone was talking at once. The other volunteers were decided, and before anyone could say much else about it, the men left to ready themselves for the journey.

"They shouldn't go," Adam said, moving to stand beside Mercy.

"But if they don't do something, we'll starve." She looked up at him. "These children are hungry."

"I know." His voice was resigned.

Since things had quieted somewhat, Mercy touched his arm. "You were going to tell me something a while back. Something about yourself that you fear will change my feelings for you. Now seems like as good a time as any to tell me."

Adam looked at her for a moment and then nodded. "I suppose you're right." He pulled her to the farthest corner of the cabin.

Mercy knew he was uneasy, but she also knew he would have to tell her whatever it was so she could assure him it didn't matter. Still, waiting for him to speak was maddening.

"So tell me already," she blurted after several long seconds of silence.

He heaved a sigh. "It's about my past. About who I am."

"Preacher! Preacher, where are you? Come quick. Big Joe's takin' a turn for the worse and is askin' for you," Shorty called from the door.

Adam gave her an apologetic look before hurrying off. Mercy wanted to scream in frustration but stood in silence. There would be a chance to hear Adam's concerns. She just needed to bide her time.

Chapter 18

Grace paled as she read the newspaper. Authorities stated that the entirety of the Rogue River region was at war. Up and down the river, the Indians were raiding, killing, and burning down any structure built by the whites. The army was hot on their heels, but the Indians kept avoiding capture. In their wake, they left atrocities too numerous to detail, according to the editor.

"Did you read this?" she asked Hope, who sat nursing her son. Hope's expression made it clear that she had. Grace clutched the paper to her breast. "Our poor Mercy. She may already be dead."

"You can't think that way," Hope countered. "It doesn't do any good. Lance said the newspapers always blow things out of proportion. They even lie outright. We both know that's true."

"Well, maybe we can go into town and ask what's happening. Dr. McLoughlin can tell us something. He's still in touch with the governor and legislators."

Hope shook her head. "Grace, you have no business leaving the house. Alex will never allow it after the labor pains you've had off and on."

"It's nothing but false labor. I still have a couple weeks before we really have to be concerned." Grace tried to sound convincing, but she knew Hope wasn't buying it. She knew as well that her time was near. "I can't just sit here and do nothing. I have no idea if any of them are alive."

She thought of poor Eletta, who would have just had her baby. Her friend had never been strong, and if she had to flee for her life so soon after delivery, she might bleed to death.

"This is why Alex wanted to keep the newspapers out of your hands," Hope replied calmly. She lifted the baby to her shoulder and patted his back. "If he finds out you went behind his back to read it, he's not going to be happy."

"I can't help it if he left it out in clear view."

Hope snorted. "Clear view, eh? You call being stashed under the cushion of his chair in clear view?"

"He had to know I'd clean house." Grace shrugged. "Is it my fault that I needed to pound the cushions and rid them of dust?"

"Well, he's your husband, and you're the one who will have to deal with him."

Grace refolded the paper. "I can't bear this. I didn't want her to go in the first place, but everyone seemed so sure it would be all right. If she gets killed—"

"If she gets killed, we'll deal with it then. Until we hear otherwise, she's fine, and we have to rest in that. We can't go rescue her or bring her home. She might even be on her way home now, for all we know. Isaac did promise that if things started looking bad he would get them all out of there."

"I know, but I just feel so helpless." A contraction tightened like an iron band around her, and Grace shifted uncomfortably. She knew she needed to remain calm for the sake of the child.

"We can pray," Hope offered.

Grace nodded. "Yes. We can pray, and I have been."

"Well, there's no limit on how many times you can petition God for the same thing," Hope replied with a smile.

"I suppose that's true enough." Grace forced a smile in return. "I'm going to go lie down for a bit and do just that. I'm afraid I've worn myself out this morning."

"Are you going to tell Alex about this?"

Grace struggled to her feet. "I'm not going to start lying to him now. I knew when I picked up that paper that I would have to tell him. Maybe if he sees that I can read the news and still be all right, he'll stop worrying about it." Pain shot through her gut, causing Grace to clutch her stomach.

"Are you all right?" Hope asked, getting to her feet. She put her son in a cushioned basket not far from her chair and went to Grace.

The pain passed, and Grace straightened. "I'm fine." She didn't think it wise to tell Hope that this pain wasn't like the others. "I'll get my rest, and everything will be just fine."

<hr>

At Fort Miner, it was decided that the seven men would leave in the morning to go for food. Mornings had been foggy the last few days, and it seemed the perfect cover in case the Indians were still out there. The men slipped out of the fort and headed for the brushy cover along the river as quickly and silently as possible. Everyone in the fort seemed to hold their breath. The sentries watched until the men were out of sight, and everyone, even the meanest-tempered miners, prayed.

But it was soon evident that the Indians were still very much on guard as the air filled with the sound of gunfire. It wasn't long before two men, one wounded, came running back to the fort. The armed men in the fort fired into the trees, hoping to give them cover. Once they were safely inside, everyone learned that they had been ambushed.

"We're the only two who managed to get away," one of the men said, holding his hand to his wounded arm. "The rest are dead."

"What are we going to do?" one of the women wailed.

Everyone started talking at once about how they might survive or even escape. Mercy walked to the back of the cabin and took a seat on the floor beside their things. Neither of the two men who had returned was Nigel Grierson. It seemed overwhelmingly sad that she should have just seen him again only to learn he was dead. Maybe that was why God put her in this place at this time. Otherwise Nigel might have died, and no one would ever have known what happened to him. She knew he had at least two brothers and wondered if there might be a way to contact them and let them know about Nigel's sacrifice.

Of course, Nigel was also guilty of killing innocent people. At least to her way of thinking. She supposed she was one of the few who saw it that way. She sighed. Their captivity here might well stretch even longer than the one she'd endured at the Whitman Mission.

"Are you all right?" Adam asked, taking a seat on the floor beside her. "I know your friend Nigel was one of the men who didn't return."

"Yes, I was just thinking about that."

"I'm sorry. It's hard to lose friends."

She smiled and shook her head. "We weren't really friends . . . just acquaintances, although he did once pledge that he would take responsibility for me when I was younger. I just was wondering if I'd have any way to contact his brothers and let them know about his death. One of them, at least, went south with him when he decided to search for gold. I don't remember about the other. I know at one time he had joined up to hunt down the Cayuse. Maybe both of them did." She shrugged. "I have no idea where they are now."

"I'm sorry. Maybe once you're back in Oregon City, you could have something published in the newspaper."

She looked at him, realizing that was probably her best recourse. "Thank you. I will do exactly that. I just hate to think of him lying out there dead and his family not knowing what happened. Despite what he did with the militia, he was a hero in his efforts to see us fed."

"Yes, he was."

"What will happen now, Adam?"

He reached for her hand. "I don't know."

"We have to have food. I heard one of the women talk about boiling shoe leather to feed her children."

He drew her hand up and looked at it as if contemplating its contours. "I've considered sneaking out and finding Tunchi."

"No, you can't do that." His words filled her with panic. "There's much too great a risk. I realize you're known to many of the Indian tribes in the area, but we're at war now. You have no guarantee the other warriors will see things Tunchi's way."

"No, but I might manage to get through or even be allowed to speak to those in charge of the warriors."

"And you might be killed." She shook her head. "I couldn't bear that, and neither could Faith."

His dark eyes held her spellbound. Mercy wanted nothing more than to throw herself into his arms. She couldn't bear the thought of him leaving her . . . of him dying.

"Please, Adam. Please promise me you won't try anything like that. Faith and I need you. I couldn't bear to face the future without you."

He drew her hand to his lips. "All right. I promise. I won't do anything without talking to you about it first." He placed a brief kiss on the back of her hand.

She sighed with relief. "Thank you."

The arguments in the center of the cabin grew louder, causing

Mercy to look around for Faith. She spied her almost immediately in the corner with several other little girls. They were playing with their dolls and ignoring the nonsense going on around them. It was so amazing how children could survive such intense situations.

"What are you going to do about Faith?" Adam asked.

Mercy shook her head. "What do you mean?"

"What do you have in mind for her? Are you planning to take her to your sisters to raise?"

Without thinking, she responded, "I won't know until I have a chance to talk to Hope." She realized at once what she'd said.

"Why would you have to talk to her about it?" Adam asked.

Mercy bit her lip a little harder than she'd intended and tasted blood. She tried to think of something she could say to excuse her comment, but then shook her head. She wasn't going to start making up excuses or lies now. Not when she'd bared her heart to this man.

"Hope is Faith's mother."

Adam looked at her like she'd lost her mind. "What are you saying? Eletta was her mother."

Mercy nodded. "Yes. Her adopted mother and the only mother Faith has ever known. But my sister Hope gave birth to Faith." She looked at Adam, hoping he would understand. When he continued to look puzzled, Mercy added, "Faith is half Cayuse."

Recognition dawned, and Adam's gaze shifted to where Faith was playing. "But she doesn't look Indian at all. She even has blue eyes like Eletta."

"I know. She's the spitting image of my sister with her dark hair and blue eyes. I see Hope in her expressions every day."

"But does she know that Eletta and Isaac weren't her real mother and father?"

"No. First, because they *were* her real mother and father.

Giving birth doesn't make you a real mother. It's the day-to-day relationship that does that. Second, Eletta planned to tell her one day but hadn't said anything about it yet. Instead, she kept a journal for Faith. I have it with me, and I'm supposed to give it to Faith when the time is right."

Adam let go of her hand and leaned back against the log wall. "I never had any idea. Isaac never told me."

"Eletta didn't even realize that *I* knew. She never said anything to me until near the end. I told her I'd known for a long time. See, my sister Grace and Eletta managed to keep it hidden. Eletta pretended to need Hope to accompany her and Isaac to California when they left Oregon City. Hope didn't want the baby. She even contemplated killing herself. Faith was a reminder of all the evil that had been done to her by Tomahas." Mercy paused. "That was Faith's father's name."

She could see Adam was doing his best to take in the news. "Hope was terrified that her baby would look like Tomahas. Not only that, but if she'd let people know she was with child, they would know that the Cayuse were responsible, and Faith would have been shunned. Hope probably would have been too, and for no fault of her own. That's the worst thing about it."

"People can be cruel," Adam murmured. His tone suggested he fully understood.

"Hope delivered Faith in California and then came home to us as if nothing ever happened. I didn't even know about it until much later, when Grace was having her first baby. Hope and I were helping with the delivery, and when I was out of the room, they started talking about the past. I was just outside the door and overheard them discussing it." She smiled and shook her head. "It all made sense, and I thought how very naïve I'd been. Hope kept me safe when we were hostages and paid a high price for it. I'll always love her for that, and that's why I won't deliberately hurt her now."

215

"I see what you mean."

"I figure once we get out of here and sail north, we can stop in Portland. I'll send Hope a letter and explain what's happened and what I would like to do. But I'll give her the right to refuse."

"If she does, what will you do?"

Mercy gave a little laugh. "Well, if you can just get your priorities straight, we can marry and raise her together."

"Are you proposing to me?" he asked, looking amused.

"I suppose I am. Goodness knows I've waited long enough for you to do the asking."

His look of amusement faded. "Mercy, you aren't being fair. You presume that I feel the way you do, but I might not."

Mercy decided enough was enough. Without warning, she leaned closer and wrapped her arms around his neck as she kissed him. She felt her breath quicken and her heart race as he responded to her kiss and pulled her close. Mercy wanted the kiss to go on forever, but she knew she needed to make her point. If not, Adam might never come to his senses and address his feelings for her.

She pulled back abruptly and jumped to her feet, leaving Adam looking stunned. She smiled down at him. "Tell me again how you might not feel the same way I do."

~~~

"I knew her worrying was going to bring that baby on early," Alex said, pacing the floor.

Hope gave him a sympathetic smile. "She's doing just fine, so stop fretting. And it's not so early. Due dates aren't an exact science. She might have been expecting longer than she realized. Either way, I'm confident everything will be all right." She looked at her husband. "Lance, I think you might have to whip up a game of chess or some other distraction to keep Alex from losing his mind."

Lance laughed. "You women just don't understand what we go through when our wives are giving birth. It isn't easy on us. We really suffer."

Hope rolled her eyes. "Oh, please. You have no idea of suffering." She headed back upstairs to tend to Grace.

When she reached the bedroom door, Grace was crying out for her. Hope rushed into the room to see that Grace was trying to deliver the baby herself.

"But the baby hadn't even crowned yet when I went downstairs!" Hope hurried to grab some towels and a basin of water and vinegar to bring to the bed.

Grace fell back against the pillows as Hope hurriedly washed her hands and then took hold of the baby as it slid out of Grace's body.

"It's another boy."

He started to wail immediately. Hope put her finger in his mouth to make certain there was no mucus to clear, but given his loud protests, she had little fear of that. She cut the cord and washed him.

"What are you calling him?" she asked Grace.

"James Edward Armistead."

"Edward after Uncle Edward, I presume, but why James?" Hope finished cleaning the baby and wrapped him up tight in a warm towel.

"Alex was studying the book of James and decided it was a very fine book and an equally fine name. I thought it sounded nice too."

"Well, James, your mother is anxious to see you." Hope smiled down at the blue-eyed boy, who had finally calmed. He looked back at her as if trying to figure out who or what she was.

Hope handed him to Grace. "I'd best go tell the very anxious father. I'll be right back to finish tending you."

She left the room as Grace cooed and fussed over her new son. When Hope reached the top of the stairs, Alex was already halfway up. She held out her hand to stop him. "We're not quite ready for you, but I wanted you to know that you have a fine, healthy son. James Edward."

A pale-faced Alex eased back against the stair rail. "And Grace is all right?"

"She's perfectly fine, but I need to get back to her. I'll have them both ready to receive visitors shortly."

She could see the look of relief that washed over his face. This man loved her sister more than life itself.

"Go rest, Alex. I'll call for you as soon as I can."

He nodded. "I'll go tell the children."

"And just so you know," Lance called from the bottom of the stairs, "our son believes it's his dinner time." He held up the fussy baby as proof.

Hope smiled. "Dampen a towel in sugar water and let him suck on that. I promise I'll get to him as soon as I can."

She continued smiling as she made her way back to Grace. Mercy would be vexed that she'd missed the delivery. She had hoped to be home by now. A shadow of doubt rose in Hope's mind, and her smile faded. She paused outside the closed bedroom door.

What if she is dead? What if they're all dead?

Her thoughts went to Faith. It was impossible not to think about the baby she'd given away. The baby she hadn't wanted. Faith was half Indian, but the warring tribes wouldn't know that, nor would they care.

She gave a heavy sigh. "Lord, please save them. Save my sister . . . and my daughter."

Chapter 19

In the days that passed, Adam mulled over what Mercy had told him about Faith and about her own feelings for him. He also couldn't help but remember that she'd proven her point when she'd kissed him. He did love her. He loved her more dearly than he'd ever loved anyone. She was the first thing on his mind when he awoke and the last in his thoughts as he fell asleep. During the day when he was working to ensure their safety, he thought of Mercy more than anyone else . . . even Faith.

It was time, he decided, to tell her the truth and let the situation play out as it would. He couldn't lie about loving her, but neither could he lie about his Indian heritage. Besides, he was almost certain the Mercy he'd come to know wouldn't care about such a thing. In the past he hadn't told Lizzy or her family about being Cherokee because he knew it wouldn't set well. With Mercy, he felt confident it wouldn't matter. So then why was this so hard?

"Could you join me outside for a few minutes?"

Mercy looked up from where she sat on the floor, helping Faith learn some new spelling words. "Of course." She looked at Faith. "You stay here and work on these words. Remember to study the definitions I wrote out as well as the pronunciation. It won't do any good to be able to spell a word if you don't know how to say it or what it means."

"Can't I come outside with you? It's been forever." Faith frowned and looked at Adam. "Please?"

He squatted down. "It's not safe, Faith. We can't tell when the Indians might decide to send a volley of arrows over the embankment. I just can't take the chance that one might hit you."

"But what if it hits you or Mercy? You might be killed."

"I suppose you're right, but I need to tell Mercy something in private, and you can hardly find much of that here."

Faith shrugged. "You can sit here with Mercy, and I'll go across the room where most everyone else is."

Adam knew that she was worried and decided it might be for the best. "Very well. Mercy and I will stay here and talk."

Faith jumped up with her journal and pencil. She kissed Adam on the cheek, then skipped across the room, narrowly avoiding a couple of women who were carrying pails of water.

Still squatting, Adam looked at Mercy. "I need to tell you about myself."

Mercy laughed. "You figured that out, eh?"

He smiled and sat on the ground. "I don't have much time, since I'm supposed to take a turn at watch on the wall. But what I have to say won't take that long."

"Then you'd best get to it," Mercy said in a stern manner, but her expression was filled with love.

"Well, you know that I went to college in Boston. I think Eletta told you that much."

"Actually, it was Isaac, but yes, I do know that much. Harvard, if I remember right."

"Yes, that's correct. When I was there, I became good friends with a man named Marcus Price. He was also attending Harvard, although his focus wasn't to study theology. After the first couple years, we became inseparable, and as we attended various events, we started including his younger sister Elizabeth." He waited to see if she might pose a question, but when she didn't, he continued.

"Lizzy was rather spoiled, but beautiful and funny. She had a great heart for the poor and often worked with the Ladies Aid Society to benefit the needy. She even helped at the orphanage. She would go and read to the little ones."

"She sounds wonderful."

"She was, and I fell in love. I asked her father for her hand in marriage, and even though I had nothing of financial means, he was delighted to agree because I was so highly thought of by the church and the college."

Mercy frowned but said nothing. Adam was hesitant to continue, but he knew the truth had been delayed far too long.

"Lizzy was popular with the gentlemen. One in particular had hoped to marry her and join their fortunes. He never cared for me, and in his desire to discredit me, he paid a man to search out my past. When the truth came out about my background and family, Lizzy's father put an end to our engagement, and all of my Boston friends turned their backs on me."

"How terrible. I'm so sorry." She looked away and seemed to study her hands. "So I suppose you're still nursing a broken heart and that's why you don't want to marry me."

Adam was taken aback. "Not at all. I did care deeply for Lizzy, but that was nearly five years ago, and she's now married with a family of her own. I will not spend another thought on her." He shrugged. "I doubt I could even conjure an image of her, not with you in my life."

Mercy looked at him, and her expression betrayed her confusion. "Then why? Why, when I know you have feelings for me, can't you admit you love me and want . . . to marry me?"

He drew in a deep breath and held it for a moment. Everything could change with what he was about to say. He exhaled and met her eyes. "Don't you wonder what made the Price family turn from me?"

"Not in particular. We all have things we've done that we wish we could undo."

"This wasn't something I did. It was something I am."

Mercy gave an exasperated sigh. "So just tell me and let me be the judge as to whether it's so terrible that I cannot love you. As if there could ever be anything like that."

He nodded. "I'm a quarter Cherokee Indian. My mother was a half-breed."

Mercy's mouth dropped open, and her eyes widened in surprise. Adam felt a sense of dread wash over him until Mercy began to giggle and then laugh.

"It's the truth. I'm not joking."

She composed herself and shook her head, still smiling. "I know you're not joking. Just as I've always known that you're a quarter Cherokee."

Adam stared at her. "But how? How could you know?"

"Because, silly, I came west with your brother. He told us about his desire to preach to the Indians because he was a quarter Indian himself. He told us all about his—your mother." She shook her head again. "Is this the reason you thought I'd turn away from you?"

"It's a pretty big reason. After all, it ended the only other love affair I've had."

"No, God allowed things to happen that way because he knew I would love you better and more completely than Lizzy ever could."

Adam could hardly believe it didn't matter to her. "But you know what people will say if we marry and they find out."

"That I married the man I love with all my heart." She

touched his cheek. "Adam, no one in my family will care, and theirs is the only good opinion I have ever sought—except for yours."

He felt his heart skip a beat and pressed his hand against hers. He cherished the feel of her touch on his face. "I don't know what to say. All of my life it's been a source of pain and suffering. When I was a boy, people knew about my mother and taunted me without end. I was called all sorts of names and cursed as worthless. When Lizzy's family turned against me, even Marcus, who had pledged his never-ending friendship, said horrible things. I figured I would never fit in in the white world."

"There are a great many cruel people in this world. Having gone through what you did, you can understand how it will be for Faith if anyone learns the truth about her heritage. In her situation it's even worse, however, because your mother was born out of love, and Faith was conceived in hatred and lust."

"I do understand. Only too well."

"I know the years have softened Hope's heart. I even know that she sometimes regrets giving Faith to Eletta. I've heard her tell Lance—her husband—that she feels as if an important part of her is missing."

"You seem to do a lot of eavesdropping." He grinned. "But I suppose I can understand why."

"I didn't seek it out. It just happened in situations where I was in the right place at the right time. Given all the events that have transpired in my life, I see it as God giving me the information I need to make better decisions. I want Hope to have a chance to reclaim Faith—if she wants to. I want Faith to have a home with siblings—flesh of her flesh. But if that cannot be, then I want us to raise her, since we both love her so dearly."

"And what of Faith?"

"I want her to be happy. If Hope doesn't mind us bringing

Faith to the farm, then I think Faith will make it clear to all of us what makes her happy."

"You've thought this all out in great detail."

"I have. The only thing that stands in the way of making me truly happy is . . . your unwillingness to marry me." She gave him a look that dared him to deny her statement.

"Who says I'm unwilling to marry you?" He stood and pulled her to her feet. "Since the truth hasn't frightened you away, I see no further obstacle to our marriage."

Mercy put her hand on his chest as he started to pull her into an embrace. "Wait just a minute. Last I heard from you, you said you might not feel the same way about me."

He brushed back wisps of her long brown hair before cupping his hands against her face. "I love you, Mercy Flanagan. I love you more than life itself. I never thought that we could be together because of my blood, but the fact that you don't mind it makes me love you all the more."

She smiled but said nothing. Adam drank in her expression of love for several moments. He was finally able to give his heart without worry of the truth ending the affair.

He grinned. "I don't know what the future holds for us, but if you'll still have me, then I'd like to accept your proposal of marriage." He gently pressed his lips to hers. Mercy's arms went around his neck and she returned his kiss with gusto.

"Are you going to marry Mercy now?" Faith asked.

Adam pulled away, feeling embarrassed at having lost track of where they were. He looked down at the child he would always consider his niece. "Would you like me to?"

Faith nodded, her dark brown pigtails bobbing. "Mama said that with a little prayer and a lot of patience, she was sure it would happen."

"What?" Adam asked. "Your mother wanted to see us together?"

The little girl laughed. "She did. She told me that she'd prayed you two together and was certain God would help you fall in love."

"Well, I'll be." Adam shook his head and laughed. "Here we've been matched by our family and didn't even realize it was happening."

"Eletta confessed it to me on her deathbed, but it doesn't matter," Mercy replied. "For once I'm glad for the meddling."

He turned back to gaze into her turquoise eyes. "I am too."

"So are you going to get married today?" Faith asked.

Adam considered the matter. "Given I'm the only pastor around these parts, I guess we'll have to wait. But in my heart, there is no one else nor ever will be."

Mercy smiled. "There's never been anyone for me . . . but you."

As the latter days of March came upon them, the people at Fort Miner were as low on hope as they were on food. Tempers were foul, and everyone was tired of living in such cramped quarters. Fights erupted on a daily basis, and often they came to blows. For days at a time, there would be no sign of the Indians, and the people would begin to believe the worst was over. Then, just as their guard was lowered, they would face another onslaught.

But by the twenty-first, their hopes were renewed with the arrival of the regular army. Troops came from Port Orford as well as from California, and the Indians were quickly driven back or killed.

At first no one dared to believe their captivity was finally at an end, but when a schooner arrived to take them back to Port Orford, everyone breathed a sigh of relief. The siege was over.

Mercy knew rescue had come just in the nick of time. Much

longer, and she was certain there would have been deadly fights among some of the men. Especially those who felt the Indian wives were worthless and there for the purpose of spying and eating valuable rations.

"I'm ready to take any and all back to Port Orford," announced the captain of the schooner, a man named Tichenor. "We should be quick about loading up, as the area is far from secure. I know many of you men have pledged to stay and fight, but anyone who wishes to leave may come aboard."

"Are we really going to go to your farm?" Faith asked Mercy. She cradled her doll while staring out at the ocean and the ship that had come to their rescue.

"Well, it's not *my* farm, but we'll see. I'd like to take you there. It's beautiful."

Adam appeared with their possessions. He'd rolled Eletta's quilts and tied them to his back once again, and carried Mercy's bag and his own pack in hand.

"What about our Indian wives?" a man suddenly called out. "I don't want to leave my woman here to die."

"Yeah, what about my wife?" another asked.

Mercy feared the tensions would escalate should the captain refuse the native women passage. Captain Tichenor seemed to consider the matter only a moment, however.

"I am a member of the Territorial Legislature with the power to perform civil unions. I will marry any man to his Indian wife in a legal and binding ceremony, and then—and only then—will I allow the Indian women to have passage on my ship."

There was a rumbling of conversation amongst the men while the captain went on to explain. "A legally wed man and wife will not face separation, nor will an Indian wife be required to leave her husband and be removed to the reservation."

Several of the men came forward. "We're willing to have you marry us," one of them announced.

Mercy noticed several men with Indian wives who didn't come forward. She could only wonder at the future of those women. It was sad to imagine the men had no more regard for their wives than to leave them behind to be captured or killed.

"Hey, why don't we see if the captain will marry us as well," Adam said, leaning close to whisper in her ear.

"That's a wonderful idea." Mercy looked at Faith. "Would you like it if Adam and I got married today?"

Faith nodded enthusiastically, but then just as quickly grew serious. "But you won't have a pretty dress and walk down the aisle with flowers. My mama used to talk about her wedding and how beautiful it was, and how she hoped someday I would have a wedding just like it."

Mercy smiled. "Pretty dresses and flowers are always nice, but the most important thing is that two people love each other and love God. Nothing else really matters." She looked back to Adam. "Nothing."

At sunset, after the last of the passengers were safely aboard and the ship was under way, Mercy and Adam held hands. Faith stood between them as if to bear witness as Captain Tichenor joined them in marriage.

Despite the chill of the ocean breeze, Mercy thought it the perfect place for her wedding. The western sky was a mottled painting of orange and pink as the sun slipped beyond the horizon.

"Will you have this woman, Mercy Flanagan, to be your wedded wife?"

"I will," Adam replied, smiling at Mercy.

"And will you have this man, Adam Browning, to be your husband?" the captain asked Mercy.

She was so happy she thought she might cry. "I will."

"Have you a ring as a symbol of your pledge?" he asked Adam.

Mercy panicked. She hadn't considered the need for such a thing.

Adam held up his hand. "One moment, Captain." He leaned down and whispered something to Faith, who nodded in return. Adam straightened and produced a small gold band. He looked at Mercy. "I will buy you another when we reach Portland, but Eletta gave me this to save for Faith. She said she'd have no need of it in heaven. Faith agrees that we may borrow it."

Mercy looked at Faith and smiled despite the tears that spilled onto her cheeks. "Thank you."

Adam slipped the ring onto her finger, and without further ado, the captain declared them husband and wife. When Adam kissed her, Mercy felt as if her entire world had finally come around right.

"I hope you don't regret this," Adam teased as he pulled away.

Mercy wiped away her tears with the back of her sleeve. "Never."

Chapter 20

Once they arrived in Portland, Adam immediately took Mercy and Faith to meet his brother's friend Reverend Matthew Beckham. He was a somewhat portly man who had recently become a widower, and he welcomed them enthusiastically.

"I'm very glad for the company. My congregants have done so much to keep me from being lonely, but now that you're here, I insist you stay with me. This house is more than big enough for all of us."

Adam looked around the neatly ordered room. The Reverend Beckham had insisted they sit as a family on a small sofa that was more like a cloth-covered pew. The old gentleman sat in a rocking chair opposite them, near the fire, where he occasionally used a poker to stoke the meager flames. It did seem the house was large enough to accommodate them all, although it had already been mentioned that there were only two bedrooms.

He glanced at Mercy for her opinion. She gave a slight nod, and Adam turned back to their host. "We'd be happy to, Reverend Beckham."

"No. No, that won't do." His round face reddened slightly as he cleared his throat. "Call me Matthew as your brother did. I would definitely like to be your friend."

"I know we would like that as well." Adam had already made all the introductions, but he couldn't help bringing Mercy to the forefront again. "My wife is quite talented at making shortbread and other delicious treats. Perhaps you would allow her to make something for you while we're here."

Matthew looked as if Adam had offered him the finest of gifts. "Since Martha's death, I've been at the mercy of the congregation. The ladies bring me shares of their family's supper, or I'm invited to their homes, but it isn't the same as having the wonderful aroma of food being cooked right here in the house. I would love nothing more. I think you'll find it a small but well-appointed kitchen, just past the dining room." He waved in the direction of an open archway, beyond which stood a table and chairs.

Mercy smiled. "I'm sure it will be more than sufficient after our meager provisions at the mission. I would be happy to take over cooking for you while we're here. It seems only right that we each do our share."

The reverend clapped his hands. "It's settled then. Make up a list of what you need, and I will fetch it from the grocer."

"Maybe you could also help me find a position," Adam said. "I don't know how long we'll be in Portland. There is a matter we are waiting to resolve." He looked down at Faith, who sat between them, and smiled. He didn't want to explain in front of her that they were waiting for a reply to the letter Mercy sent as soon as they landed.

"I'd have you work at my church, but there would be little

money in that. However, I know several men who own mills, and they're always in need of extra hands. I'm sure we could secure something there, if you're not afraid of hard work."

"That would be fine. I'm neither afraid of nor a stranger to hard work. Living in the Rogue River country, it was necessary to do physical work on a daily basis."

Matthew's expression changed to one of sadness, and his already ruddy face darkened. "It's a bad situation, that Rogue River business. There's been nothing but conflict and controversy in the newspapers regarding the fighting."

"It is a bad situation," Mercy responded before Adam could speak. "The army and volunteer militia are using it as an excuse to commit murder, as far as I'm concerned. We've lost dear friends because of it—even Isaac and Eletta's deaths could be said to be a result of this heinous conflict."

"The newspapers back east make it clear that many easterners find Oregonians to be barbaric, money-hungry murderers," Matthew replied. "They believe we could have all lived peaceably if the government weren't paying men to eliminate the Indians."

Adam shook his head. "Given that so many people have come west in the last ten years, I doubt we could ever have been completely at peace. The white man would have insisted on taking over the land, and the Indians would have been left with no choice but to fight."

Matthew sighed. "It is to my deepest sorrow that such evil takes over the hearts and minds of men."

"Such evil?" Mercy asked.

"Greed. Greed for land and possessions," Matthew replied. "Men went wild at the promise of gold in California, and when that played out false for so many, they turned to the land. The various land laws give away thousands upon thousands of acres to those who will work the land and improve it."

"And for the most part, it's land the whites have paid nothing for," Alex added. "There have been a few token payments to some of the tribes, but overall the attitude has been that the Indians own nothing and therefore it's there for the white man to take."

Matthew studied Adam for a moment. "You sound like quite an advocate of the natives. Have you considered trying to get in with Indian Affairs? You would make a wonderful agent."

"Mercy and I have talked about some sort of continued ministry. We've even thought about helping at the new reservation. We could both teach school, and I could share the gospel as well."

Faith yawned and leaned against Adam. No doubt she was as uncomfortable on the stiff bench-like sofa as he was.

"I think that would be marvelous," Matthew replied. "Your heart is such that the Indians would see you as their friend."

"They did once, anyway." Adam couldn't help but be saddened at the loss of so many lives. "After the wholesale murder of so many, I'm not sure they'll ever see a white man as a friend again."

"It will be hard, but in time there will be healing."

Adam hoped Matthew was right, but he doubted it would come anytime soon.

The room grew dark and chilly as the sun began to set, and Adam knew Mercy and Faith were probably hungry. He had a little money left from helping Captain Tichenor onboard the schooner, although he'd been trying to hold on to it in order to buy Mercy a ring.

"What say I go buy us a few groceries, and maybe Mercy could whip something up for us?" he said.

Faith straightened.

Matthew got to his feet. "I have a better idea. There's a boardinghouse just a few doors down, and the woman there serves a mighty fine supper. She always has extra and has encouraged me to join in anytime I like. I'll speak with her and see if we might all join her. Then tomorrow I will lay in a supply of food." Without waiting for Adam's reply, Matthew headed for the door and took up his coat and hat. "I won't be but a minute."

Once he'd gone, Adam stood. He reached down and pulled Mercy into his arms. "How are you feeling? I know we've done nothing but be on the move all day."

"I'm fine. Tired, but fine." She smiled and then laid her head against his chest. "So long as I'm with you, I'll always be just fine."

"Are we going to live here?" Faith asked.

"For a short while," Adam said, pulling back. He continued holding on to Mercy. "Would that be all right with you?"

Faith closed her book and shrugged. "I really want to see the farm."

"And we will. First, however, I need to make a little money so we can buy some of the things we need."

"Yes," Mercy said, nodding. "You need at least one new dress. You've all but outgrown that one. I swear you must have added six inches to your height since that dress was made for you."

"And Mercy needs a new dress, and I'm sure both of you need other more personal garments—maybe even new shoes." Adam glanced down at Faith's well-worn boots. "I recall you saying your boots were pinching you. My guess is you've outgrown those as well as your dress."

Faith got to her feet. "Do you think we'll be here long?"

Adam dropped his hold on Mercy and lifted Faith in his arms. "We'll be here for as long as the Lord desires us to be. We must always remember to pray and seek His guidance. Our own plans are fine, but if they don't line up with His, then we must rethink them."

"Mama always said that when we commit our ways to the Lord, He will direct our steps."

"And God will definitely see us through this and show us what to do," Adam replied.

Matthew returned, his face redder than ever from his hurried journey. "Come! Come! Mrs. Norris says she'd be delighted to have us all to supper. She's serving chicken and dumplings." He waved them forward. "She was just calling everyone to the table."

~~~

Reverend Beckham's house made a cozy home. Since there were only two bedrooms, Mercy and Adam shared their room with Faith, just as they'd done on the schooner. Mercy wondered if they would ever be alone to have a true wedding night. Nevertheless, she was grateful for a roof over her head and a real bed.

They had been with the reverend for nearly a week when Adam found a job at one of the local mills. It paid well enough that, given they were living rent-free, they would soon have enough money to buy what they needed. The reverend wouldn't hear of them paying to share his house, since Mercy was more than happy to cook and clean for them. Not only that, but Adam helped the reverend by cutting firewood and fixing anything that needed attention. Matthew declared them to be a gift from God to ease his loneliness and poor housekeeping.

Mercy was glad they could help, but she was also concerned about the letter she'd sent to the farm. She had told them everything that had happened and let them know she was safe in Portland. She had also enclosed a separate letter for Hope. She could only pray that the news hadn't upset her sister too much.

Faith thrived in the safety of Portland. She no longer had bad dreams at night, and her focus on schoolwork was much better than before. Mercy wondered when it would be the right time to share the truth with her. It would be a hard truth to learn, but Mercy knew that one day, Faith would be grateful for the knowledge. At least Mercy hoped that would be the case. She figured that if she were in Faith's shoes, the truth would be important to her.

"You look deep in thought," Matthew said, joining Mercy in the kitchen as she made bread.

"I suppose I was." She finished kneading the bread and separated it into several bread pans while she talked. "It's been a very long journey in a short few months. So much has happened that I can scarcely put it all together."

"I can understand that. Adam tells me you went through the attack on the Whitman Mission as well. That couldn't have been easy."

"No, it wasn't." She put the bread pans aside to give the dough a chance to rise. Wiping her hands on her apron, she turned. "It was, however, a valuable experience."

"And then you endured the Rogue River wars." He shook his head. "Few women could go through so much and still maintain such a joyous countenance."

Mercy smiled and leaned back against the counter. "As Nehemiah eight, verse ten states, 'The joy of the Lord is your strength.' I would not have a pleasant demeanor without the Lord."

"To be sure. It would seem," he said, taking a seat at the table, "that you have come full circle in some ways."

Mercy considered this for a moment. "I suppose I have." She nodded. "Would you like some coffee? There's still some on the stove."

"No. I'm only here for a few more minutes. I must make sick calls today. Several of my congregants are suffering from illness."

Mercy wondered if Matthew wasn't also the victim of some physical malady. He had more than once mentioned frequent headaches. She was glad to have vinegar once again at her fingertips. She felt so much better taking her daily doses than she did when vinegar had been unavailable. Perhaps she could encourage the pastor to do likewise.

"I hope they're not suffering too much. My sister is a healer and taught me some of her remedies. For instance, we take vinegar every morning to help our constitution. Perhaps you would like to try it as well. We never suffer headaches, so it might be useful."

He nodded, looking intrigued. "I might very well do that. I know my Martha had cures for such things, but I never bothered to find out what they were. Just one more reason I regret her passing."

"Well, I can help you with several remedies if I can get my hands on certain ingredients. I don't want you to suffer." She turned her attention to the small roast that one of the church members had given to the reverend. "Do you have a preference how you'd like this cooked?"

Matthew chuckled. "I have no preference whatsoever. Martha would sometimes roast it in the oven with vegetables, and other times she would cut it up to make stew or beef pie. I can honestly say that I will eat most anything, as my thick waist suggests."

"Your wife sounds like she was an amazing woman."

"She was a good wife, and her loss is greatly felt." His expression changed, and worry lines furrowed his brow. "We came west with one of the earlier groups, and we both fell in love with Oregon Country. We found the people here hungry for the Word of God and eager to civilize this great land. They are certainly a hardworking people."

"And what of the Indians?" Mercy turned back to him again. "Adam and I have talked about working with the native peoples. He's even written to the man in charge of the Indians here, Joel Palmer." She felt as if she were rambling and paused before asking, "Did you ever work with the natives?"

"From time to time we encountered some of the local Indians, back when they were still fairly at ease mingling among the white people. Things weren't always so difficult. When we first arrived, the Indians were incredibly helpful. Years ago, they would come into town to trade. Unfortunately, with more and more white families coming into the area, there was bound to be trouble. The natives often just took what they wanted if the whites refused to trade. There were some attacks on homes out away from town, but now the local Indians are far less inclined to fight—even before the project began to put them all on reservations."

"It seems cruel to take them from the land they love and force them to move to a place like Grand Ronde. I've heard it's very different than the southern part of the territory."

"I've never been to the Rogue River area," he replied.

"It's beautiful and not nearly as rainy as it is here. Eletta said the summers were quite lovely. I doubt the Indians will adjust very well to the damp and cold."

"I suppose it will be difficult."

Mercy grew thoughtful. "The river was such an important part of their life. Will they live near a river now? Will they be able to fish for salmon and make their plank houses?" Her emotions surged and threatened to spill into her conversation, so Mercy turned back to the meat. "I think I'll make stew."

"Mercy, you have a tender heart," Matthew said, coming up behind her. He cleared his throat. "Never be ashamed of that."

Mercy faced him and sighed. "I can't hate them, even after the siege. They seem so alone in all of this. Even the people who are supposed to be their advocates steal from them and cheat them."

He nodded and put his hand on her shoulder. "You and Adam will no doubt be of great use to them."

"We've talked about going to Grand Ronde to live among them. Adam knows many of the Rogue River Indians, and at one time they respected him and called him friend. If it's possible they can still do that, then I think we can make a difference."

Smiling, Matthew patted her shoulder. "I must be going, but I'll be back to sup with your little family tonight."

Mercy smiled as he took his leave. He was such a kind man. And though she worried about his health, she knew they were blessed to share his home.

"Mercy, I finished all the problems you gave me. Do you want to check my work?" Faith asked, coming into the kitchen.

"In a bit. I need to get this meat started for our supper. Would you like to help?"

"Sure." Faith put her work aside. "I used to help Mama." She paused for a moment. "I miss her." Her words were matter-of-fact.

"I do too. Your father as well. They were good people, and they loved you a great deal."

"Do you think they know I'm all right?"

Mercy knelt next to Faith. "I know they do. I made a promise to your mother that I would make sure you were cared for. She knew I would keep my word. I hope you know that too."

Faith nodded and wrapped her arms around Mercy's neck. "I love you."

"I love you too." Mercy held her close. "I will always love you, Faith. You're a part of my family now and always will be."

"I just wish they hadn't died."

"Me too."

Faith pulled back. "Do you think they're in heaven right now? I can't remember, but I thought Papa told me that we won't go to heaven until the final judgment."

Mercy shrugged. "I'm not sure how it all works or where exactly we go when we leave this earth. Jesus told the thief on the cross that he would be with Jesus that very day in Paradise. So we must go somewhere lovely, and if it's not heaven, then it's surely very close to heaven."

Faith nodded. "And will the baby be born there?"

Mercy smiled and pushed back one of Faith's pigtails. "I'm sure the baby is there with them, and you will one day see him . . . or her."

"I hope it was a girl. I always wanted a sister."

Mercy thought of Hope's two boys and wondered if Faith would enjoy having little brothers. Mercy had always wanted a brother.

"Maybe you'll have a baby, Mercy, and I can pretend it's my brother or sister." Faith began to dance around. "Maybe you'll have a whole bunch of children, and I can play with them all and help you take care of them."

Mercy laughed. "If I have a whole bunch of children, I'll need all the help I can get. But for now, you are more than enough for me."

She stood and watched a moment while Faith twirled. How could Hope do anything but love this child? How could anyone not love her?

Chapter 21

After a full ten days with Reverend Beckham, Mercy was beginning to fret. There had been more than enough time for her letter to reach the farm and for them to send a response back. But there had been no letter. No sign whatsoever that her sisters knew she was in Portland, awaiting their blessing to return to the farm.

"I've written down ten new spelling words," Mercy told Faith. "I want you to look up each word and write down if it's a noun, adjective, or verb, as well as the pronunciation and meaning. Pastor Beckham said you could use his dictionary, but treat it with respect. It's a fine book, much nicer than any we had at the mission."

"When I'm done, can I read one of Reverend Beckham's books? I was telling him about the problems in England with the church and King Henry the Eighth. He said he had a book on the Puritans and the witches in Salem, Massachusetts. He said it was also a sorry time in the history of Christian people."

"Yes, I'm sure it was. I don't know, however, if it's appropriate for you to read. I'll have Adam take a look at it first."

Faith frowned and sighed. "What's the use of being able to read if nobody will let you read?"

"God has given us the job of caring for you. That care includes being cautious in exposing you to things that might cause you harm."

"I don't think learning about those people would cause me harm."

Mercy nodded. "Maybe not, but the stories related to witchcraft and Devil worship might give you horrible dreams and perhaps even troubled thoughts throughout the day. Let Adam read it first, and if he thinks it's all right, then you may read it as well."

Faith settled herself at the dining room table. "I guess I'll just do my work then."

"I'll tell you what. I know how much you love writing stories. When you finish these words, you can write a story for me about something you remember from when you were a very little girl."

Faith instantly perked up. "Can I write about anything?"

"Absolutely. It will be fun to see what you came up with. But first you must do the work I gave you. When you're finished, we'll go over the spelling words together to see if you have the proper definitions and pronunciations."

"I'll get it done really fast."

Faith picked up the dictionary and immediately started searching for her spelling words. Mercy smiled. Faith loved to learn, but she loved writing even more. Going to their shared bedroom, Mercy opened a box of school supplies Adam had purchased, including paper and pencils. Paper was a luxury, so Mercy was careful not to use it for just anything. Usually a slate board served their schooling purposes, but Mercy wanted to keep Faith's stories to give back to her when she grew up. She thought it might be a pleasant way to remember the good things of the past.

She returned to the dining room and gave Faith a pencil and a piece of paper before heading into the large front room to clean the fireplace. It looked as if it hadn't been cleaned in a month of Sundays. Probably not since Mrs. Beckham had been alive.

Mercy shoveled out all of the ash and put it in a bucket to discard outside. It wasn't pleasant work, but since she was already on her knees, it did provide ample time for prayer.

While she worked and prayed, Mercy thought about Hope. She prayed that her sister would understand about Faith. She knew she was asking a lot. Seeing Faith again would bring back the past and all they had endured. Hope would no doubt remember John Sager, the boy she had fallen in love with—the boy who'd died in her arms. Hope would have to relive the horrible things Tomahas had done to her and the fears they all had for their very lives.

Perhaps it was wrong of me to even suggest bringing Faith to the farm.

Mercy couldn't help feeling guilty. Had she been completely insensitive? She had never wanted to cause Hope pain, but how could this situation do anything but hurt her?

"Are you all right?" Lance asked Hope.

She had spent the morning in the field with the sheep while Grace cared for the children. She had sought the serenity of the herd and silence of the field in order to contemplate the news Mercy sent.

"I keep trying to figure out what's right." She looked up to find Lance watching her with concern. He had come to find her out in the fields. "You needn't look at me like I'm going to fall apart. I'm stronger than you think."

"I know you're strong. Sometimes I think you're too strong

or that you try to be strong all on your own. You do remember that I'm here to share the burden, don't you?"

She smiled and stepped into his arms. "Of course, silly. Haven't I been talking to you about Faith these last few years?"

He tilted his head and gave her a look that told Hope he could see beyond her façade. "Yes, but I know too that you bury a lot down deep in your heart and won't share."

Hope sighed. "Some things aren't worth sharing. Some of those old thoughts and feelings need to die." The sun broke through the clouds overhead, and the whole field was bathed in brilliant light. It refreshed Hope's spirit. "I want to think about good things—the present and future. To bring up past troubles would only give them power over me, and I won't have that."

"You know I'll agree with whatever you decide is right, don't you?"

Her heart was touched by his sincere words. Lance had always been patient and generous with her. "I do know that. Whether Faith ever knows the truth about me and her father, and I'm not sure she should, I believe I'm all right seeing her—having her here on the farm. At first I wasn't at all sure, but I've given it a lot of thought."

When he didn't say anything, Hope looked up. "What are you thinking?"

He shook his head. "I can't imagine what that poor child has gone through. She's lost the only parents she's ever known, endured mass killings and a siege. Seems to me you two have a great deal in common."

"I suppose we do—in many ways." She heaved a sigh. "God knows she's never far from my thoughts."

"She'll have to be strong to recover from all that violence and loss."

"God will help her. He has a way of helping us through

those times." Hope put her head on her husband's shoulder. "It doesn't always seem like it at the time, but He does."

"I just want to make sure this is something you can get through without too much pain. I love you, Hope, and I don't want anything to hurt you." He hugged her close.

"There will always be pain in life. I've matured enough to know that much. I don't like the idea of suffering and misery for anyone, and I think refusing to let Faith come here would be cruel. Mercy can hardly turn her out to strangers. Besides, you know how I've felt over the years."

"The regret?"

Hope straightened and stepped back. "Yes. The regret of giving away my child. I told myself I hated her—that she would be a constant reminder of Tomahas, but now . . ." She looked back at the sheep. "I can't explain my heart. Something changed with the birth of Sean. It set me on a different road. Holding him and nursing him, I couldn't help but remember doing the same for Faith. The more I thought about her, the bigger that hole grew in my heart—the hole left when I gave her to Eletta and Isaac." She shook her head and turned back to Lance.

"Then Eddie was born, and instead of diminishing that emptiness, it only seemed to make the loss all the more evident. I can't explain it any other way but to say a part of me is missing—our family is incomplete."

Lance nodded. "I'm happy to welcome her into our family. I'm happy to take her as my daughter—because she's a part of you."

"And you don't think you would find it troubling that she's also a part of Tomahas?"

"She didn't choose her parents nor the circumstance behind her conception. I would never punish a child for the sins of her father. She is your daughter, Hope, and I will gladly make her mine as well."

Mercy's back ached by the time she finished scrubbing out the fireplace. She'd even managed to clean some of the soot from the lower chimney. It looked far better and wouldn't smoke so much when Matthew lit the fire that evening. She tossed her scrub brush into the pail of dirty water, then got to her feet. Only then did she notice the time. It had taken her two hours, and in all that time, she hadn't been interrupted by Faith even once.

Grabbing several logs, Mercy quickly laid them in the grate to be ready later when the chill of the evening made a fire necessary. After that, she picked up the pail and wet rags and headed to the kitchen through the dining room. She was surprised to find that Faith wasn't there. She had filled both sides of the paper she'd been given for her story, but she was nowhere in sight.

Mercy quickly disposed of the dirty water and left the rags and brush in the empty pail. She washed her hands and dried them on a fairly clean spot of her apron, then discarded the apron as well. Perhaps Faith had gone to the privy. Turning her attention to the dirty rags, Mercy went outside to the pump they shared with the neighbors and refilled the bucket so the rags could soak.

She glanced toward the privy. "Faith?"

Mercy listened for a response. Nothing.

She went back inside. There was still no sign of Faith in the kitchen or dining room. The only place left to check was the bedroom.

She found the door open just a crack and peered into the room. Faith sat on the edge of the bed, reading. It was impossible from Mercy's vantage point to see what the child was reading, but Mercy suspected it was the book on the Puritans.

She pushed open the door, and the sound caused Faith to look up.

"I'm sorry," Faith said. Her voice was barely audible. "I was looking for another piece of paper, and I found this." She held up Eletta's journal. "I thought it was a new book to read, and when I opened it, I saw that my mama had written it for me, so I thought it would be all right to read it."

Mercy could tell by the look on her face that Faith had already read the entire journal. There was no use trying to conceal the truth.

"Yes, she wrote it for you. I had thought it would be some years, however, before I gave it to you to read." Mercy crossed the room to sit beside Faith on the edge of the bed. "I wish you would have asked me first."

"I'm sorry, Mercy. I didn't mean to snoop, and I wouldn't have read it, but . . ." She shook her head and looked so troubled that Mercy couldn't be mad.

"It's all right, Faith. I understand." She put her arm around the little girl. For all her maturity, the contents of the journal were no doubt difficult to understand. "It's just that what your mother wrote is hard enough for an adult to read, much less a child. Do you want to talk about it?"

Faith nodded. "Is it all true?"

Mercy drew a deep breath. "Yes."

"Your sister Hope is my first mama?"

"Yes."

"And that bad Indian man was my first . . . papa?"

"Yes." Mercy heard the trembling in Faith's voice. "But none of that matters anymore. What is important is that Eletta and Isaac loved you and raised you to be their own. They wanted you more than anything else in the world."

"But my first mama didn't want me?"

Mercy could see the pain in Faith's expression. "Oh, Faith, it wasn't that. Hope didn't even want to live after the attack on the mission. She had fallen in love with a special boy there, and when he was killed, she wanted to die too. Then the Indians were . . . well, they were mean to her and abused her terribly."

"But the Indians at our mission were good people. They loved us and would never have hurt us."

"I know, but the Cayuse were different. The measles had killed many of them and their children. They blamed the white people because they brought the sickness west. The Cayuse were angry, and their desire for revenge was the reason they attacked."

"Did they hurt you too?"

"Not like they hurt Hope." Mercy could see it as if it were yesterday. The smells and sights weren't easily forgotten. "I was very frightened. I thought they would kill me in my sleep."

"I was scared when that mean Mr. Caxton wanted to kill everybody at our mission."

"Then you can understand how frightened we were."

"Did the Cayuse keep you a long time?"

"About the same amount of time we were under siege at Fort Miner. Every day they tormented us. They thought it great fun to hurt us. We were prisoners, and we didn't know how long the Cayuse would allow us to live."

Faith considered this for a moment. "Did you give away a baby too?"

"No. I didn't have a baby." Mercy gave Faith's cheek a stroke. "Hope kept me safe."

"But she didn't want me to be her daughter."

Mercy was taken aback at how quickly Faith changed the subject. She couldn't lie to the child. That would be more cruel than the truth. "No. At that time, she knew she couldn't be a good mother to you. She didn't want you to suffer because of her."

Faith seemed to think about this for several minutes, and Mercy remained stock-still and silent. News like this was far more disturbing than reading about witches and Puritans putting them to death. Mercy found herself almost wishing she'd given Faith permission to read the book. Perhaps she wouldn't have gone venturing.

Finally, Faith looked up. "Mama wrote that I look like my first mama. Is that true?"

Mercy nodded. "Yes. I don't know what Hope looked like when she was your age, but you remind me of her now. Hope was always the prettiest of us. Our older sister Grace is quite pretty too, but there is something special about Hope, just like there is about you."

Another few minutes passed by in silence. Mercy had no idea if she'd handled the matter well or not, but she knew it wouldn't be long before Adam came home. Perhaps if Faith was still troubled then, Adam could speak to her in private.

"I need to get supper started, but I want to make sure you're all right. Do you have any other questions I can answer?"

Faith looked at the journal and then back to Mercy. "Just one."

Mercy gave her a smile. "What is it, sweet girl?"

"Am I a bad person since my first papa was such a bad Indian?"

Chapter 22

The question took Mercy by surprise. She could see the pain in Faith's eyes—pain born of a very difficult truth. How could she hope to ease the situation?

Lord, please help me say the right thing.

"No, Faith. You aren't a bad person. You love Jesus. Remember when your mama and papa taught you about God and the sacrifice Jesus made for us on the cross?"

"Yes." Faith's troubled expression persisted.

"And you asked Jesus to take away your sins? He did. He came into your heart and lives there still."

"But will God punish me because of my bad father?"

"No, precious child. Let me show you something it says in the Bible." Mercy got up and retrieved Adam's Bible. She sat back down beside Faith and turned to the eighteenth chapter of Ezekiel. "Here's what it says in verse twenty, 'The soul that sinneth, it shall die. The son shall not bear the iniquity of the father, neither shall the father bear the iniquity of the son: the righteousness of the righteous shall be upon him, and the wickedness of the wicked shall be upon him.'" Mercy looked at Faith. "Do you understand? It's saying that each person will answer for their own doings. A child won't be punished for the sin of their parent. You do not bear the sin of Tomahas."

Faith's furrowed brow relaxed and she sighed. "I'm glad God loves me."

Mercy sighed as well and closed the Bible. "I am too. His love is all that gets me through sometimes."

Faith placed her small hand atop Mercy's as it rested on the Bible. "I love you, Mercy. I'll always love you."

"And I love you, Faith. No matter what happens, always remember that. Adam and I love you, and we will do whatever we can to keep you safe and happy."

Faith nodded. "But I still want to know my first mama. Do you think she would want to know me?"

That was the question Mercy had been asking herself for weeks. "I can't answer that question. It's something only Hope can tell us. I think very soon we shall know the answer."

"But I can pray that she'll want to know me—can't I?" Her gaze held a mix of expectation and uncertainty.

"Of course. We can pray about anything, and we should definitely pray about this." Mercy drew Faith into her arms. "God wants us to bring all of our needs to Him."

"Then I'm going to pray about this, 'cause I need to know my first mama."

"I could pray with you, Faith."

The little girl pulled away and shook her head. "No. Right now I want to pray alone. Later we can pray together."

Mercy nodded, then kissed the top of Faith's head. "I'll be happy to pray with you later. Why don't you just stay here? It'll be nice and quiet, and that way when the reverend and Adam come back, they won't disturb you."

Faith nodded but said nothing more. Her eyes were fixed

on the journal, and her expression was gravely serious. Mercy sent a quick prayer heavenward asking God to ease the child's worries, then left the room to see to supper.

A part of her was relieved to have the matter out in the open, but an equal part was more concerned about what it would mean should Hope agree to let them come to the farm. She had told Hope that Faith knew nothing about her, nor would she unless Hope wanted to share that information with her.

"Well, there's nothing to be done about it now."

She pulled on a clean apron and started to peel potatoes and pray. It seemed these days she did a lot of praying while tending household chores.

Lord, I know You care about all of our needs, about the desires of our heart. I know You watch over the tiniest sparrow. Because of that, I know You are watching over Faith at this very minute—Hope too. Lord, we just need to know what You would have us do. We need guidance.

A knock on the front door startled Mercy. She put the potato and knife aside, then wiped her hands on her apron as she went to open the door.

"Is this where I might find Mr. Adam Browning?" the man on the porch asked.

Mercy smiled. "Yes, it is. He's not here at the moment, but I'm his wife, Mercy Browning."

He returned her smile. "I'm Joel Palmer."

"Won't you come in, Mr. Palmer? I'm glad to meet you." She knew their points of view were different where the Indians were concerned. Palmer had set up the reservation systems and promoted it as the only means of settling the war. However, he was also the man who might allow her and Adam to minister to the Indians with the government's blessing. "May I offer you some coffee or tea?"

"No, nothing." He held his hat in hand. "Your husband's

letter came as a great surprise and joy. I'm intrigued by his desire to minister—even live among the savages at Grand Ronde."

"Won't you sit?" she asked.

"No. It would hardly be proper for me to stay. However, I would very much like to speak with your husband. I'm heading across the river to visit one of the generals at the Vancouver barracks. If time permits, I'll return."

Mercy nodded. "My husband and I are both experienced at living among the Indians, and many of the people you plan to move to Grand Ronde are our friends."

"Truly?" He looked surprised by this declaration.

"Yes, truly. We both lived at the Browning Mission on the Rogue River among the Tututni. We taught school to the native children—even a few adults—and Adam preached among many of the tribes. I was one of the hostages at the Whitman Mission, so I feel I understand more than most. We believe it is God's calling on our lives to help the Indians. God knows this relocation is going to be devastating."

Palmer looked uncomfortable. "It's for their own good. They're prisoners of war at this point, but the day will come when peace will again reign, and they will need to be safely contained for their own protection."

Mercy shook her head. "I find that very sad. I'd like to think that the government knows what they're doing, but I cannot."

"You're quite an outspoken woman, Mrs. Browning."

She paused, fearing she'd offended him, and softened her attack. "I care deeply for those people, and while it has never been my desire to see them moved, I understand your reasoning. They would not be safe nor welcome where they are, and that would only lead to more killing on both sides."

This seemed to assuage Palmer. He smiled again. "I'm glad you are a woman of reason. These affairs will be decided by men, but I find your insight helpful. If possible, I will return soon to discuss the matter with your husband. If we cannot meet, however, please tell your husband that I will address all of this in a letter to him."

Mercy smiled. "I will do that. Thank you, Mr. Palmer, for your consideration of our desire to help."

He left, and Mercy could only lean back against the closed door and beat down her anger. He, like most of the government officials, had no idea what they were doing to the Indians, nor did they care. In fact, if these men had their way, the Indians would die out at the reservation, never again to be a problem to anyone.

~

Adam didn't mind the hard work at the sawmill. He worked at the most menial of tasks, loading and unloading lumber, but it was work, and it paid an honest wage. The job also gave him time to think about the past and the future. Everything had happened so fast in the last days at the mission. He hadn't even had time to mourn his brother's death. Since learning about Isaac, Adam had been running on sheer nerve and gumption. Fears for the living had consumed him, and thoughts of his brother had to be put aside.

Now, however, he had more than enough time, and the loss was painful. Ten years Adam's senior, Isaac had always been there for him. Adam had shadowed his brother as soon as he could walk, and Isaac had patiently endured it. When their father passed away, Adam had only been twelve. Isaac, although newly married, had stepped up to keep the family going. Eletta had been so beloved by Adam's mother and sisters that it seemed only natural they should move into the family house. That had given Adam a few more precious years with Isaac.

Isaac was also the reason Adam had gone into ministerial

studies. When Isaac and Eletta announced they were going west to Oregon Country, Adam had even told Isaac that he might join them one day. When things had fallen apart in Boston, it seemed like the logical thing to do. But now Isaac was gone, and Adam hadn't even thought to write their sisters and let them know what had happened. No doubt word had reached Georgia about the Rogue River wars, and they would be worried.

He also needed to let them know about his marriage to Mercy, even if it was a marriage in name only at this point. He smiled at the thought that he had married a woman who didn't care one whit that he was a quarter Cherokee. His heart was near to bursting with love and desire for his wife, and he looked forward to the day when they could consummate their marriage and live as true man and wife. But for now, there was Faith to contend with, and given the close quarters at Matthew Beckham's house, it was necessary to wait for his wedding night. It wasn't easy, but Adam reminded himself that there were so many more important things on which to focus his attention.

For one, he knew Mercy was worried about her family not yet responding to her letter. He knew it was a delicate situation and wouldn't be easily resolved. Yet Mercy felt it important to reunite her sister Hope with the child she'd given away. He couldn't understand it himself, but he believed Mercy did, and because of that, he was willing to go along with whatever she decided.

"Browning, I'd like to speak to you when you finish up there."

Adam looked up and gave his boss a nod. "Sure thing, Mr. Cochran. I just need to tie down this load for delivery."

"I'll see you in my office then."

Mr. Cochran left Adam to finish his work and ponder what his boss wanted. Adam knew he'd done good work, so he had no reason to fear a reprimand. He tied off the load and made his way inside the mill to Cochran's office. He'd no sooner reached the open door than Mr. Cochran was waving him inside.

"Have a seat."

Adam smiled and did as he bid.

Cochran pushed aside a stack of papers and leaned his elbows on his desk. "I'll get right to the point. I was happy to give you a job, but the fact is my cousin has just returned from California, and . . . well . . ."

"You need to let me go so he can have the position?" Adam asked.

Cochran looked uncomfortable. "Yes. Although between you and me, I doubt he will work half as hard."

"It's not a problem. As I told you before, I'm a preacher at heart. And I'm not sure how much longer I'll even be in Portland."

Cochran's no-nonsense expression remained fixed. "You're a good man, Browning." He pushed forward a piece of paper. "Here's your final credits."

Adam had agreed to work for store credit, so it came as no surprise that Cochran would settle up in such a manner. What was a surprise was the amount listed on the voucher.

"This is a lot more than what you owe me."

Cochran nodded. "I realize that, but I know you have a family to provide for, and even if you aren't here much longer, they'll need food—maybe other things. I want you to have it. I guess I feel it's the Lord's doing, so don't try to give it back."

Adam grinned. "Well, I can hardly refuse the Lord's blessing." He put the piece of paper in his pocket. "I appreciate it." He extended his hand.

Cochran nodded. "Well, that's that." He shook Adam's hand. "I'll see you in church."

"I'm much indebted to you, and I won't forget your kindness."

Cochran grumbled something as he pulled his stack of papers to the center of his desk but didn't respond. He'd never shown himself to be a talkative man.

Adam picked up his hat and coat before heading for home. He knew the store credit would allow him to buy several things Mercy wanted, as well as some candy for Faith. It had been a long time since she'd had a treat. But more importantly, Adam felt confident there would be enough money to get Mercy her own wedding ring.

He walked toward the heart of town, passing the docks where steamers and freight boats were taking on goods and passengers. Hopefully the day would come soon when he and Mercy would board one of the ships with Faith and make their way to Oregon City. After that, Adam hoped, word would come from Joel Palmer, the man in charge of Indian Affairs in Oregon Territory. Adam had sent him a brief letter asking to speak to him in regard to the reservation at Grand Ronde. Given that most white men hoped to avoid the Indians, Adam figured his request to live at or near the reservation would at least intrigue Palmer.

Ahead of him on the walkway, Adam caught sight of a big bearded man. He looked at a piece of paper in his hand and then looked up to gaze around him. Given the small bag at his feet, it was almost certain he was a lost traveler.

"May I help you find someone or some place?" Adam asked.

The big man turned, and a broad smile broke across his face. "I'd surely appreciate it if you would."

"Who are you looking for?"

"A Reverend Matthew Beckham. Do you know him or where I could find him?"

Adam laughed. "I should say so. He's just up this way." He

pointed and kept walking. The tall man kept pace with him. "I'm Adam Browning. I happen to be staying with the reverend. He took my wife and my niece and I in for a time."

This caused the older man to stop. "Browning, you say?" The stranger laughed. "Well, if that don't beat all. I guess the Good Lord always knows how to put folks together. I'm Mercy's uncle, Edward Marsh."

Chapter 23

Adam looked at the big man for a moment. "Edward Marsh. Truly? We had despaired of ever hearing from Mercy's family."

Edward nodded. "I can understand that, son." He extended his hand. "I'm mighty glad to finally meet you. I was sorry to hear about your brother and his wife. They were fine folks."

Adam shook the older man's hand. "Yes. They were. I miss them terribly."

"And the Indian wars down that way, I heard they were pretty bad."

"They still are, as far as I know. It's a sad time, to be sure." Adam shook his head. "It got completely out of hand. The volunteers answered to no one and the regular army still can't figure out the nature of men who would rather fight and die in the face of superior warriors than give up their home."

"Seems that ought to be an easy enough matter for any man to understand," Edward Marsh replied. "It hasn't been that long since our fight for independence."

"You would think they'd remember, but apparently not. Or

at least it's no longer important to understand the Indian. The goal at this point appears to be elimination and nothing more."

"It would seem that way." Edward glanced around them at the busyness of the town, and they began to walk again. "Portland's a lot bigger than it was even a few months back. Still have plenty of tree stumps to remove, though."

"Yes." Adam looked around at the muddy streets. "Someday these roads will be paved stone, and the entire place will look like the cities do back east."

"I've no doubt you're right on that account. The development of Oregon Territory is going to change life for everyone west of the Mississippi."

"Still, I can't support the government-sanctioned killing of the natives, just because they lived here first."

Edward fixed Adam with a sober gaze. "The two races just conflict, and there doesn't seem to be any common ground on which to meet. I've lived here for a long time—long before the rest of the country had any interest in being here. We got along pretty well with the Indians, mainly because we tended towards their way of life. We didn't seek to own property, and we shared the resources of the land. Of course, there were bad men on both sides."

"There still are." Adam frowned. "I know the Indians have done their fair share of attacking and killing indiscriminately, but I think the cause for this round of battles has more to do with the white man than the Indian."

"Could be, but neither is blameless."

"That's true enough. Especially regarding the attacks of the last few months. The whites pressed in, and the Indians took a difficult situation and pushed it over the top. I can't say they're without blame, but I know for a fact that the start of all of this was egged on by the white government and men who didn't want to share a territory rich in resources."

"We must remember what it says in Romans thirteen." Edward fixed him with a stern expression. "'Let every soul be subject unto the higher powers. For there is no power but of God: the powers that be are ordained of God.' The government officials may be making a wagonload of mistakes, but they are there by God's will."

Adam considered those words for a moment. He was right, of course. "'Wherefore ye must needs be subject, not only for wrath, but also for conscience sake.'" Adam looked at Edward and nodded. "It's pretty clear, eh?"

"Clear enough," Edward Marsh said, smiling. "But politics and theology can wait. Right now I want to know more about you."

"There's not a lot to tell." Adam pushed aside his worries about the future. "I'm a seminary-educated pastor with a heart for the Indians. You already know that I'm Isaac Browning's brother."

Edward nodded. "And on top of all that, you got yourself hitched to my niece. I hope you know what you've gotten yourself into." He grinned. "There are a whole lot of family members who want to make sure Mercy gets treated right, what with her being the baby of the family. You've got to answer to me and her two brothers-in-law, but even harder will be meeting with her sisters' approval."

Adam smiled, but inside he felt a bit nervous. "They needn't worry. I love Mercy, and I am blessed beyond words that she agreed to be my wife."

"Well, I know her sisters have been praying she'd settle on a husband."

"I hope she didn't just settle on me."

Edward laughed. "There's difference between settling on someone and settling for them, son. I know my niece well enough to know she wouldn't settle *for* anything. She's had her fair number of disappointed would-be suitors, believe you me."

"I have no difficulty believing that. Her beauty alone would cause a man to gravitate toward her."

"Mercy will make a loyal and capable wife. She isn't afraid to get dirty or work hard."

"I know. I've seen it over and over. She's unafraid too. That impressed me even more. At the mission, she was clearly uncomfortable on many occasions, but she pushed through her own feelings to be a benefit to others."

They were nearly to the small house where the reverend lived, so Adam slowed his pace. "The house is just up the road, but before we get there, I wonder if you would tell me why you've come. We've been worried about the reception we might receive."

Edward sobered. "There's a lot of concern to be sure. I suppose you know all about Faith and Hope?"

"I do. I wasn't sure that you did. Mercy indicated it was a great family secret."

"It was until recently. I wasn't aware of the situation, but Grace filled me in. I can't imagine the suffering Hope went through, but my pride in her only grew after hearing of her ordeal."

"Yes, I felt the same, and I don't even know her. Still, we're worried about how the family feels about having Faith around. I won't see her hurt. She's lost her parents—at least the ones she knew—and it has taken a big toll on her."

"I've no doubt about that, son, but never think that we would cause that child to suffer. She's innocent of anything her father did."

"I agree, but I'm sure others wouldn't. I know what it is to be cursed for your blood."

"When I first came out west, many a trapper had an Indian wife. Most stayed with them until the end of life—either their own or the woman's. I would never look down on someone for their heritage."

"But a lot of people would, and Faith, although she looks white, is a half-breed."

"And you're worried about the family looking down on her for that?"

Adam could hear a bit of offense in Edward's tone. "I don't mean to insult anyone. I just know from experience that it can cause deep pain to be rejected for something you can do nothing about."

Edward put a hand on Adam's shoulder. "You don't need to worry. We aren't like that in our family. Hope was taken by surprise at the news, but after a few days of prayer and discussion with her husband and the others, she decided it wouldn't be right to refuse. After all, Faith doesn't know anything about the past. So you can come and stay as long as you like, and Faith too."

Letting go of nearly two weeks of tension, Adam smiled. "Thank you. I know that will be a great relief to Mercy."

Mercy went back to the stove to check on the stew. She'd mixed the roast given to the reverend with potatoes and carrots. The aroma was pleasing, and the bubbly brown broth made it visually pleasing as well. She pulled the pot from the hot part of the stove and set it aside to cool before going to slice some bread.

The reverend had sent word that he was taking supper with one of his parishioners after all, so Mercy knew it would just be the three of them. And given what Faith had learned that afternoon, she was glad. Hopefully Adam could reinforce the things she'd said and help Faith know that she had nothing to fear from God nor her loved ones regarding her blood.

It angered Mercy to imagine that people would blame Faith for her heritage and make her suffer for something she had no control over. She thought of Adam and how the woman he'd planned to marry had rejected him because of his Indian blood. It was all so cruel.

She finished slicing the bread, then set the table. Adam would be home any minute, and she knew he'd be famished. She always sent him with a lunch to eat at the mill, but he worked so hard that by evening he was half starved.

Mercy went back to the stove to check the coffee, which was ready. Now she just needed to carry the food to the table. She had just reached for a potholder when there was a knock on the front door.

"Perhaps that's Mr. Palmer returning." She hurried to the door, not bothering to remove her apron. She opened it with a smile only to find Adam waiting there. "What are you doing knocking on the door? Goodness." She stretched up on tiptoe and pressed a kiss to his lips.

"I have a surprise for you," Adam replied and turned just enough to reveal the man standing behind him.

"Uncle Edward!" She squeezed past Adam and threw herself into the older man's arms. "I'm so happy to see you! How are you? How are my sisters and the rest of the family? Are you hungry?" She couldn't contain the flow of questions despite his laughter.

"I'm happy to see you too. Everyone's fine, and yes, I'm hungry enough to eat a full-grown bear by myself."

Mercy hugged him tight, then stepped back. "I don't have a bear to feed you, but supper is ready." She looked at Adam. "Where did you find him?"

"He was looking for us. Just came off the boat from Oregon City."

Edward nodded. "It's true. I was mighty glad for the Lord providing direction through this young man of yours."

"Well, come in. I want to hear all the news." Mercy smiled up at Adam. "I'm so glad you were there to show him the way."

She gave him another kiss. "Glad too that you're home. I have some things to tell you."

"I do as well." He followed her into the house with Uncle Edward bringing up the rear.

"So who is this reverend you're staying with?" Uncle Edward asked.

"He was a friend of my brother," Adam replied.

"He's been so good to us. He lost his wife a short time ago and is happy for our company."

"I look forward to meeting him." Edward dropped his bag by the door.

"He won't be with us for supper, since one of his church families invited him to share the evening meal with them," Mercy explained. "But you'll no doubt see him later tonight."

She felt like dancing at the sight of her uncle, but then it dawned on her that she had no idea why he'd come. Perhaps her family had decided against Mercy coming home with Faith in tow. Maybe they'd sent Uncle Edward to deliver the news.

She bit her lip and grew quiet as she went to the stove. If they didn't want her back, what would she do? She couldn't imagine a life that didn't include her family, but she could hardly abandon Faith.

The pot of stew felt almost too heavy to carry as Mercy brought it to the table. Suddenly everything seemed to weigh down on her. She couldn't just continue pretending nothing was wrong. She placed the stew on the table as Adam showed her uncle where to sit.

"I'll grab another bowl," he said, heading to the kitchen.

Mercy took that moment to pose her question. "Uncle Edward, why have you come?"

He met her gaze with a look of confusion. His eyes narrowed. "Why? I thought that was pretty evident. I came to bring you home. We figured you probably didn't have much in the way of funds, so I bought us all tickets to return to Oregon City on the steamer. We leave tomorrow morning."

"All of us?" Mercy felt certain he would understand the meaning of her question, but then Faith entered the room.

"Is it time for supper?" Faith asked. Then she realized the man seated at the table wasn't Matthew Beckham. "Who are you?"

Edward chuckled. "I'm Edward Marsh, Mercy's uncle. Now how about telling me who you are?"

The child smiled. "I'm Faith."

Adam returned with a bowl and some silverware. "She has a loving heart and a good head on her shoulders. Not only that, she loves Jesus." He put the dinner things on the table and held out his arms to his niece.

Faith ran to him and squealed with delight as he lifted her in the air and tossed her upward. She wrapped her arms tightly around his neck as he settled her against his chest.

Edward smiled and gave a nod. "She reminds me of another little girl I once knew."

Mercy met his gaze and knew he meant Hope. She noticed, however, that her uncle hadn't answered her question.

Adam gave Faith a kiss, then put her down. "I don't know about the rest of you, but I'm famished. Let's say grace and eat." He plopped down in his chair while Faith hurried to take her seat beside Uncle Edward.

Mercy took her chair and bowed her head. It was hard to focus on even the brief prayer for all the worry flooding her mind. When Adam said *amen*, she quickly decided to get an answer to her question.

She fixed her gaze on Uncle Edward. "All of us?"

He understood and nodded. "Of course. All of us."

Mercy felt a wave of relief wash over her and smiled. "Faith, guess what. We're going on the boat tomorrow."

"Where?" she asked, looking at Adam and then back to Mercy.

"We're going to the farm." Mercy smiled and pushed aside the matter of Faith knowing who her mother really was. "We're going home."

Chapter 24

Faith fell asleep early. Her excitement about the next day's travel had completely worn her out. Mercy was glad for this, as it gave her the opportunity to discuss the situation with her uncle and Adam.

Matthew had returned home nearly an hour earlier, but after a brief exchange with Uncle Edward, he too excused himself and went to his bedroom, saying he felt it important they have time alone to make their plans. Mercy knew he was saddened at the news that they would leave the following day, so she didn't try to encourage him to remain. Instead, she planned to get up very early and bake him some shortbread as a thank-you for all he'd done for them.

"I'm so glad you're here, Uncle Edward. I was beginning to fear the worst when I didn't hear from Grace or Hope."

"Well, it was difficult news to hear." He smiled as Adam took a seat beside Mercy. "Not the marriage or your safety, of course. But Eletta and Isaac, and Faith."

"No, I understand. No one anticipated Faith being with us."

Mercy bit her lower lip and gazed into the fire. "How did Hope take the news?"

"It was hard on her," Uncle Edward admitted. "Grace said she kept to herself for several days. She needed time to sort through her feelings and thoughts, I suppose. Your Aunt Mina does the same thing when issues weigh heavy on her heart."

Mercy nodded. The three sisters had always been that way—keeping their thoughts buried deep until they had time to sort through them.

"But she came around?" she finally asked.

"Yes. She had a long talk with Lance and then with Grace. She couldn't believe it would be right to leave the child in the hands of strangers. She reasoned that Faith didn't know who she was, so it would be all right to have her at the farm."

Mercy's head snapped up at this. She met her uncle's gaze with an expression she had no doubt betrayed her worry. "That's not exactly the case."

Adam and Edward both looked at her in confusion. "What are you saying, Mercy?" Adam asked first.

She drew in a deep breath. "Earlier today, Faith found Eletta's journal."

"Oh." Adam nodded slowly. "That does change things." He ran his hand through his black hair. "It changes everything."

"I guess I don't understand," Uncle Edward said, looking back and forth between the couple. "How about you explain it to me from the beginning?"

Mercy twisted her hands in her lap. "You see, Eletta kept a journal for Faith. It was something she started when Faith was born, and Eletta wanted her to have it when she was older. Only Faith found it today and read it. She thought it was just another book. When she opened it and saw that her mother had written it for her, Faith figured it was all right to continue reading."

"But why does that change things?" her uncle asked.

"Because Eletta told Faith about her birth—about Hope and Tomahas."

Uncle Edward frowned. "She knows all that?"

"She does. We had a long talk afterwards. Faith was worried she was a bad person because her father was bad. I had to explain to her that no one thought her bad and that the Bible said we would each answer for our own sins."

Edward rubbed his bearded chin. "Well, I'm not sure what we should do."

Mercy shook her head. "I wish I'd kept that journal hidden. I hate that this has happened. We had planned to keep the information from her until she was older and better able to understand it."

"But she knows." Edward leaned back in his chair. "I suppose we could go to Oregon City as planned, and the three of you could stay in my old cabin while we explain to Hope what's happened. I'd have you just stay at our place, but we're busting at the seams already."

Mercy longed for the matter to be resolved quickly. "If I could just talk to her first, I think I could help her understand. It won't take long to reach Oregon City. Once we do, maybe you could drive me out to the farm, and Adam and Faith could wait in town. That would give me a chance to speak with Hope. She needs to understand that Faith is already set on knowing her. If Hope wants nothing to do with her, Faith will lose yet another person in her life."

"But Hope isn't in her life," Adam interjected. "Faith only knows about Hope from the pages of Eletta's journal. It isn't fair to force Hope to see her, nor would it be good to take Faith there and have Hope learn the truth after the fact. I think you're right. You should go first while we wait in town. It would be best if we give Hope the choice."

"And if Hope refuses to see her . . . well, I imagine we'll just have to cross that bridge when we get there." Mercy couldn't imagine how much pain that would cause Faith.

"I don't see how we can do it any other way," Adam answered. "I'll talk to Faith about it. We've got a longer history than you two, and I think she might better understand if it comes from me."

Mercy nodded. He was probably right.

The clock on the mantel chimed.

"Goodness, it's ten." Mercy got to her feet. "Are you sure you want to stay here, Uncle? I don't like the idea of you sleeping on the floor."

"I won't be sleeping on the floor. You and the reverend saw to that by giving me that nice stack of blankets. Believe me, after some of the places I've slept in my day, a pallet by the fire will be just fine."

"Well, if you need anything, just knock on our door. Faith sleeps deeply, so I doubt you'd rouse her." She kissed her uncle on the top of the head. "I'm so glad you've come. Even if our situation is complicated, it's good to see family again."

Later that night, Mercy lay awake. She felt terrible, knowing the burden she was about to put on her sister. Hope had done so much for her during their captivity at the Whitman Mission. It had created a special bond between them, and despite their different opinions of the Indians, she and Hope shared a closeness Mercy didn't have with Grace.

She sighed and stared out into the darkness. She knew Hope had her regrets and sorrows, and the last thing she wanted to do was add to them. She sighed again.

"Are you going to do that all night?" Adam asked in a whisper.

Mercy startled, not realizing he was awake. "Do what?"

"Sigh. Toss and turn." He pushed himself up on one elbow.

"You make it very hard to ignore that there is a beautiful woman lying in bed next to me." He ran his hand down her arm.

Mercy shivered at the wonderful way Adam's touch made her feel. They'd been married for weeks now but might as well not have bothered with vows for all the obstacles that kept them from truly becoming man and wife.

"Sorry. I'm just troubled about all of this."

Adam pulled her close and wrapped his arms around her. "It won't solve anything to fret all night. Tomorrow we'll go to Oregon City, and you'll have plenty of time to worry. Let it go for tonight. You need your sleep, and so do I."

"I know. I just keep praying and praying. I want so much for things to go well. I don't want Hope or Faith to be hurt by this."

"Do you trust God to know what He's doing?"

"Of course."

Adam kissed her temple. "Even though it's not the way you would have done things?"

"You know I do. I know nothing happens that He doesn't already know about."

"So just accept that Faith reading that journal was exactly as it was meant to be. God will help you to break the news to Hope, and who knows—in the long run, this could turn out to be the best possible solution to the entire situation."

Mercy relaxed in his arms. "You're right, of course."

"Of course," he echoed. "I'm nearly always right."

She giggled. "I wouldn't go that far, but you do have a good head on your shoulders, and I need to trust your insight and wisdom."

"Spoken like an obedient wife. Now go to sleep."

He kissed her again, this time on the lips. It was a brief kiss, but it reminded Mercy of how much she loved this man.

"You're making it hard to ignore that there's a handsome man in my bed," she whispered.

He gave a muffled laugh as he buried his face against her neck, but Mercy didn't laugh. Now she felt wide awake for an entirely different reason.

~

"You really used to live here?" Faith asked as she danced around the main room of Uncle Edward's first cabin in Oregon City.

"I did." Mercy looked around the room. "But things were very different back then."

"The flooding and repairs that followed made some changes to the place," her uncle declared, "but the structure is sound. That's the benefit of digging it into the ground a bit. You can't tell from the outside, but the first layer of logs is under the dirt. Learned that trick from an old timer."

"Well, it served you well," Adam replied. "Seems quite cozy."

"It is." Edward looked toward the door. "Let's get your things out of the wagon and into the house, and then . . . well, Mercy and I should be going." He walked outside to fetch a load of their belongings.

"I'll go help him." The look on Adam's face suggested he had misgivings about letting her go to the farm alone.

Mercy put her hand on his arm. "It will be all right. I shouldn't be gone long. It'll take no more than half an hour to drive out to the farm, and then another to drive back. I won't spend too much time there. Just long enough to explain the situation."

Faith stopped midtwirl. "Will you tell my first mama about me?"

Mercy nodded. "I will. I need to tell her that you know who she is."

Faith frowned. "I wish I hadn't read it."

"There's no sense making a wish like that now," Adam said, heading for the door. "It's done, and we'll just handle things the best we can."

Mercy went to Faith and knelt in front of her. She took her niece's hands. "Faith, I don't know how this is going to turn out, but I want you to know that no matter what happens, Adam and I love you and always will."

Faith smiled. "I know that." She threw her arms around Mercy's neck. "I love you too."

The child's response gave Mercy the courage she needed to face the task at hand.

Once their things were safely in the cabin, Uncle Edward handed her up into the wagon. "Adam, I'll drop you and Faith off at my house. That way you can have something to eat while you wait. Faith, you can help Mina with my two little girls, Maribelle, who happens to be two, and the new baby, Analiese. The boys will be at school, but when they come home, I'm sure my son John would be happy to show you his puzzles and games. Maybe even take you on a grand adventure." He smiled.

Mercy looked at her uncle. "I didn't know you had a new baby. You said nothing about it last night."

He chuckled. "Well, given all our other topics, it just never came up. Mina had Analiese in January."

"I didn't even know she was expecting."

"Neither did she for a time. In fact, she had figured her child-bearing years to be done, and then lo and behold, Analiese was born. It was a pleasant surprise for the both of us."

It was a short drive to Edward's home in the heart of town. Adam and Faith were introduced to Aunt Mina and sufficiently fussed over. Faith nearly danced a jig at the sight of the new baby. Her enthusiasm made it easier to leave her behind.

"Can I hold her?" Faith asked Mina.

"Of course. Let's wait until we're back inside, though," Mina replied.

Mercy and Edward bid them good-bye and headed out. They

drove in silence for several minutes while Mercy looked at all the changes in town. There were several new buildings and even more businesses along the river.

"It's hard to believe there's been so much change in just six months."

"It's been busy, to say the least," Edward replied.

Mercy gazed down at the Willamette River and the falls. Spring was always a beautiful time in Oregon Territory. "It feels so good to be back among the familiar, but at the same time, I miss the Rogue River. Does that sound silly?"

Edward, ever his jolly self, laughed. "Hardly. You're allowed to love more than one place, you know."

Mercy smiled and drew in a deep breath. "I do love more than one place. I still love the little farm we had in Missouri. Sometimes I miss it for all the sweet memories I had there of Mama and Da. No doubt there will be more places in my life that provide such memories."

"I have at least a hundred places like that. All sorts of little nooks in the wilderness I found hunting and trapping. In fact, I hope to take my two oldest boys to some of them this summer. Then there are little towns and settlements where I stayed a short time . . . all with memories sweet and bitter." He snapped the lines so the horse would pick up speed as the road rose up and away from the river. "I never figured I'd settle down, but I have to say Oregon City agrees with me."

Mercy nodded, but her mind was elsewhere. She had ridden this way hundreds, if not thousands of times, but never had she done so with such a feeling of trepidation. "I've prayed and prayed about this. I hope I say the right things."

"Stop fretting. Hope loves you, and she's a strong soul. She'll figure out the right way to deal with all of this."

Mercy nodded. "I know you're right. I guess . . . I just want everything to turn out happily."

"And what would make you happy?" His expression bore great tenderness.

"I don't know exactly. A part of me wants to keep Faith and raise her for my own, but at the same time, I feel a strange . . . pull on my heart to bring her and Hope back together. I've prayed a lot about this, and I believe Faith belongs with Hope."

"Would that be so bad?"

"No, of course not. I mean, I'd miss having Faith around every day, but if she were with Hope, she would at least have her blood mother, and then there are the children—her brothers. Faith needs to have a family."

He smiled and gave a slight nod. "I know you, Mercy. You'll do the right thing and you'll be happy for it. Some folks go begrudgingly into God's will, but I've never known you to be that way. Trust Him."

Mercy considered her uncle's words as they drew closer to the farm. Ahead, a large open field stretched out across the hills. This was one of the pastures where they often took the sheep.

"This fencing is new." She noted the rail fence that ran the full length of the road.

"It is. Alex and I worked on it all winter. Lance, too, when he wasn't too busy with his legal practice. With you gone and Hope having just given birth, it was work to keep the sheep well fed and happy. I let Phillip come out and help when time permitted. At seventeen, he needs to be trying things to see where his interests lie. We now know for sure that it isn't in sheep."

Mercy laughed. "I always figured Phillip would be too caught up in adoring girls to think much about a job."

"He'd like it that way, but I won't have it. I told him he wasn't allowed to court anyone until he had a job. Thankfully, he sees himself working at the mill once he finishes school. Which won't be much longer. Before we know it, it'll be June."

"It seems like I've been gone so much longer than half a year."

"Maybe it's not the days so much as the experiences that make it so." Edward glanced over with a smile. "I always found that to be true."

"A lot has happened, to be sure." Mercy thought about it for a moment. "I've never packed more experiences into such a small amount of time." She smiled. "But despite losing Isaac and Eletta and enduring all the trouble with the Indians, I wouldn't trade it for anything. It gave me Adam and Faith."

They rounded the bend at the top of the hill, and there in the distance was the big house Grace and Alex had built, along with the smaller house where Lance and Hope lived with their children. There were multiple outbuildings, including a large barn and a lambing shed.

"It's so good to be home."

Mercy's eyes welled with tears. How she had missed this . . . missed her sisters. It had always been the three of them, for as long as Mercy could remember. The sight of the sheep grazing across the field made her smile. They wouldn't be spaced out like that if they didn't feel safe. And then she spied Hope and knew the reason for the contentment of the sheep.

"Uncle Edward, let me out here. I want to speak to Hope before I talk to any of the others."

He pulled back on the reins, and the horse came to a stop. Mercy climbed down unaided and went to the rail fence. Hiking her skirt, she climbed over as gracefully as possible, certain it was one of the least ladylike things she'd ever done. But it removed the obstacle between her and her sister.

She began to walk across the field, picking up her pace as she went. She might have run but for the sheep. She didn't want to frighten them. It was all she could do not to laugh out loud. Hope would think her mad for sure if she came barreling across the field as if being chased by a bear.

"Hope!"

Hope turned and froze for a moment, then gave a wave. She left the sheep and began to walk as quickly as she could toward Mercy. When they were no more than ten feet apart, Hope burst into tears. They embraced as if they hadn't seen each other for years.

"I was so worried about you. We kept hearing all of the horrible things that had happened and feared the worst," Hope said, hugging her tight.

"There was plenty of danger, to be sure, but there was also the beautiful and rewarding." Mercy pulled back and wiped her eyes. "I thought of you so often."

It was only then that Hope seemed to realize Mercy had come alone. "Where are the others? How did you get here?"

"Uncle Edward brought me. I had to see you first." There was no sense in delaying her reason for coming. "Faith knows who you are."

Hope's face paled. "How? Why?"

Mercy took a step back. "Eletta had written her a journal. She started it when Faith was born. She wanted Faith to know the truth someday and figured when she was older, she would give her the journal. But as Eletta grew weaker, she asked me to keep it for Faith."

"But that doesn't explain how Faith found out." Hope looked panicked.

"Eletta taught her to read at a very young age, and she devours books. She's so smart and . . . well, she looks just like you."

"Like me?" Hope repeated as if she hadn't heard correctly.

"Yes. Anyway, she found the journal by accident, saw it was addressed to her, and . . . It was hard for her to take in."

"I can't even imagine." Hope closed her eyes. "So she knows everything?"

"Yes. Eletta was thorough. She explained about Tomahas

and the mission attack, and what a sacrifice it was for you to give her life."

"And how did Faith deal with that?"

"She wanted to know if she was a bad person because her father had been bad."

Hope fixed Mercy with a look of disbelief. "How could she even think such a thing?"

"I suppose it's easy enough when you learn you're the child of a man most people hated . . . a man who savagely murdered innocent people. She doesn't understand in full all that happened to you, but she knows you were treated horribly. Eletta explained all of that, but she also wrote of your great sacrifice and love. She said there weren't many women she admired more than she did you."

"Eletta said that?" Hope shook her head. "I . . . I can't imagine why. I was such a bitter thing when I was with them. Angry and unable to bear company. I'm sure I was a misery to live with."

"Perhaps, but Eletta saw you differently. Remember, you were giving her the one thing she longed for most and couldn't have. A child."

Mercy felt sorry for her sister. Hope looked stunned, and Mercy couldn't even be sure what all she was comprehending, given the difficult topic.

"I left Adam and Faith with Mina and the boys, and Uncle Edward drove me out here. I wanted you to know what had happened . . . in case . . ." She left the rest unspoken.

Hope closed her eyes again. "This is so much harder than it was supposed to be. I thought she'd come here with you, and I would see her and get to know her, but she wouldn't know me." She shook her head. "I suppose that sounds selfish, but it's so hard to sort through my feelings." She began to walk back toward the sheep, and Mercy followed, giving Hope time to deal with the news.

After several long silent minutes, Hope stopped and looked at Mercy. "What of Faith? What does she want?"

Mercy smiled. "That's easy. She wants to meet you. She said she needed to know her first mama."

Hope bit her lip, and tears streamed down her cheeks. "But why? What does she want from me?"

"I can't be certain, but right now her biggest fear is that you hate her." Mercy squared her shoulders and asked the question she'd been dreading to even think. "You don't hate her—do you?"

For a moment Hope didn't reply, and Mercy feared the worst. She stood silent while Hope considered her answer.

Lord, please help her find peace about this.

"I don't hate her," Hope finally said. "Lance and I have been praying about Faith and what it might mean to see her and have her here. We both agreed that God must have a plan in it, so there's a reason it has happened this way."

"Adam and I have prayed about it too."

Hope met Mercy's gaze and let go of a long breath. "Bring her to the farm."

Chapter 25

Arm in arm, Hope and Mercy walked to the house, where Grace anxiously waited. When she saw Mercy, she ran across the lawn to greet her and crushed her in a fierce hug.

"I feared I'd never see you again." For several minutes, Grace did nothing but hold her.

"You're going to squeeze the life out of her, Grace," Uncle Edward finally said, coming up behind them.

Grace released her hold and stepped back. "I'm just so glad you're all right. I kept worrying that I sent you off to your death."

"You didn't send me anywhere. I'm a grown woman capable of making my own decisions." Mercy fixed her sister with a look that dared her to refute that statement. Uncle Edward laughed heartily, and even Hope had to smile.

Grace gave a reluctant nod. "I suppose you are. And married! How could you go off and have a wedding without us?"

"I knew I'd never hear the end of that." Mercy crossed her

arms. "We exchanged vows on the steamer as the sun set over the ocean. It was very beautiful and romantic, even if we were starving and filthy from the siege."

"And you love him?" Grace asked.

Mercy rolled her eyes. "I think you know me well enough to know I wouldn't marry for any other reason. Yes, I love him. I love him dearly. He's all I could ever want in a husband. Kind and considerate, generous and wise, and He loves God."

Grace's expression relaxed. "I'm so glad. When Eletta told me she intended for the two of you to meet and fall in love, I didn't dare say anything about it." She put her hand to her mouth with a gasp and then lowered it slowly. "Oh no, I wasn't supposed to say anything."

"Faith already spilled the beans, and it's all right. I'm glad, in this instance, that someone was planning out my life."

Grace glanced toward their uncle. "He said you left Faith and Adam in town. He said there was a very good reason, but he wouldn't say what it was." Her green eyes narrowed. "Who's going to tell me?"

"I will," Hope answered. "Mercy wanted to see us first. She wanted me to know that Faith realizes I'm her mother."

"What?" Grace looked from one sister to the other. "How?"

"I'll explain later," Hope said. "Given the hour, I'm sure Mercy and Uncle Edward want to get back to town."

Mercy glanced at her uncle. "We'll come back in the morning. Uncle Edward gave us his cabin to use tonight. Tomorrow we'll come to the farm with everyone, and you can all get to know each other." She smiled. "I think you'll be very pleased."

The ride back into town was easier on Mercy's conscience. Now that things were cleared up with Hope, she'd rest much easier that night.

"I'm glad things went well," Uncle Edward said as they approached the town.

"I am too. More than I can say. I never wanted either Faith or Hope hurt in this matter."

"I can tell you have something on your mind, though."

"I do. I'm praying about it and hope you will as well."

He glanced over. "And what is it I'm to pray about?"

"Hope accepting Faith into her family as her daughter."

"I'll pray God's will in the matter, but this won't be easy, no matter the decision."

"I know." A light rain began to fall, and Mercy rubbed her hands together to ward off the damp chill. "I've been praying about it a lot already, and I'll continue to pray. But I think they belong together. They share so much that they don't even realize."

"I'm sure that's true, Mercy, but you can't force it."

"I won't. Faith will always have a home with me and Adam, and if Hope needs more time to come to terms with this, then she'll go on living with us."

Uncle Edward looked ahead to the road. "I'll definitely be praying. Ain't never known anything that wasn't made better by prayer."

Back in Oregon City, Mina insisted Mercy come inside and eat supper before they returned to the cabin. "I won't have it said that any of my guests went hungry," she told Mercy as she served her a plate. "I kept this warm for you." She straightened and smiled at her husband. "And I kept two plates warm for you."

He rubbed his stomach. "Good. I'm starved. All this rescuing of wayward relatives has given me a big appetite." He sat at the table as Mina went to the kitchen for his food. "Adam, I hope you're always as happily married as I have been."

Adam had taken the seat opposite Mercy. He held a cup of coffee and met Mercy's gaze with a smile. "I'm sure we will be. We've already had so much conflict and trouble that the rest of our lives will be calm and serene."

Edward laughed. "If you say so."

Mercy looked around the room. "Where's Faith?"

"She's upstairs with the children," Mina answered. "She's quite smitten with the baby and Maribelle. In fact, she asked me if she could stay with us tonight. I assured her it was all right with us, but we would have to talk to you and Adam."

Mercy shrugged and looked to Adam. He merely raised a brow as though it were entirely up to her. She lost herself for a moment in his eyes. "I'm sure . . ." She shook loose of Adam's gaze. "I'm sure she's delighted to be with children again. I think that's fine. Adam and I can just walk here from the cabin in the morning to collect her, then make our way to the farm."

"First you'll have breakfast with us," Mina declared. "Then you may go."

"You might as well not protest," Edward threw out. "Mina is used to having her way."

There were chuckles all around the table. Mercy sighed happily. It was so good to be with her family again.

It wasn't long after that when Faith skipped into the room with Maribelle doing her best to keep up. "Did you ask them?" she questioned Mina in a conspiratorial tone.

"Did do ask dem?" Maribelle did her best to mimic.

"I did, and they agreed you could stay," Mina replied.

Faith's face lit up. "Did you hear that, Mari? I get to stay tonight." The little girl clapped her hands while Faith went to Mercy and nearly choked her with a hug. "Thank you." She let go, then leaned down to whisper in Mercy's ear. "Did you tell my first mama about me?"

"I did." Mercy touched Faith's cheek. "She's looking forward to meeting you tomorrow."

Faith's eyes widened. "Truly?"

Mercy smiled and nodded. "Truly."

An hour later, after bidding her aunt and uncle good night, Mercy looped her arm through Adam's as they walked back to the cabin. The rain had stopped, but it left a definite chill to the air.

"I wonder if you've realized something," Adam said after they'd walked nearly half the distance in silence.

"What?" Mercy snuggled closer.

"This is our first night alone."

She straightened and stopped midstep. She felt her heart skip a beat. "No. I hadn't even thought of that."

He put his arm around her. "It's all I've been able to think about since Mina announced that Faith wanted to stay the night with them."

Mercy couldn't think of anything to say. She wasn't completely unaware of what this night would mean to them, but she suddenly felt shy.

He cupped her chin and tilted her face upward. "It's been worth the wait. Now I have you all to myself, and we have the entire night together." He lowered his mouth to hers and kissed her.

For a moment, Mercy forgot all about where they were. She turned and wrapped her arms around his neck. The warmth of his touch spread like wildfire through her body as the kiss deepened. The wonder of the moment filled her mind with all sorts of thoughts and feelings that until now she'd not allowed herself to consider. Intermingled with those thoughts, however, came the realization that they were kissing in plain sight of anyone who cared to watch.

She quickly pulled away. "Goodness, you made me forget my upbringing. I won't have it gossiped that we were spooning and making moon eyes at each other in the middle of Main Street. Let's go, unless you mean to stay here all night." She started down the street, doing her best to keep her wits about her. All she could really think about was the man behind her and the love she bore him.

Adam easily caught up with her and pulled her hand through the crook of his elbow. "You can be a bossy little thing at times."

She laughed at his teasing. "Only when I'm determined to have my way."

"I see. Well, since our thoughts are obviously leaning in the same direction, I suppose I can overlook it this time."

～

"Are you all right?" Lance asked Hope. "I've been worried about you ever since you told me what Mercy had to say."

"I'm fine." She sat looking in the mirror as she combed out her long brown hair. Lance stood behind her with an expression of grave concern. She put the brush down and turned. "Really, I'm fine. I don't know how things will be tomorrow or what I'll say to . . . Faith, but I feel strangely at peace."

He pulled a chair close and sat down. "As long as you're sure."

She looked past him, fixing her gaze on the bedside lamp. Flickers from the flame caused shadows to dance along the wall. Not far from her bed, Eddie slept soundly in his cradle, while Sean was in the room next door. How she loved her little family. They meant so much to her. Could she risk their happiness by including Faith?

"I'm not sure about anything except that God is in control of everything, and therefore I have to rest in that and trust Him for the outcome."

"I'd do anything to keep you from reliving the pain you went through." He took her hands. "Anything."

She looked into his eyes. "I know you would, and I love you for that. Sometimes I think you're the only person who truly knows me. We have no secrets, you and I. I can't say that about anyone else."

"I pray you never feel the need to keep things from me."

"You've seen me at my worst, when I was about to shoot Tomahas. I can't imagine there could be anything quite so bad after that."

"That wasn't your worst—it was one of your better moments, Hope. You came face-to-face with the man who had killed your friends and taken your innocence, and you didn't kill him. That took a lot of courage." He smiled, and for a moment Hope could only sigh.

"This is going to take even more courage," she finally whispered. "I want it to happen—I really do. I didn't want Faith to know who I was just yet, but now it seems wiser that we meet on an even footing. Still, I can't help worrying about how it might affect our family."

"Just remember, nothing has to change unless you want it to. I will support your decision no matter what and never think less of you for your choice. If you want to raise Faith as our own, I will do that. But if you find you cannot, I will understand and abide by that as well."

"Thank you." Hope stood, and Lance did likewise. She put her arms around his waist. "I love you very much."

Lance pulled her close, and Hope laid her head against his chest and listened for the steady beat of his heart. So many times she had done this when she was afraid. It always offered comfort and reassurance.

"You are my life, Hope. Nothing would make sense in this world without you."

Mercy could feel Faith trembling as she presented the child to her extended family. Leaning down, she whispered, "Don't be afraid. They already love you." She straightened and smiled. "And this is Faith."

Faith looked around the room at the gathering of people and then looked back to Mercy and Adam. "There's a lot of people. Are they all part of the family?"

"They are." Mercy took Faith's hand and led her to Grace. "This is my sister Grace and her husband, Alex."

The couple smiled, and Grace bent down. "I'm very glad to meet you, Faith. These are our children, Gabe and Nancy. Our baby James is sleeping just now, but you can meet him when he wakes up."

"I'm five," Gabe said, coming close. "How old are you?"

"I'm seven." Faith sized him up. "Can you read?"

Gabe nodded. "My mama said it was important to know how to read."

"It is. I love to read."

Shy Nancy peeked out from behind her brother. She watched Faith with dark eyes that seemed to miss nothing.

Mercy knelt and held out her arms to Nancy. "Surely you haven't forgotten me."

Nancy considered Mercy for a moment, then skittered behind Alex. She took hold of his leg and peered around him.

Mercy shook her head. "Well, that's what I get for going away."

"I remember you, Aunt Mercy!" Gabe threw himself at her so quickly that Mercy fell backward and landed with a thud on her backside. Everyone laughed, including Mercy.

"I'd forgotten how strong you are, Mr. Gabe!" She hugged him close, then got to her feet with Adam's help.

Faith was already looking across the room to where Hope waited with baby Eddie in her arms. It was clear that Faith realized who she was, so Mercy took her hand and led her to her mother. Hope handed the infant to Lance and smiled.

Slowly, as if fearing she'd frighten Faith, Hope sank to her knees. For a moment, the two just looked at each other as if trying to figure out what to say. A hush blanketed the room, and even the children were silent.

Mercy felt Adam come up behind her. He put his hands on her shoulders as if to give her strength.

Finally, Faith spoke. "You're my first mama, aren't you?"

Hope nodded. "I am, and I'm very glad you've come to see me."

~~~~~

Adam found Mercy standing by one of the rail fences, looking out across a field of peacefully grazing sheep. The evening air was chilly, but she hadn't thought to bring a wrap, so Adam pulled off his coat and put it around her shoulders.

"Out here contemplating the events of the day?" he asked.

She turned, pulling the coat close as she did. "I am. I think things went well, don't you?"

He pushed back an errant strand of her brown hair. "I do. I think everything is going to be all right."

She nodded. "It felt like all the pieces were finally in place."

"Do you think Hope will be able to love her?"

"I think so. I know Faith already loves her and the rest of the family. She seemed so happy this evening, playing with all the children. It's like she should have always been a part of us."

"Yes. I can see that too." Adam studied her face for a moment. "You know, I can never get enough of you. Those beautiful turquoise eyes have captivated me from the beginning. Do you suppose our children might have eyes that color?"

"It's possible. Look at Faith, she has blue eyes just like Hope." Mercy smiled. "But I wouldn't mind if our children had dark hazel eyes like yours. I think they're very handsome. They've always made me feel as if you could look past all my pretenses and see the truth in my heart."

"I've never known you to put on pretenses. You've always just said what you were thinking."

"I suppose that's true, but I haven't always wanted to reveal my feelings. Like when I first realized I was smitten with you. I thought it was a bad idea to fall in love with a man I hardly knew."

Adam chuckled. "Some things are just meant to be."

"I was just thinking about that before you came." She looked back at the field. "I spent a lot of time out there praying and thinking about life and what I wanted. I thought about the past and all that had happened. There are so many things I wish might have been different, but then I wonder—if they were different, would everything I know and love now also be altered?"

"I've contemplated the same thing. While there were a great many difficulties and some deeply felt pain in my past, I wouldn't risk what I have now by altering what happened then."

Mercy nodded. "Nor would I. Even the attack at Whitman's, because had it not happened, Faith wouldn't exist. I can't imagine my life without her in it."

"Will you be able to part with her if Hope decides to raise her?"

"I'm not pretending it will be easy, but I remind myself that she'll still be a part of our family. Even if we do go to Grand Ronde, it's not so far away that we won't be able to come back here for visits."

"True enough." Adam pulled her into his arms. "Besides, by then we might have some of those babies with turquoise blue eyes, and you'll be far too busy to miss Faith."

Mercy lifted her face to him. "I hope we have a lot of children together, Adam. I think you'll be an amazing father."

"And I know you'll be the perfect mother." He gave her a chaste kiss, then turned her loose. "I nearly forgot why I came out here in the first place. Grace said supper is ready."

Mercy looped her arm through his. "Then we'd best get back. Grace runs a very orderly house. She'll soon be bossing you around with the rest of us—making you take your morning vinegar and drink plenty of boiled water. You will find her in every detail of your day."

Adam laughed. "So long as you're there beside me, I can bear up under just about anything."

Chapter

26

In early June, word came to Adam that Joel Palmer wanted to see him. Since they had left Portland so quickly, there had been no chance to connect with the Indian Affairs agent, but Mercy knew that, given his interest in Adam, he eventually would be in touch.

Palmer had been all over the Territory, trying to deal with the affairs of the Rogue River Indians, and still he made plans to discuss Adam's request.

Adam's departure cast a gloom over Mercy, but she did her best to ignore it. It would have been madness for her to accompany Adam, given that he might very well end up back in Port Orford before everything was said and done. The danger there was still very real, and even if she'd wanted to put herself in the middle of that, her family would never have approved.

The weeks they'd spent at the Armistead Farm had drawn Faith and the family close. Mercy watched her niece flourish as she began to establish herself with her siblings and cousins. As the eldest child, she became the leader of their little band, and even Gabe adored her.

Mercy hadn't yet posed the question to Hope as to whether or not she intended to raise Faith herself. Until now, Faith had been incorporated into the group of children as just one more of their number. Mercy, along with Grace and Hope, gave direction and correction as needed, almost as if there were some unspoken agreement.

But at night, when everything settled down and the families separated to their own sleeping quarters, Faith was rather displaced. She stayed in Grace's house, because that's where Mercy and Adam were staying, and while she never said anything about the arrangements, she seemed out of sorts. With Adam gone, Mercy finally decided to address the matter.

Once she had Faith tucked in for the night, Mercy sat on the edge of her bed as she usually did to hear Faith's prayers. "Before we pray, I want to talk to you about something."

Faith sat up. "What about?"

"You seem happy here. You seem to enjoy being with your cousins and . . . your little brothers."

She nodded. "I like them very much. I like to read to them. Only Gabe can read, and he doesn't read very much. Sometimes I just tell them stories about when I lived at the mission."

"I'm sure they enjoy that." Mercy smiled as Faith's head bobbed in agreement. "But there's something else I want to talk about."

"About my mama?"

Mercy had noted over the last week or so that Faith had dropped the title "first mama" and started referring to Hope simply as "mama." She didn't call her that in front of anyone. In fact, she didn't call Hope anything at all in the company of others. No doubt she wasn't sure what to call Hope, and since no one was saying otherwise, it remained unaddressed.

"Yes. I . . . I want to know your feelings, Faith. As you know, Adam has gone to see about us moving to the reservation to work with the Indians. I don't know how soon he'll be back, but we should start thinking about what will happen after that."

"I don't know what will happen," Faith said. "Do you?" She blinked several times as if her eyelids were growing too heavy to stay open.

Mercy shook her head. "No, but I want you to know that everyone here wants only the best for you. I think it's obvious that everyone cares about you. They all loved Eletta and Isaac, and they can't help but love you too."

Faith yawned and eased back against her pillow. "I love them too." Her words were murmured almost too low to be heard.

Mercy decided it was probably not the best time to sort through all the particulars of their future. She leaned down and kissed Faith on the forehead. "We can talk more about this tomorrow. Let me hear your prayers."

Faith was usually detailed in her prayer requests and praises, but not tonight. "God bless everyone." She yawned. "Keep Adam safe and help him to help the Tututni. Be with my friends . . . and don't let . . . anyone kill them." She yawned again, and her words grew fainter. "Thank You . . . for . . ." She fell silent.

Mercy opened her eyes and looked down at the sleeping girl. She was so petite and doll-like, almost fragile in appearance, yet Mercy had never known someone quite so strong and enduring. She pulled the cover up to Faith's chin, then picked up the lamp and stood.

"God, please keep her safe—don't let her be hurt by the decisions of the adults around her. Please give us clear direction where she's concerned." She went to the door and paused again. "Thank You for giving us this beautiful little girl, Lord. She has been a blessing to so many."

Instead of going to her own bedroom, Mercy placed the lamp on the table at the top of the stairs and then went down to see if anyone else was still awake. The downstairs was quiet, and as Mercy walked through the rooms, she found herself missing Adam more than ever. She paused by the fireplace and hugged her arms to her body. The fire had burned down to embers but still gave off warmth.

"I thought I heard someone down here," Alex said, holding up a glass. "I decided to have some milk. Want a glass?"

"No, thank you. I was just wandering around."

"Missing Adam?"

Mercy smiled. "Yes. Very much."

"I can tell you," he said, leaning against the doorjamb, "it did my heart good to see you two together. I worried that maybe the circumstances of the siege had thrown you into marriage without any real love between you, but when I saw the way Adam looked at you, I knew you'd be fine."

"And how does Adam look at me?"

Alex's expression grew thoughtful. "Like I look at Grace. She makes me complete—she's my hopes and dreams—my life." He smiled. "I know Adam feels that way about you just by the way he looks at you. But just to be sure, I had a nice long talk with him."

Mercy laughed. "About me?"

"About this family. I felt he had to be warned." Alex grinned. "You three Flanagan girls constitute a mighty army."

"Goodness, Alex. You make us sound like overbearing, demanding tyrants."

He shook his head. "Not exactly, but you're all very good at getting your own way. I've grown used to it, but I knew Adam would feel overwhelmed. Grace figures she has the right to manage anyone who comes through her door. Then there's Hope, who always seems to know what you're thinking before you even say a word."

His comment made Mercy laugh again. "And what about me, brother-in-law?"

Alex smiled. "You just love everyone. You're kind and generous and very much as your name suggests—full of mercy. You
easily forgive and never hold a grudge. It's always amazed me
that you can so easily let it go when someone wrongs you. I've
always envied your ability to do that."

Mercy shrugged. "I can't see carrying it around when there
are so many other things I'd rather embrace."

"Well, I believe God has given you a special gift in that. I
admire you for how you handle yourself."

"Don't admire me too much." Mercy shook her head. She
easily remembered attitudes and actions that were less than admi-
rable. "I do find that I can forgive with a fair amount of ease. Even
with what happened at the Whitman Mission, I just felt better
letting it go and putting my thoughts on better things. When I
was south at the Browning Mission, however, and a man named
Billy Caxton attacked the place with his men, I knew more anger
and ugly thoughts than I'd ever known before. It took a lot prayer
to forgive him—especially after learning that he killed Isaac."

"Adam told me about that. I can't imagine a man so filled
with hate that he would do such a thing."

"Neither could I. Isaac and Eletta were kind to him and his
friends." Mercy felt tears come to her eyes. "I wish so many
things could be different, but then, I suppose if things hadn't
happened the way they did, I wouldn't be here, and neither
would Faith."

"And her being here is important to you, isn't it?"

Mercy took a seat on the settee. "It is." She sighed. "I feel
certain that she and Hope are destined to be together—that
God wants them together. I don't want Hope to feel forced
into it, but Alex, Faith needs her. I'm not sure Faith will ever
be whole without her."

Alex smiled. "If this is truly God's doing, Mercy, then it will
come together in His time. Hope puts her trust in God, and

because of that, she'll listen to His voice and prodding. Just give her time."

"Are you certain you don't mind looking after all the children?" Hope asked as she tied on her sunbonnet.

"Grace asked me the same thing before she headed to town. I'll be fine." Mercy looked at the children. "We're going to have fun making cookies, aren't we?"

Gabe and Sean clapped their hands, while Nancy just gave a nod. Faith, however, stood in the doorway and said nothing.

Hope glanced across the room to where the two babies were sleeping. "I shouldn't be gone long. I'm just going to check on the lambs and move the flock to another pasture."

"Take your time. We'll be fine."

"Can I go with you?" Faith asked Hope.

Her request surprised Hope, and she did her best to hide her discomfort. She had always interacted with Faith while in the company of others. Still, the child's request tugged at her heart. "I don't see why not."

Faith brightened and looked at Mercy. "Is that all right?"

"Of course." Mercy looked at Hope for a moment and nodded. "I'll expect to see you both in a few hours."

Faith followed Hope from the house without saying a word. Hope stopped to pick up her shepherd's crook and then whistled for the dogs. The two collies came bounding up, eager for attention.

"Good dogs." Hope whistled, and they took off at a run toward the fenced area where the ewes and lambs grazed.

The dogs easily slipped under the lowest fence rail while Hope and Faith entered through the gate. The ewes took more protective stances as the dogs arrived, and the lambs bleated and crowded closer to their mothers.

"There sure are a lot of lambs," Faith said in wonder.

"Yes, we've had over two hundred born. There were a lot of twins this year." Hope walked at a slow pace toward the far end of the pasture where another gate would allow her to move the flock out of the enclosed field.

"Mercy said that men were going to come next week to shear them. Can I watch?"

"We're late getting to the task this year, but it's a lot of work, and we'll need everyone to do their part. Including you. Do you think you might like to lend a hand?"

"Yes," Faith answered, jumping up and down. "I want to help. I want to learn all about the sheep."

Her reaction made Hope smile. "I think we can arrange that." She reached the gate and opened it. "Come over here and then stand back. The dogs will bring the sheep through in a hurry."

She whistled again, and the dogs went quickly to work. They were adept at herding the sheep and a wonder to watch. Hope could see how enthralled Faith was with the process. Watching her, Hope realized how much her feelings for Faith had deepened. She thought back to when Faith had first been born. Hope had been terrified to even lay eyes on the infant for fear she would look like Tomahas. Instead, Faith looked no more like that murderer than Hope did.

It wasn't long before the sheep were secured in the larger pasture, and Hope motioned to Faith. "Come on. We'll leave them to feed."

"Will they be all right here without us?"

Hope smiled and nodded. "They're very self-sufficient when it comes to eating. And the way the land has been settled around here, with more and more people coming in all the time, wild animals are less of a worry. The dogs will keep watch and let us know if there are problems."

Securing the gate was quickly accomplished and Hope started back toward the house. Before they'd gone very far, Faith spoke up.

"Why did you give me away?"

Hope stopped and looked down at her. "Mercy told me you read the journal. I thought that told you everything."

Faith nodded. "I know that the Indians hurt you and that they hurt a lot of people and killed your friends." She frowned and looked away. "I know you didn't want me, but . . . why? Did you think I'd be bad like my first father?"

Her question pierced Hope's heart. Without concern for the damp ground, she knelt. "Not bad. I never thought you were bad. I was afraid, Faith. I was very afraid."

"Of me?"

Hope sighed. "Of you. Of my life. Of everything. I wasn't sure I could ever be a mother to you or anyone." She looked past Faith and prayed for the right words to say. "I know this will be hard for you to understand, but I want to try to help you." She looked back at the little girl and felt a deep tenderness for her. "I really didn't walk with God back then. I knew who He was and I'd been raised to respect and fear Him, but I didn't read the Bible or pray, and I certainly didn't think about living the life God would have me live.

"When all those bad things happened at the mission—when my friends were killed, and we women and children were taken hostage—I blamed God. If He was all-powerful and good, then why had He let this happen?"

Faith nodded. "I don't understand why He let those men attack our mission. They killed my friends."

Hope reached out and touched Faith's face. "Then you probably understand better than anyone else how I felt back then. Once we were rescued, I thought I could forget about it ever happening. I thought I could put it behind me and never have to remember those awful things. Then I found out I was going to have a baby."

"Me."

Hope nodded. "Yes. Knowing I was going to have a baby meant I'd never be able to forget what happened."

"I don't think I can ever forget what happened to my friends." Faith shook her head. "Even without a baby to remind me. But . . ." She paused, and her brows knit together as if she were pondering something very difficult. "I don't know that I want to forget. Maybe if I forget what happened, I'll forget them too."

Her words gave Hope pause. Her simple statement touched Hope deeply. "See, I didn't think like that back then. I guess I was just fooling myself. I believed that if I could just stop thinking about what happened—stop hearing anything about it or having anything to do with anyone who reminded me of the attack—then I'd be all right. But you know why that didn't work?"

Faith shook her head. "No."

"Because I still had to live with myself. I was my own constant reminder of all that had happened and all that I'd lost." Hope sighed. "I couldn't get away from the memories, because I couldn't get away from myself. It made me want to die. Then, when I found out I was going to have a baby, I didn't think I could bear it. I figured we'd both be better off . . . well, it's not important now—because it wasn't true. Eletta—your mama told me how much she wanted a baby and couldn't have one, and I felt bad for her. But when she reminded me that what happened wasn't your fault just like it wasn't my fault, I knew she was right. You and I . . . we were in the same position in so many ways. It wasn't our fault, and therefore, we didn't . . . we don't need to carry the guilt."

"Did you hate me?"

Hope shook her head. "No. I never hated you, Faith." She smiled and got to her feet. "I could never hate you. God made you—only He has power over life and death. I didn't understand why things had happened like they did, but I never hated you, and I never will."

Faith's expression changed from concerned to happy. "I'm so glad you don't hate me."

It was Hope's turn to grow serious. "You don't hate me, do you?"

"No," Faith replied, laughing as she began to dance around. "I love you."

Adam returned by the end of July. Mercy had never been happier to see anyone in her life. With Adam gone, she hadn't felt a moment's peace. Nothing felt right.

"I thought you might never come back." She hugged him close. "I missed you so much."

He chuckled and kissed her forehead. "I missed you too." He straightened and looked around. "Where is everybody?"

"Getting ready to eat. Alex and Lance arrived just ahead of you. I'm surprised they didn't realize you were back and wait for you."

"I didn't come by way of town, so they wouldn't have seen me." He put his arm around her. "I need to put the horse up, but why don't you walk with me and I'll tell you everything that happened."

"I'd like that." Mercy clung to his arm as if he might disappear if she let go. "I want to know how everything went. What of the Tututni and Mr. Palmer? Is the war finally over?"

"I doubt the war will ever really be over. There's a lot of bitterness between the Indian and the white man, and I don't know how it can be healed. Both sides are so wounded and angry."

They reached the horse pen, and Mercy stood back as Adam unsaddled his horse. He looked tired but healthy. His skin was tanned from hours spent outdoors, and his clothes looked like they'd seen better days. Still, she thought he'd never been more handsome.

Adam turned the horse out and closed the gate to the pen. "I'll come back and see to him after supper." He once again put his arm around her waist. "As for the outcome of my meetings with Palmer, it's all very good. We're approved to teach and preach at the reservation. Of course, it will take time to win any kind of trust with the people there, but some of our friends are already at Grand Ronde, and others are making their way there. We'll join them as soon as we can pack up our things and go."

"You mean right away?" Mercy stepped away and turned to face him. "Tomorrow?"

"If you can pack that fast." He grinned. "I know you can do most anything you set your mind to."

Mercy shook her head. "I suppose I just thought it would take more time."

"It's already been weeks. Meanwhile, the government shipped several hundred Rogue River Indians north to the reservation. And, Mercy," he paused, "they aren't doing very well."

"What's happened?"

"Sickness, lack of food, exhaustion from the trip. Many have died, and I fear many more will do the same." He frowned. "Most of the people who have any say over the matter simply don't care whether the Indians die or not. In fact, I believe they hope the hardships will decrease their number."

"That's terrible. Is there anything we can do?"

"I don't know. We'll do what we can and act as advocates to anyone who will listen, but given the general attitude toward the Indians, I fear it will fall on deaf ears."

Mercy heard the pain in his voice. He cared so much about these people—as did she. "Well, I guess we'd best go break the news to everyone."

"What about Faith?" He asked the question that was already on her mind.

"I don't know. Things have gone well here. Faith fits in nicely and enjoys the younger children. Still, Hope and I haven't had a chance to discuss the matter. I suppose we'll have to do that now." She squared her shoulders and threw him a smile. "I know God's already made provision."

After a long kiss, they joined the others in the house, and everyone was delighted to welcome Adam back. Faith flew into his arms. Adam gave her a big bear hug while she dotted his face with kisses.

"I missed you, Uncle Adam."

"I missed you too." He kissed her nose. "Have you been helpful while I was away?" He put her back on the ground.

She nodded. "I helped with the sheep and the little children. I even helped in the kitchen."

"That she did," Grace said, coming from that direction. "Supper's on the table."

"Before we go in, Adam and I have something to say." Mercy looked at her husband and then back to her sisters and their families. "We've been approved to teach on the reservation at Grand Ronde."

"That's wonderful," Alex declared. "When will you go?"

Mercy looked again to Adam.

"Right away," Adam said. "They need us as soon as possible. We intend to pack up tonight and leave in the morning."

Grace looked startled. "Tomorrow? So soon?"

"They aren't going to give you a chance to rest?" Lance said, moving to stand by Hope.

"No, they're sending in more Indians every day. I know a great number of the people from my work along the Rogue River. Some of them are very sick, and the rest are discouraged. I'm hopeful we can make a difference."

"I'm sure you'll be an answer to prayer," Alex threw in. "I don't have any doubts you're doing the right thing."

"But what about me?" Faith interrupted. She looked around the room, her eyes wide. "Where am I going to live?"

Mercy had anticipated the question but felt no more capable of giving an answer than she had weeks earlier. Before she could answer Faith, however, Lance spoke up.

"Where would you like to live?"

Faith looked at Mercy and then at Hope.

Hope stepped forward and smiled down at Faith. "You mean a great deal to us. In fact, we want you to know that we love you, and you are welcome and wanted here in our family."

Mercy could see there were tears in Hope's eyes, just as there were in her own. Faith stood biting her lower lip as if trying to reason through it all. Hoping to ease the situation, Mercy stepped forward and knelt beside her.

"Faith, we want you to be happy, so the decision is up to you. We love you too. In fact, everyone here loves you, so you needn't be afraid. No matter what you decide, you'll always have Adam and me in your life. We'll come and visit whenever we can. And if you'd rather come with us, then we'll see to it that you can come here and visit too." She smiled and stood. "You will always have a home where people love you. You'll never be without a family."

Faith's eyes filled with tears. "I love you, Mercy, but . . ." She turned back to Hope and began to cry in earnest. "I want to stay with my mama."

Hope opened her arms to Faith, and the child didn't hesitate. Both were sobbing, as were Grace and Mercy. The moment of healing seemed to wash over the entire gathering.

Adam put his arms around Mercy and pulled her back against him. She felt his warmth and the strength of his embrace. She watched as Hope and Faith held on to each other and prayed that

God would bless this mother and daughter. She cried silently, continuing to pray and praise God for all that He had done.

Adam led Mercy outside and held her while she regained her composure. He pressed tiny kisses along her hairline and stroked her cheek.

"I understand now," he whispered. "I can see you were right all along. She belongs here. She's always belonged here."

Mercy nodded and looked into her husband's eyes. "Just like I've always belonged with you."

"I couldn't agree more. Nothing in my life felt quite right until I met you." He reached into his pocket. "I almost forgot, I have something for you. Something I promised you."

Mercy waited as he fished something out of his pocket. When he held up a small gold band, her eyes filled with tears. "It's perfect."

"It's simple and small, like you." He took hold of her hand and pulled Eletta's ring from her finger. "But also like you, it stands for something mightier . . . something powerful and enduring." He slipped the new band on Mercy's finger. "It's truly a token of my love. A circle that never begins or ends." He drew her hand to his lips and kissed her finger.

"Oh, Adam. How I love you." She wrapped her arms around his neck. "I wasn't sure I'd ever fall in love with anyone. None of the boys who came courting appealed to me. There was always something missing, and now I know what it was . . . you."

He pressed a kiss to her forehead. "After what happened in Boston, I figured God meant me to be alone, and the thought terrified me. But then He brought you into my life. He gave me mercy . . . my most cherished Mercy."

She sighed and smiled. "I'm happier than I could have ever thought possible. I found my place. I finally know what God wants me to do, and nothing has ever felt so right."

"And just what is it God wants you to do?" he asked.

"Love you."

Tracie Peterson is the award-winning author of over one hundred novels, both historical and contemporary. Her avid research resonates in her stories, as seen in her bestselling HEIRS OF MONTANA and ALASKAN QUEST series. Tracie and her family make their home in Montana. Visit Tracie's website at www .traciepeterson.com.

More from Tracie Peterson

Visit traciepeterson.com for a full list of her books.

Within the mountainous regions of Montana in the 1890s lies the promise of sapphires and gold for those who seek it, but danger and deception are also found there. When three women are separately pushed into that world, can they and their hearts survive?

SAPPHIRE BRIDES: *A Treasure Concealed, A Beauty Refined, A Love Transformed*

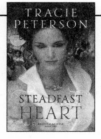

Brought together by the Madison Bridal School in 1888, three young women form a close bond. In time, they learn more about each other—and themselves— as they help one another grow in faith and, eventually, find love.

BRIDES OF SEATTLE: *Steadfast Heart, Refining Fire, Love Everlasting*

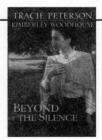

Nanny Lillian Porter doesn't believe the dark rumors about her new employer. She feels called to help the Colton family. But when dangerous incidents begin to plague the farm, will she find the truth in time to prevent another tragedy?

Beyond the Silence by Tracie Peterson, Kimberley Woodhouse

⬥BETHANYHOUSE

You May Also Like . . .

After being unjustly imprisoned, Julianne Chevalier trades her life sentence for marriage and exile to the French colony of Louisiana in 1720. But soon she must find her own way in this dangerous new land while bearing the brand of a criminal.

The Mark of the King by Jocelyn Green
jocelyngreen.com

When unfortunate circumstances leave Rosalyn penniless in 1880s London, she takes a job backstage at a theater and dreams of a career in the spotlight. Injured soldier Nate Moran is also working behind the scenes, but he can't wait to return to his regiment— until he meets Rosalyn.

The Captain's Daughter by Jennifer Delamere
LONDON BEGINNINGS #1, jenniferdelamere.com

When an 1850s financial crisis leaves orphan Elise Neumann and her sisters destitute, Elise seeks work out west through the Children's Aid Society. On the rails, she meets privileged Thornton Quincy, who suddenly must work for his inheritance. From different worlds, can these two help each other find their way?

With You Always by Jody Hedlund
ORPHAN TRAIN #1, jodyhedlund.com

When the man who killed her father closes in, Grace Mallory tries to flee—again. But she is waylaid by Amos Bledsoe, who hopes to continue their courtship. With Grace's life on the line, can he become the hero she requires?

Heart on the Line by Karen Witemeyer
karenwitemeyer.com

BETHANYHOUSE